THE
REUNION

JAMES CAMPBELL

The Reunion

ISBNs
978-0-9966076-9-8 (print)
978-0-9966076-8-1 (eBook)

Spafford, Horatio G. Lyrist. "It is Well with my soul," 1873
United Methodist Church Hymnal 337

"And Aubrey was her name.
A not so very ordinary girl or name."

David Gates, 1972

THE
REUNION

CHAPTER ONE

S itting in a worn thatched rocking chair that had been on the front porch for as long as I could remember, I slowly rocked and sipped my coffee as the first grayish-blue hint of dawn began to transform the last traces of night into day.

On cue, the squirrels began their descent from their nests high in the Georgia pines, and a gathering of birds in a nearby holly tree began to chirp.

As light filtered through the tops of the trees, I looked past a small patch of grass just beyond the porch. The faded white tags still attached to the newly planted cedar trees were swaying slightly in the wind. There were ten in all, and they served as a buffer between the lawn and woods. The trees that were there before, along with most of the yard, part of the porch, and most of the windows on the front of the house, had been blasted away during an extraordinary chapter of my mostly normal life. I stopped rocking, thinking about the early morning raid that had ended so explosively.

It had been a few years earlier when my wife, Aubrey, our buddy Nathan, and I got tangled up in a situation that almost cost us our lives. Millions of other lives, in fact, could have been lost as well.

As so often happens, trouble came to find me at a high point in my life. Aubrey and I had just reconnected after nearly twenty-five years apart. As I took another sip of coffee, I thought about the serendipitous night in Madison when I went to my neighbor's house for a wine-club meeting, which is where Aubrey and I found each other once again. All eyes had been on me as I began to introduce the wine I'd brought for the evening. It was at that moment that I spotted Aubrey in the back of the room. When our eyes met, I froze. She was just as beautiful as she had been when I walked away from the love and commitment I had pledged to her in our teenage years.

There was an uncomfortable moment in the room as the host finally walked over to refocus my attention on the wine bottle in my hand. I mumbled something—who knows what—and when I looked up, she was gone. According to my neighbor, she was living in Madison and owned an art and furniture shop downtown.

The next morning, I was at her shop when she opened the door. Not surprisingly, she was a bit formal and a little distant—as she well should have been. From her expression, I could tell I had twenty-five years of hurt I needed to repair.

Our story goes back to the time we met as teens at our fathers' hunting camp in Jewell, Georgia. The first time I saw her was after an opening morning hunt. It had been brutally cold, and she was dressed in heavy camouflage overalls with her hat pulled down as far as it would go. When I walked into the cabin, she tilted her head suspiciously as she watched me from across the room. I was sure she'd heard plenty about the new city boy who'd joined the club. I was not impressed, and neither was she—at first.

Later that evening, we dropped by her house to return a map my father had borrowed from her father, Mr. Reese. I was ready to get home and not happy about the detour. But that all changed the second she opened the door.

She was dressed in jeans with a gray flannel shirt, and her long auburn hair was no longer bound by the ball cap. Her eyes, previously half hidden by the hat, were the color of emeralds, and she was without a doubt the prettiest girl I had ever seen. I stood motionless and stared.

During that hunting season, we became great friends and were inseparable. Our fathers became good friends as well, and after deer season ended, I found myself in Jewell almost every weekend, fishing the river with the Reeses.

Aubrey and I turned sixteen that summer and fell in love—as much as anyone that age can fall in love. On the dock down by the Ogeechee River, we pledged our love that summer, but that promise would only last through my first year of college.

Our story took a turn with my ill-fated decision to enroll at the University of Georgia while she was still in Jewell finishing high school. I should have never gone to college early; my priorities quickly turned to academics over her. She tried her best to nurture our relationship, but with increasingly fewer phone calls and even fewer visits, I allowed us to drift apart. It was the biggest mistake of my life, and I had always hoped I would get another chance to be with the only girl I had ever loved.

After I talked with her that morning at her store, we began seeing more of each other. She was cautious at first, and I didn't blame her. Things moved slowly until the weekend we took a trip back to Jewell to her parents' house. We walked down to the dock on the Ogeechee River where we first professed our love, and the rush of feelings overwhelmed us both. It was like we'd never been apart. We'd had our first kiss on that dock, and twenty-five years later, we embraced and kissed again.

Over the next month, we found ourselves recommitting to the promises we made when we were sixteen. She was giving me a second chance.

Our relationship continued to grow. Then—as much as I didn't want to—I had to leave her for a trip to Paris. My business partners and I had planned the trip to celebrate the recent sale of our company. The idea for that business had been born when I was working with my dad right after college at Norfolk Southern Railroad. He and I discovered a unique opportunity to start a logistics company to support the intermodal operations of the Canadian railroad. Since he was close to retirement and didn't want to move to Canada, I talked a few friends at the railroad into joining me. The sale had proven to be very profitable and we had chosen Paris to celebrate.

I would have liked to have taken Aubrey, but it had been planned as a guys' trip. We were all history buffs, and none of the wives had an interest in our plans to follow the Normandy invasion up to Belgium and to do some camping. I told Aubrey I would make it up to her and take her to Paris the next spring.

While I was gone for two weeks, a series of events escalated into calamity. Aubrey and I talked most nights, but we had skipped a few days when the guys and I were camping and lost service on our cells. I knew she was excited about something she was doing with a movie, but she wanted to surprise me when I got home with the details. But she had seemed upset when we talked on my last night in Europe. Something had happened, she said; she'd tell me when I got home.

But when I got home the next day with flowers and Parisian perfume, Aubrey wasn't there. After some time had gone by with me unable to get in touch with her, I called her mom and checked with her friends, but no one knew where she was.

Knowing she had been worried about something, my fears began to mount. Not knowing what to do or where to go, I went to a wine event where I was hoping someone might have some information about where she might have gone. I did, in fact, get lucky and overheard a few ladies saying Aubrey was involved with a movie. It was apparently being filmed in Porterdale, a town not far from us. I asked them for more details, but that was all they knew. So I jumped in my truck and headed straight to Porterdale. It was bitter cold that night, around ten degrees, and the whole town looked frozen and abandoned. I searched for hours in the sleet and freezing rain. Late in the morning, I finally found her Tahoe parked at the end of a gravel drive, next to what looked to be an old, abandoned motor home. Seeing that she wasn't in the truck, I rushed into the motor home, where I found her in a back room badly beaten.

CHAPTER TWO

Aubrey is an accomplished artist who can create something new from old pieces of furniture and discarded objects, some of which she finds on the side of the road. She can take a half load of junk to the dump (and if she is taking it to the dump, it is truly junk) and come back with a full load of what she calls treasures.

She makes coffee tables from antique doors, dining tables from slabs of ancient heart pine, and eclectic bookshelves from collages of different types of wood. After she has distressed and painted the pieces, no one can tell they aren't hundreds of years old. This talent is what led her to be lying on the floor, almost dead, in the back of a motor home on a dark street in a town where she did not belong.

Over the years as she developed her craft, she had become a favorite with the movie-industry types who regularly worked on antebellum films and documentaries in the historic town of Madison. It was her specific talent for creating props that caught the attention of Mark McClure, a megalomaniac who was producing a movie as a front to carry out an attempted plot that was beyond sinister. His plan was to commit what could have been one of the greatest mass killings the world would ever know. A group of biogenetic engineers who met while in school at Georgia Tech had created a virus (N1N7) that was capable of infiltrating city water systems for the purpose of timed-release mass killings. Their goal was to reset the course of evolution, which they felt had been altered in an unnatural way.

Aubrey became involved when McClure asked her to be part of a documentary he was filming in Porterdale. He'd met her while shopping for movie props in her store, and, like most men, he became smitten with her unique blend of beauty and intelligence. He told her he was looking for someone to locate and create props and said he would pay her a nice fee to consult on the documentary. He also said he would like her to play a role in some of the scenes. Bringing Aubrey in was his big mistake.

Later, despite the concerns of his group, Mark insisted that she be inducted into their secret society. That happened in the eleventh hour of an operation that had been years in the making. The group tried to convince him not to bring her in, but he refused, and the decision ultimately cost him his life.

His downfall, other than insisting that Aubrey be involved, was being too cavalier about a plan he thought no one would be smart enough to figure out. The FBI figured it out, however, and the plan was foiled, thanks to information they received from Aubrey. That is when McClure sent an assassination team to go after her.

After I got Aubrey out of the motor home, she rejected my attempt to take her to the hospital, insisting she was fine. We argued about her needing medical attention, and as a compromise, I took her to the condo of my good friend Nathan Roark. He had experience treating wounds from his days in Vietnam, and he was the only person I trusted who had those kinds of skills.

Nathan dressed her head injury and gave her some pain medicine, then we put her to bed. When we got back to the den, he had a thousand questions. I filled him in on what little I knew, and all we could do was guess about the rest until she woke up. When she did, it took her about an hour to explain, and that is when the assassins showed up at Nathan's house.

They shot their way through the front door, throwing canisters of tear gas into the kitchen. We quickly ran to the balcony and down the fire escape, dodging bullets as we ran from the condo to my truck. We were all baffled over how they could have tracked us to Nathan's condo. We figured they must have followed us from Porterdale but didn't understand why they had not attacked us sooner.

As we left Madison, we had to figure out a place to go, and the only place I knew was my farm in Warthen. The farm is about an hour's drive from Madison, and we were extra careful to be certain no one was following us. My place is deep in the middle of the country, and it was dark with zero traffic as we made our escape; it would be impossible for them to follow us or to find us there.

But I was wrong. They did.

We found out too late they had put a tracking device in Aubrey's backpack. We did manage to escape from the farm with the help of the explosion—which was caused by me, not them. As a retirement present from my Canadian friends, who'd gotten caught up in the disaster-prepping craze, I had received a detection system for the farm, complete with semi-illegal explosives. Not a gift I thought I'd ever use! But the explosion (which caused way more destruction than I ever thought it would) gave us time to exit my property and make it to the airport, where we climbed into my Cessna 182 and managed to escape. The three of us have had an inseparable bond since then.

It took us a while, but our life slowly returned to normal. Aubrey was making furniture, and I was giving flight lessons at the airport in Sandersville. Then less than a year later, another event rocked our world, disrupting our honeymoon. And this time it was Nathan who needed help from us.

The last time we'd seen him had been a week before, at our wedding. After the reception, he shook my hand, hugged Aubrey, and, without either of us knowing, hopped on an airplane for Haiti.

It turned out he had received a desperate call from his friend Charles during our reception. The friend's daughter, Marti, had been kidnapped, and Nathan was the only person Charles felt he could trust to find her.

Nathan's goddaughter Marti had risen as a grassroots presidential candidate in Haiti and had quickly taken the lead in a field of 139 candidates. Her new popularity with the Haitian people had upset some powerful and corrupt men. This group was intent on securing victory for the candidate they favored, and Marti had become a threat. Then suddenly she disappeared.

Nathan and his friend Reagan found Marti in a military camp hidden in the jungle in the eastern part of the country. Once they had rescued her, the only way out was by air. Knowing Aubrey and I were just a few hours away in the Caymans, he reached out to us. We were in my Cessna 310, which was capable of holding six people. He needed us to meet him at a grass airstrip in the town of Jérémie.

Nathan had never asked me for anything and was one of the most selfless people I knew. I wanted to help him, but being a new international pilot, I didn't know if it was even possible for me to fly to Haiti. After an intense conversation with Aubrey and doing some checking on the internet about airspace requirements, I loaded up the 310 and the two of us headed to Haiti. It was a three-hour flight, and we were both relieved to get there. We waited for Nathan and his friend, but they never showed.

What was supposed to have been a normal pickup at the airport turned into a rescue mission on a narrow road in a canyon after dark. Nathan called us to a location less than a mile from the security compound where he and Reagan had snuck in and grabbed Marti. Her captors had found her missing and caught up with Nathan's group about the time I was landing. As we were loading them into the airplane, the soldiers began firing.

Departing the dark, narrow road and clawing for altitude, the airplane was an easy target. The scene became surreal as the bullets moved through the airplane with no sound of gunfire from below. The hail of bullets sounded like bees buzzing around the fuselage. I'm not sure how many times we were hit, but Reagan tragically was killed after taking several bullets to the chest. We would have made it out had they not disabled the right engine with a fiery explosion.

With no other choice, I had to crash-land into a canopy of trees. We knew that whoever was shooting at us would soon be trekking to the crash site. We removed everything from the airplane and tearfully placed Reagan in the pilot's seat before we set it on fire. We hoped that would cause our attackers to think we had all perished in the crash—or at least buy us time before they found only Reagan in the aircraft.

With what I am sure was divine intervention, we made it on foot to Jérémie, where I contacted a pilot friend from home to come get us in his company jet.

Within a few months, the corrupt men were caught and held responsible for the death of Reagan and the kidnapping. Jeanne-Marti Lamartine would return to Haiti and become the first female president of the impoverished island nation. Aubrey and I keep up with Marti through the news and the occasional phone call. One day we plan to return to Haiti—for a very different kind of trip.

I'm aware that anyone hearing either of those stories would think we are a trio of renegades or spies. Well, Nathan, in fact, *is* a spy, but Aubrey and I are not. I worked almost thirty years developing logistics software, a career in which the only excitement came when a computer—and not an airplane—crashed. Aubrey may have ruined a piece of furniture by applying paint or stain when the weather was too humid, or maybe she's gotten a few painful cuts or splinters, but that has been about it. We are two normal people who became not so normal for brief periods of time.

With all of that behind us, my days now consist of giving flight lessons at the Washington County airport. Aubrey is still making cool eclectic furniture from her landfill treasures and things that someone else threw out to the curb. Nathan, under threat by his wife, retired from his clandestine career with the CIA and is now living in the mountains of North Carolina.

It had been an extraordinary couple of years. As I sipped my coffee on the porch, waiting for Aubrey to wake up, it seemed like those events were from another life. But the faded white tags on the trees reminded me that they were not.

Hearing the front door open, I turned to watch the woman of my dreams walk across the porch and sit down beside me.

"Good morning," she said with a little squeak in her voice.

"Good morning. Sleep well?" I asked, reaching over and squeezing her hand.

She nodded and looked out over the yard while taking a sip of her coffee. Although we never talk about it, the things that happened here were hardest on Aubrey. And as much as I love this place, I told her we would move if the memories were too difficult for her. She would not consider it.

To give her more room for her projects, I built her a little cedar cabin with a workshop overlooking the pond. We also kept her house in Madison. It's a nice place to get a break from the country life and to stay in touch with friends.

After we finished our coffee, I followed her back into the house and into our bedroom. I eased up behind her and placed my arms around her waist, kissing her neck gently. She turned, bringing her lips close to mine, and I was thinking this could be the morning (she is *not* a morning person) when she promptly put an end to that illusion. She gave me a quick peck and moved toward the bathroom.

"Maybe later tonight if you're lucky." With a sultry smile, she closed the bathroom door.

Chapter Three

Our spoiled-rotten dogs, Hannah, Savannah, and Bella, were in the kitchen, lined up in a row and patiently waiting for their favorite—Aubrey. They only gave me attention if I was holding food.

"Good morning, ladies," she said, walking into the kitchen and dressed for the day.

It was part of the dogs' routine to watch her pack my breakfast. I had to watch as well. After finding honey bun wrappers from the vending machine at the airport stuffed into the console of my truck, she had begun making what she called a heart-healthy breakfast—more like a "heartless" breakfast, really, which is what I called it. Even the stray dogs at the airport wouldn't touch Aubrey's flaxseed muffins with their cardboard taste. Watching her, I reminded myself that I would need to do a much better job hiding the honey bun wrappers.

She then made me a sandwich for lunch, consisting of a mix of weeds and vegetable mush called tofu. I was trying my best to get used to the stuff. As unpalatable as the sandwich was, it was better than the muffins. She put the muffins and the sandwich in a cooler bag and poured some coffee into a thermos. I grabbed my flight bag from my office, and on the way out, she wrapped the cooler bag over my shoulder so I wouldn't conveniently "forget." I did have a habit of leaving it on the counter.

With a smile, she gave me a kiss and a hug. "Have a great day, and I'll see you this afternoon. Be sure and eat your muffins today. It will be a life-changing experience, I promise. Also, I think there is a one-hundred percent chance that you will get lucky tonight." She reached around to pinch my backside.

Sugar and icing, I thought, were the only things that could make those muffins change my life, but her promise of me getting lucky was all I needed to have a little skip in my step. I would need it with the day I had scheduled, and I might just eat the muffins after all.

The dogs followed me to my truck as they did every morning. I kept a bag of dog treats in the side door and threw one out to each of them. I scratched behind their ears to say goodbye and then jumped in my truck and headed to the airport, my mind on the frustrations that lay ahead for me that day.

About three months earlier, a couple of millennials had shown up at the airport to ask about flight lessons. They were waiting in front of my hangar, arms folded and leaning smugly against a white Toyota Prius.

I got out of my truck and greeted them.

"Are you Colby Cameron?" one of them asked.

"I am."

"I'm Alan, and this is Mitch." With his arms still folded, the speaker nodded toward the guy next to him. After what I had been through over the past few years, I would normally have my suspicions up about what they were doing there. But these guys were wearing skinny jeans with old-school Converse tennis shoes, and to use an expression from the sixties, they were kind of nerdy. Plus, they were leaning up against a *Prius*. So I just stood and waited.

Then Alan asked the question: "Are the stories true about what you did in Haiti?"

Not too many times in my life had I been caught off guard, but this was one of them. How could two kids who looked like they were still in high school show up in Sandersville, Georgia, asking me about things that happened in Haiti? It had been an international incident, but not one that made the headlines or got any attention in the States. Now, they had my full attention.

"Why don't you tell me what you know about Haiti?" I leaned against my truck.

"Mitch and I have decided we want to become commercial pilots. And we don't want to go to some lame flight school that is all about dragging out the time to get more of our money. So, we've been following pilots' forums and came across a blog about how you landed your Cessna 310 with one engine out and the other one on fire—at night and in a jungle, saving everyone on board. Then we did some research, and we saw you were an instructor here, not far from where we live in Atlanta. If all that is true, we want you to teach us." This guy was apparently the spokesperson for the two.

They were not entirely correct. I did not save everyone on board, but that was not anything I wanted to discuss with them. However, I was a bit intrigued that they had done their research and driven two hours from Atlanta. They might just be in luck. A couple of my students had just completed their flight courses, so I had some time. I invited the boys into the hangar to discuss the long, difficult, disciplined process of becoming professional pilots.

I had them take seats in my makeshift office and began telling them about the levels of instruction from private-pilot training to the process of becoming professionals in the field.

I was about to make a point when, with a self-assured smirk, Alan raised his hand and stopped me. He said that all they needed from me were a few lessons to get their solo permits. And then on their own, they could build the needed hours and get my sign-off to take their private-pilot tests. Alan informed me that they were already very experienced pilots. Their "flying" had been done on a flight-simulator game on their computers over the past year. Now, they just needed to "duplicate" the experience in a real airplane.

I had just taken a sip of coffee and almost spit it out trying not to laugh. I've had some cocky student pilots who saw themselves heading into elite *Top Gun* careers, but never anyone who thought his skills on some computer game could turn him into a pilot. I regained my composure and told them I would be glad to assist them in achieving their goals. I could not wait to get them in the air and teach them a lesson about how virtual reality compares to real reality. I asked them if they were ready to start, and with confident nods, they said they were.

First I pulled my prized 1976 Cessna 182 out of the hangar. I began the lesson with the technical aspects of the 182, which I had rebuilt from the wheel skirts up. This was not a trainer, I said to the boys. I explained to them it was a complex aircraft and much more difficult to fly than the Cessna 150 they should be starting with.

Speaking for the first time, Mitch informed me that wouldn't be a problem since they both had flown many hours in a 182. I tried not to roll my eyes and continued with the preflight inspection.

Since Alan seemed to be the big shot, I put him in the left seat and put Mitch in the back. I took the right seat up front and decided to keep quiet and see what they knew.

Alan taxied to the runway, made the correct announcements, and pushed the throttle full forward. Halfway down the runway, he pulled back the nose at precisely the right speed and rotated the airplane into the air. I had him do a few turns and then line back up for landing. I had my hands near the yoke, ready to take control if needed.

Surprisingly, he landed like he had done it a hundred times. I didn't say a word and had him pull the airplane to the ramp.

I then put Mitch in the left seat, and he pretty much duplicated what his buddy had just done. I tried my best to hide my astonishment. Unless I was too old-school and had missed a briefing about computer pilot training, I was thinking this might be the first-time students had taken off and landed by themselves. And not just in a trainer but in a complex airplane.

Over the next week, I put them in every kind of adverse flight situation I could think of, and they had no problems. So just as they had asked, I signed off for them to do their solo training. Then, after a month of hard work, they completed enough hours to take the FAA private pilot's exam. I sent them to the FAA flight examiner in Macon, and they both passed with no issues.

The next part of their training was learning to fly the airplane with only the instruments and no view of the sky outside. IFR (instrument flight rules) is by far the toughest rating to achieve. The difficulty lies in taking the numbers from the gauges and computing them to navigate and fly, all while having to struggle with the challenges of spatial disorientation.

Without any reference to the ground or the horizon, a pilot loses the ability to determine angle, altitude, or speed. There are plenty of stories about pilots who have flown their airplanes straight into the ground or ocean, never knowing they weren't flying in the right direction. One must trust what the instruments are telling them and not what they feel.

Both Alan and Mitch once again proved proficient and excelled in their training. After they completed the minimum number of hours, I scheduled them for an IFR-check ride in Macon, and again they passed with no issues.

It was rare for pilots not enrolled in a commercial flight school to excel so quickly. I was proud of them and was beginning to think there might be something to this idea of learning by playing games on the computer. But then we started multi-engine training, and the confidence that came with having "flown" on the internet came to a sudden end.

Flying a multi-engine aircraft is not much different than flying a single-engine plane—until one of the engines fails. With the control issues and loss of power that come with engine failure, a pilot is thrown into a dire situation. If a pilot does not take corrective action within seconds of the engine failing, he or she may not be able to recover, especially if the loss occurs at night or in IFR conditions.

The new Cessna they were flying should not have given them much of a problem. On the other hand, it could be physically demanding to control an older aircraft if one were to lose the critical engine. But that was not the case with my airplane. It had counter-rotating propellers and was not difficult to fly on one engine if the pilot took control in a timely manner.

Over and over I would set them up for an instrument approach then shut down an engine about a mile from the runway. Every time I had to bail them out. What was interesting is that the operation of the Cessna 310 was mostly computer based compared to the 182, which had no computers and whose gauges were all analog. Since they were computer flyers, one would think they would have done even better in the 310, but after many failed attempts, we brought the airplane and their egos back to the ground.

After a debriefing and a little pep talk, they silently sulked toward their car. They had done really well until now, and after all their bragging, I could not resist giving them a piece of parting advice.

"Hey," I yelled before they got into their car.

They turned around and looked.

"Go home tonight and consult with the Mario Brothers, and let's get this right tomorrow." I said it with a smile, and they laughed as they climbed into the car. They knew they had it coming.

Chapter Four

I t was approaching noon, and after pulling the 310 into the
hangar, I was feeling hungry. I was not in the mood for muffins, so I grabbed the sandwich—although it seemed more
suitable for a goat than me. It was either the sandwich or walking
to the FBO and eating from the vending machine, and I was tired
from instructing the kids all morning. I pulled the sandwich from
my cooler and settled on the couch. Facing west, the couch was a
great place to have a beer and watch the sun set after a long day of
flying. Or to try to stomach whatever Aubrey had concocted and
put between two pieces of bread.

As I sat with my feet propped up on a coffee table Aubrey had
made from old pallets, I heard a pilot announce his arrival into the
Sandersville air space. Like most pilots who have hangars there,
I have a radio at my desk, which I use to monitor my students as
well as any flights in and out of the airport. In an airport without
a control tower, it is a courtesy to respond to inbound aircraft with
current weather conditions and information about traffic around
the airfield. The pilot stated he was ten miles out from the west
and asked about traffic.

I put down my sandwich and walked to the desk to respond. "Inbound traffic into Kaolin Field, winds are light and variable, favoring runway thirteen. No traffic reported in the area."

Since we were a small county airfield, we didn't have an airport manager or a fuel worker. There was a general understanding that the flight instructors and airplane owners would assist the city with the airport operations. The fuel pumps were accessible and activated by credit cards, but it was always a nice gesture to help with the hose and ladder.

"Winds light and variable for thirteen, and no traffic reported," the pilot repeated.

"Roger that."

I'd barely had a chance to return to the couch and pick up my sandwich when the pilot announced a one-mile final for runway thirteen.

That got my attention; it had to be a jet if he had covered ten miles in just a couple of short minutes. We didn't get many of those, so I walked out of the hangar to get a good look.

It didn't take long for it to come into sight. It was indeed a private jet and a large one. With several lucrative Kaolin companies in the area, we would occasionally have a Cessna Citation or maybe a Lear jet fly in, but nothing the size of the one that was on its final approach.

As it landed and taxied toward the terminal, I could see it was the new Gulfstream 650. I'd recently read in a flight magazine that the 650 had achieved the highest rating in several areas. It had a range of seven thousand miles and could fly 650 miles an hour with a price tag of sixty-five million dollars.

To my knowledge, we had never had an airplane of that caliber fly into our airport. It would be interesting to see who it was and why they were there.

From outside my hangar, I couldn't see the ramp. I could, however, hear the powerful engines of the big jet whine down. I'm not usually one to be nosy, but as I said, it's not often we see a jet like the 650. I quickly choked down my weed sandwich and hopped into my golf cart to get a closer look. I thought about riding up to the ramp and asking if they needed anything, but I highly doubted they had stopped for fuel. A jet like that takes high-quality fuel, and the operators don't usually take chances at small airports without franchised, reputable fuel dealers. And I knew they hadn't stopped to make a bathroom run. So, trying not to be too obvious, I parked between two hangars with a clear view of the jet and the FBO.

It took a few minutes, but the hydraulic cabin door swung open and lowered. Three people exited. Two of them were in uniform and were obviously crew. The third was a tall, older gentleman in a light-blue well-tailored suit. He was wearing dark sunglasses. The crew members walked down the steps ahead of him. He paused for a few seconds, surveying the airport. Then, carrying a brief-case, he descended and began walking with purpose toward the airport office.

What I found odd was that there was no one waiting on him at the airport. Judging by his appearance and the aircraft he arrived on, this was not a man someone would pick up late. Also, there were no Uber or taxi services in Sandersville, so he could not have ordered a car. Possibly he was early. I continued to watch from my golf cart.

Just before reaching the office door, he stopped and pulled a piece of paper from his jacket pocket. He studied it for a second and then turned and looked down the row of hangars. He paused when he saw me and stared directly at me. I felt like a deer caught in the headlights. I didn't know whether to give a casual wave or ride up and ask if I could help him.

Before I could decide, he pulled out his phone and appeared to make a call. Since it was none of my business, I reached down to put the golf cart in reverse and return to my hangar. But it was at that very moment that my phone rang in my pocket. I pulled it out and answered.

"Mr. Cameron?" the caller asked.

"Yes, this is Colby Cameron."

It took about two seconds for the "coincidence" to hit me. Speaking into his phone, the man continued to stare at me. "May I speak with you for a few minutes?" he asked in a formal tone.

"I'll be right there." I had no idea why he wanted to speak with me or how he had gotten my number. But the first thing that came to mind was a possible connection to the events I had gotten swept into along with Aubrey and Nathan. As much as I wanted all of that to go away, I knew it never would. There would always be someone from the military or national security dragging up the old events. We would be asked to repeat the things we had told them a hundred times. Since the last event had been just a little more than a year before, I assumed he had come with some questions about Haiti.

The man entered the office, and I slowly drove up the tarmac, trying to decide if I should call Nathan. But then I remembered Nathan was in class. With too much time on his hands in retirement, he had decided the military policy on the Middle East and the outdated rules of war needed his attention. So with the blessing of his wife, who would have liked him home more in North Carolina, he enrolled in an international warfare doctorate program at the University of Virginia.

He spent most of his time in class arguing with liberal professors and millennials who had never spent a day on a battlefield. Lately when I called him, he didn't pick up but texted back like all the other kids. I was expecting him anytime to start wearing skinny jeans and calling me dude.

I parked the golf cart and entered the office, where the mystery man was seated on a couch. He smiled as I walked in. Since he did not get up, I sat in a chair next to the couch and returned his smile.

"Good afternoon, Mr. Cameron. I hope you are having a good day," he said with the air of someone who is confident and always in control.

"I am. Thank you for asking," I replied, thinking, "Here we go." We would get the pleasantries out of the way, and then he would pull a transcript or deposition from his briefcase, and the interrogation would begin. "Do you recall that on the date of . . .?" Or "In your opinion, did . . .?"

I decided I would save us both some time. "Before you get started, we have answered every conceivable question about the operation in Haiti. It's all in the files, and I really don't have anything else to add to the matter."

Still calm and smiling, he replied, "Mr. Cameron, I am not here representing the military or the government. I am here on a personal matter, and I promise to be brief."

Surprised and not knowing what to say, I simply nodded.

He opened his briefcase and pulled out a large brown envelope. He held it a second before speaking. "My employer sent me to hand-deliver this letter to you. It's rather confidential, and I was going to ask for some type of ID, but after seeing you, I don't think it will be necessary." He closed the briefcase, stood, handed me the letter, and made his way to the door.

Just before walking out, he turned and gave me a final look. I had a feeling he knew what was in the letter and was wondering what my reaction would be.

"Good day, Mr. Cameron." With that, he left the office and began walking back to the jet.

I looked down at the envelope, having no idea what this could be about. All I wanted was to retire, enjoy my time with Aubrey, and spend my days in the air. I had an unsettling feeling that whatever waited in that envelope would change all of that.

CHAPTER FIVE

Just before heading to her shop, Aubrey reminded Colby to grab his cooler and thermos. He had a habit of forgetting, and today was not the day for him to forget. She smiled, thinking about the extra "ingredient" she had added to the muffins. The surprise would merit a phone call the second he figured out what it all meant. She was nervously excited, anticipating his reaction.

"Ready to go, girls?" she asked, grabbing her bag from the couch. As usual, as soon as she opened the door, they shot out in different directions in search of unsuspecting squirrels. The odds were highly in favor of the squirrels, but every now and then the dogs would find one paying too much attention to a hickory nut, and the squirrel would be a goner. Hannah in most cases was the victor. She would pridefully carry her catch around most of the morning with the other two sulking behind her in defeat.

They left the yard, sans squirrel, and walked past the barn and Colby's racing shop to the trail that led to Aubrey's workshop at the pond. Colby had started racing while he was in Canada, and when he returned to Georgia, he bought a Porsche 911 and continued with the hobby, this time racing at the Road Atlanta racetrack in Braselton. He did well, winning a championship, but after he and

Aubrey got back together, he decided to give it up and stick to flying. The race shop was now a storage facility for Aubrey's landfill finds and roadside treasures as they awaited transformation.

The sky was slightly overcast, and the humidity was heavy. Not good, she thought. Today was the day she was planning on putting the final coat of lacquer on two tables she was making for a family from Atlanta. The Downs family had recently found, with Colby's help, an ancestor's old mercantile store in the Downs community, not far from Davisboro, a town close to Warthen. The store owner's great-grandson Scott was Colby's friend from childhood, and he had commissioned Aubrey to make a couple of tables from the front doors of the old store. Scott was going to surprise his family with them at an upcoming family reunion.

On the way to the pond, she came upon a couple of homesites that dated back to the 1800s. Aubrey was always drawn to them because of the spring flowers. Although the homes had been gone for more than a hundred years, the flowers returned every year as a living memorial to the people who had once lived there.

Continuing on her walk, she noticed the deep, hand-dug wells on the property. To keep someone from falling in, Colby had placed poles around them and wrapped the poles with barbed wire. Her eyes also fell upon a piece of blue feather edge pottery lying on the trail Colby had cleared with his tractor. She leaned down and picked it up. Holding it, she thought about the families who had lived there and what their daily lives must have been like. The homesites were at least several hundred feet from the wells, and she thought about the families having to draw water and carry it back to their small homes several times a day. She imagined how isolated their lives must have been. She and Colby had always wondered who had lived on the property all those years ago. Farmers, probably, who lived hard and simple lives, trying to make a living so far from everything.

Aubrey wondered if they were happy. She imagined the men laboring all day in the fields and the women doing chores until sundown. And then what? Prepare supper, eat, and then go to bed. They didn't have electricity, and they probably had few connections with the community.

She imagined herself as a little girl living in that world, and she wondered what she would have done for fun. With nature so abundant, she might have walked the river and the ponds collecting feathers from the blue herons and wild turkeys. She might have learned to paint the tree-filled landscape; she imagined hunting crawdads and fishing for bream and white perch. She could have planted a garden and grown food for the family and maybe had a few hens and collected their eggs every morning.

Maybe it had been a good thing, not being attached to the world in the way of modern families. Maybe that lack of outside connections had deepened the love of family. Family members, she imagined, were there for each other whenever needs arose. Now, with television, smartphones, social media, and the stresses of careers, few had the time or patience to explore life beyond the superficial.

As she moved past the homesites, the cabin workshop came into view, sitting on a bluff that overlooked the pond. After all the trauma they'd endured, Colby had built the cabin so that Aubrey could get back to doing what she loved.

Normally her mind would be on the weather and what that meant for her projects, but now, that was not the case.

Over the past week, she had been trying to think of a clever way to surprise Colby with the news. Looking at her watch, she felt a little smile stretch across her face, thinking it was about time for him to open his cooler and enjoy—or at least endure—his healthy breakfast. She expected a call at any time.

Inside her cabin, the tables for the Downs project appeared to be drying as they should. When they had completely dried, she did a little light sanding. Then she applied the final finish and was happy with the outcome. Looking at the time, she noted Colby should have finished with his flight lessons; he must have already found the surprise she put in his cooler.

She brewed a cup of tea and had just settled in on the porch when her phone rang. Seeing it was Colby, she took a deep breath and, feeling both nervous and excited, she answered.

CHAPTER SIX

I just sat there, staring at the envelope. It wasn't very thick, and if the man was not from the government or the military, I had no idea who it was from.

Hearing the massive engines of the Gulfstream jet revving up, I got up from the chair and walked out to see the jet taxiing to the runway. I made a mental note of the numbers on the tail so I could check out who owned it later. Then I watched as the aircraft departed runway thirteen and quickly disappeared into the clouds.

With the envelope in hand, I eased into the golf cart and headed back to my hangar. I was anxious to find out who had sent the letter and why it was so important that it had to be hand-delivered by an enigmatic man in one of the world's most expensive airplanes.

I parked the golf cart, plugged in the charger, and being a little hungry, thought I would get something to eat while I read the letter. I set it on the table in front of the couch while I checked the cabinet for some cookies or a bag of chips. I had no luck with that, but I did see the muffins Aubrey had packed for breakfast. Next to the bag of muffins was an FAA regulations manual, and I laughed, wondering which one would taste better. Since I would be needing the manual, I grabbed the muffins and a Coke and sat on the couch to check out the contents of the envelope.

I pulled a muffin out of the bag and noticed Aubrey had done something different with the wrapping. The muffin was wrapped in foil, which Aubrey had shaped like a cone. When I pulled out the muffin, it was colored half blue and half pink. Sticking out of the top was something that most males, especially in our younger, irresponsible days, would recognize immediately. I stopped breathing. As much as I loved to prank Aubrey, this had to be her pulling one on me. There was no way she could be pregnant. Maybe it was one of the dogs.

I pulled the stick from the muffin and held it to the light, and just as clear as could be, in the little window was a plus sign that meant a positive result.

She was pregnant? There was no way! I tried to breathe but couldn't. Then I began to feel a little light-headed and had to force myself to take deep breaths. I immediately went into denial. There was no possible way she could be pregnant. We were too old to have children. I would have thought it was a false result, but knowing Aubrey, she had probably taken the test ten times before she believed what it said.

With wobbly legs, I got up from the couch and found my phone then collapsed back into the cushions. I pulled up her number and, with apprehension, pressed the button. She answered on the first ring.

"You're *what?*" I managed to spit out.

"Tin roof rusted!" she yelled, and that was followed by a little giggle. I caught the reference to the B-52's "Love Shack" song but was in no mood for her cleverness.

"How did this happen?" I asked desperately. "That ship has long sailed, and we are too old to have children."

"Well, technically, 'we' are not too old to have a child since I haven't hit menopause. I thought that I had when I skipped my last two periods—until the morning sickness started. But after several home tests and an appointment with Dr. Howell, we are definitely pregnant!" There was excitement in her voice.

As for me, I was stunned. My mind was racing a thousand miles an hour. "When and how did this happen?" I asked in an accusatory tone that I soon regretted. I obviously knew how it happened. It had probably been on one of the mornings I offered her a back rub that turned into something else.

"What do you mean, when and how did it happen? You know exactly how it happened. Are you trying to say you don't want this?" Her tone let me know I was traveling fast down the wrong path and needed to change course.

"Of course I want this. I'm just a bit overwhelmed with the suddenness of it all. Yes, I definitely want this!" I repeated with a little more enthusiasm. "Look, I'm done with the students for the day, and I don't have anything else planned. I'll put the airplanes away and be home as quick as I can, and we can discuss . . . this," I said, not sure what to call it.

"Okay. I'm down at the shop. Hurry home and be careful," she said, sounding better.

"I'm locking up now and will be home in thirty." I lay back on the couch and stared at the ceiling. How could she possibly be pregnant? People our age did not get pregnant. *Our kids* got pregnant, and we had *grandbabies*. We were starting to get gray hair, and we did not have babies! Aubrey had just turned forty-seven. Maybe it had been a miracle that she conceived, but the chances of the pregnancy coming to full term would have to be astronomical, I decided.

I got up from the couch and, still in a confused state, secured the airplanes, grabbed my flight bag and cooler, and was just about to switch off the lights when I noticed the envelope on the table. As much as I wanted to know what was inside it, nothing in my life could be more important than the news that I could possibly become a father at the age of almost fifty.

Spinning my tires as I headed home, I knew I only had about twenty-five minutes to rehearse my "positive" reaction to the news. I would have liked to have said I was excited, but I wasn't. I was worried about Aubrey.

Aubrey had wanted to be a mother all her life. Babies, children, teenagers—all of them were drawn to her. She would have been a great mother, but fate got in the way, and it was just too late. If she carried this baby to term or near term and something happened, I wasn't sure she would recover, and maybe *we* would not recover.

Although she had never said it, I knew she believed that had I not broken off our relationship in college, we would have been married for thirty years by now with a house full of kids. I needed a few answers before having our discussion, and I knew just who to call. The phone only rang once.

"Well, hello. I've been expecting your call. I'm assuming you just found out the wonderful news about the forthcoming bundle of joy. Congratulations. I couldn't wish it for a nicer guy. Maybe we can work you in for a hip and knee replacement before your darling starts playing sports," Dr. Frank Howell said in a sarcastic tone with a little chuckle.

Frank is one of my closest friends, and our whole relationship was built on who could be the cleverest or "out-banter" the other one. I knew he had been waiting for days to zing me with that one.

After I moved back to Georgia from Canada, one of my first stops had been the local airport. I had been flying and instructing for years at the James Armstrong Richardson Airport in Winnipeg and was looking for somewhere to keep my airplane and maybe take on a couple of students.

I met Frank at Kaolin Field in Washington County, and we became fast friends. He'd been working on his instrument rating and was having trouble finding the time or instructor to help him finish. He asked if I could help. I did, and he turned out to be the biggest pain of a student I'd ever had. He questioned everything I told him, and when I asked him a question, he always answered with another question. I had to remind him often that he was the student and I was the instructor.

After a few months of training, I sent Frank to Macon for his instrument flight rules exam and check ride. Usually, the examiner would tell the pilot right away if he passed or not. On that day, however, the examiner was in a hurry to do his next check ride and told Frank he would get back to him that evening.

As soon as Frank landed back in Sandersville, he nearly accosted me, wanting to know if I had heard from the examiner. I remember telling him I was not the one who took the exam and the examiner had no reason to call me. I told Frank to calm down, that he would call. He did later that evening, and Frank had passed.

Now, with Frank's smugness about the pregnancy, I couldn't let it go. After a few seconds of silence, I replied. "I wasn't ever going to tell you this, but the examiner did call me right after your check ride. He wanted to know if you were a competent pilot and having a bad day or just a total idiot. I thought seriously about telling him you were a total idiot, but that would have looked bad on me. He said he was going to fail you unless I promised him that you had done better during training than you'd done on the check ride. I told him that you had the skills but had a weak, nervous stomach and did not test well." It was all I could do not to laugh.

Frank waited a second, taking in all that I had told him before he replied. "Bullshit! He didn't call you."

I remained silent.

"Did he really call you and say that?" he asked in a high-pitched tone.

"No, you moron. They don't call the instructor and ask if they should pass the student. If you had failed, he would have stopped the flight and told you as soon as you landed. Also, they give you a slip of paper if you fail. He wouldn't have let you leave without knowing." Now it was my turn to be smug and chuckle.

"That was not nice, but I guess I deserved it. Maybe I'm relishing this news a little too much that you won't be spared from the financial burden of raising a kid, from waiting up all night for them to come home, or from the hormonal years when they won't speak to you," Frank replied.

"I don't think adolescent problems are our immediate concern. You know Aubrey's age. What are the chances that the baby could make it full term and if it did, be healthy when it's born? I'm on the way home and about to have a conversation with her. What do I say? What do I tell her? Have you ever had a patient become pregnant this late in life?"

"Forty-five is the oldest I've seen with a natural pregnancy. And it was the woman's eighth child, so her body was accustomed to the process. I have seen in-vitro and heard of natural pregnancies into the late forties, so it is possible," he replied.

"Colby, I really don't know what to tell you," he continued. "I've already set her up for an appointment this week with Dr. Bradley, the best and most experienced obstetrician in Augusta. He has delivered more babies than would fit in Sanford Stadium, and he has published several articles on late-in-life pregnancies. Let's wait and see what he has to say."

I thanked him for his advice and for taking care of Aubrey.

During our conversation, I had completed the twenty-minute trip home, and after hanging up and pulling down the driveway, I could feel the butterflies fluttering in my stomach. I said a quick prayer and put on my positive and confident face.

CHAPTER SEVEN

I decided to park the truck at the house and walk the trail to the cabin. I still needed a few minutes to think about what I was going to say. On the way down, I caught sight of an old shooting platform my father and I had built at least twenty-five years before. He had just bought the land, and I had recently graduated from college. My first purchase after landing a job at the railroad was a new deer rifle. We built the platform with used crossties and laminated flooring from old railroad trailers. He taught me on that platform how to set the iron sights of a gun and zero in a scope. Now, the sight of that platform reminded me of all the wonderful times we had together. It also made me think about what Frank said when he joked about the emotional and financial burdens that came with parenthood.

I knew I had been the cause of many stressful days for my father, and it had not been cheap to send me to college. He assured me many times how thankful he was to have the bond we had and to be my father.

It's interesting how things can show up and change our perspectives. Seeing that old shooting platform just before meeting Aubrey had certainly changed mine. I now understood that if she and I were blessed with a miracle baby at our age, I would embrace that gift completely. I stepped up on the porch of the cabin with a smile, no longer having to pretend I was excited.

Opening the door, I was greeted by a herd of wagging tails. I had to give each dog equal attention so there would be no sulking or hurt feelings. Satisfied, they ran out the door toward the pond as I walked further into the cabin.

Leaning against the mantle on the fireplace was the most beautiful girl I had ever seen. I said that a lot, but I truly felt it every time I saw her. As happened so many times, I had to pause to take her in. I was always taken aback by the way she subconsciously brushed her hair from her face and by the allure of her almond-shaped eyes that could launch a thousand ships.

She smiled at me shyly, knowing what I was thinking.

"Hey, baby—and baby," I said, taking her into my arms and feeling the power of our love. I could never understand how or why I had lived for so long without it. During our separation, a day rarely went by that I didn't think of her. Why had I spent most of my life by myself and not ever tried to get her back? Maybe it was partly as a punishment for leaving her, and there had been the possibility she might not have taken me back. But I should have tried.

I was filled with emotion over all I had lost in the past and what I might have in the future—a miracle baby with the love of my life. I felt tears flow down my cheeks. And when we faced each other, they were streaming down hers as well. Maybe she was thinking the same thing.

Silently, she took my hand, led me to her daybed, and began slowly undressing me. My breathing became heavy, and I could feel my heart beating rapidly. The same feelings of anticipation surged through me every time, and I couldn't imagine that they ever wouldn't. Count Basie was playing in the background as she softly swayed to the music. I leaned in to kiss her, but she gently stopped me. She was in full control of the seduction.

She slipped out of her jeans and pulled off her shirt. With her hands on my chest, she eased us to the bed, never taking her eyes off me. She lowered her small, lithe body onto mine, and our expression of love was powerful and passionate, natural, and pure. As I watched her, I wondered how I could ever live without her.

We held each other for a while with no need for words. She slowly stroked my hair, and we both fell asleep. We would have probably slept all afternoon had the dogs not started collectively whining at the door.

Happy and content, we got up and dressed. I let the dogs in and gave them treats while Aubrey made coffee. We both knew it was time for the discussion about the pregnancy, and I felt a sense of peace that everything would be okay.

Taking our cups to the table overlooking the pond, we stared out the window, watching two blue herons. The birds stood motionless in the shallows of the pond, and I could tell they were a breeding pair, the male being larger with a longer bill. They stood side by side, hunting for small fish by the bank. Just like us, they were preparing for offspring who would continue the circle of life.

After a few seconds, Aubrey turned to me with more of a gaze than a look. Her chin was cupped in her hand. "What are you thinking?" she asked me.

I knew I had to be careful. My concerns about her age and the odds against the baby making it to full term could be construed as negative—and neither of us needed that. I took a sip of coffee to stall.

"Maybe the better question is, how do you feel about all of this?" she asked, redirecting.

"After the first five minutes, when I was in shock, I felt a little angry. I know it was a selfish thought, but I wanted nothing more than time for me and you—to make up for the years we lost. I pictured our life for the next thirty years going on just as it is—me giving flying lessons and you making art here in your studio, listening to bands from the fifties while waiting for the paint to dry." I smiled as I glanced over at her old record player.

"I planned on us traveling to places we'd always dreamed about," I said, "and just enjoying the ebb and flow of life. That was until I made the walk from my truck to your cabin. I started to think then about all the wonderful times I spent with my father and all the lessons that I learned from him. He was so patient and taught me things about life that I might never have learned on my own. I suddenly had a feeling that I could have that same experience with my child."

"You think we need to make up for lost time," she said, "and I understand why you feel that way. All those years apart were hard on us. But we can't ever make up that time. All we have is here and now, and whether we are working, traveling, or having a baby, we are going to love each other and be together," she said, putting her hand over mine. "Let's embrace our journey and look forward to the future and let go of the past. This child will be an amazing part of that future, Colby. I know in my heart that's the way it's supposed to be."

I leaned up and kissed my bride. She was right. I had carried the guilt of the past too long, and it was time to let it go.

"Let's go home," I whispered to her.

Chapter Eight

G athering the dogs, we walked hand in hand back to the house. Our discussion had turned out much better than I had hoped for, but we still had not discussed the concerns about her age and the high-risk pregnancy. But since we were riding high, I knew that was a talk for another time. Hopefully, at our appointment with Dr. Bradley, we would find out more about what was ahead.

Aubrey took a shower while I fed the dogs and put them out for the night. I pulled a much-needed bottle of wine from the rack, uncorked it, and poured it into a decanter. Then I started supper.

Pork chops being Aubrey's favorite, I pulled a few from the refrigerator, rolled them in flour, and put them in an old iron skillet her parents had given us from the house in Jewell. It had been her grandmother's, and she treasured it. Since we were trying to eat healthy, I added asparagus and mushrooms to the meal, but I couldn't resist frying the pork chops.

About the time I had the meal in full swing, Aubrey walked into the kitchen while drying her hair with a towel and then putting it in a ponytail. "Pork chops for supper! I must have really done a good deed this afternoon," she said, easing up behind me and placing her arms around me.

"You did indeed," I replied smartly as I reached for two glasses and began pouring wine from the decanter. But when I went to hand her a glass, she gave me a sideways look.

"I'm not sure it's a good idea for me to have wine while I'm pregnant," she said, setting the wine down on the counter.

"I don't think one glass would hurt, but I certainly understand." I poured both glasses back into the decanter.

Aubrey set the table while I finished the meal. I served our plates and poured two wine glasses of tea. Before we began our meal, I said a blessing as I usually did—and that's when things went wrong.

"Dear Lord, we come to you today with wonderful news about the blessing of a child and to thank you for the honor of being chosen as this baby's parents. We ask you to give us strength and courage to face any challenges or obstacles this pregnancy may bring. No matter the outcome, we hold you high. Amen."

I lifted my head and looked at Aubrey. Her eyes were still closed, but I could see concern spread across her face. When she opened her eyes and looked at me, I knew things had taken a bad turn.

"What was all that about?" she asked and then continued without waiting for an answer. "It seems you are already planning for the worst. I am very aware it's a high-risk pregnancy, but we both need to believe it's going to happen and that everything will be normal. The last thing we need is the stress of waiting for something to go wrong. Can't you see that, Colby?"

Once again, I'd handled things the wrong way and should have left things alone, but we were past that point.

"Aubrey, I'm sorry. On the way home from the airport, I talked with Frank about being pregnant at our age. He had never heard of anyone having a natural, healthy delivery at the age of forty-seven. I want this baby more than anything, but the odds aren't in our favor, and I just don't want to get our hopes up in case things go bad. Can you please understand where I'm coming from?" I asked her softly.

She buried her head in her hands and was silent. I didn't know if the reality of what I said was sinking in or if it was something else. When she raised her head and looked at me with a fierce expression, I knew it was something else.

"Colby, you have gone through most of your life being cautious and rationalizing everything. I don't think you understand what it is to have faith and trust in anything that you can't control. I will always wonder what might have happened if I had been on board with your first response when Nathan made that call to us from Haiti, asking for our help. It was way over our heads, you said. It was your opinion he should let the professionals handle it, not us. If I had agreed, would you have really let your friend and the best man in our wedding handle that crisis on his own?" Her voice rose as she stood up.

"What have you ever really fought for?" she continued. "You know the reason we spent twenty-five years apart was that you never fought for us! I'm tired of having to push you. I will not spend the next six months watching you wait for something bad to happen! You need to go to the woods, go fly your airplane, or do whatever it takes to get your head straight," she said in a broken, tearful voice. Then she stormed into the bedroom, slamming the door shut.

I was glad she left because my first reaction was to tell her that she and Nathan needed a few lessons in rationality and caution. She seemed to conveniently forget during her little lecture that I was the one who saved her when she got tangled up in the incident with Mark McClure. Had she been a little more cautious, she would not have ended up almost dead in a shot-out motor home in Porterdale!

Also, I had risked both our lives by flying into Haiti in the middle of the night and getting shot out of the sky—when all I had been asked to do was pick up a couple of people at an airport.

I was tired of bailing her and Nathan out whenever they got in over their heads. Sooner or later, their leaps of faith would leave them at the bottom of a mountain, broken.

I thought about going into our bedroom and trying to talk to her, but I was upset and would only make matters worse. Instead, I filled an ice bucket, grabbed a tumbler, a bottle of Scotch, and a cigar from my humidor and headed out the door to the pond.

It was just before dusk, and the sky was a canvas of orange, red, and yellow. Drifting stratus clouds reflected the brilliant colors, bringing a sense of peace to the landscape below. As I approached the cabin, a skein of geese flew over in perfect formation, headed to a nearby pond for the evening. This usually was part of my evening walk with Aubrey, but not today. It was anything but peaceful back at the house, and I needed the tranquility of the water and the woods to figure out what she thought I needed to figure out.

I walked out onto the long dock that goes almost to the middle of the pond, and, as usual, the fish were there, excited and swimming around in circles. I also noted that the daily race of the turtles had begun from the marsh end of the pond. Part of our routine was to feed the fish and the turtles. They were always waiting for us, having grown accustomed to hearing the sound of my boots on the dock at this time of the evening.

But this evening I didn't have any food, only Scotch. So I pulled an Adirondack chair next to a small table and set down the ice bucket, glass, and Scotch before I took a seat. I poured a generous amount, lit a cigar, and prepared, as Aubrey had instructed, to get myself straight.

As dusk faded to dark and the night sky began to appear, I noticed my old friends beginning to show up for my therapy session. During the spring in the Northern Hemisphere, Venus, Mars, Jupiter and Saturn are easy to spot. I had begun this contemplative practice as a boy, lying back on the wet night grass and staring at the sky, wondering what it was all about and how far it might go. And now here I was, a man of almost fifty, sitting on a dock in Middle Georgia, still wondering what it was all about and how far it might go.

As I stared into the forty-five billion light-years of space, I began my musings by putting things into perspective. Some of the distant stars in view could have disappeared millions of years ago. They are so far from us that even at the speed of light, it takes millions of years to extinguish the light from our view. Thinking about the timeless nature and vastness of the universe had a calming effect on me. I thought about Aubrey and the pregnancy. I had no idea why I thought it was a good idea to bring up the risks and ruin a joyous time that could have been one of the happiest days of her life. I felt like a fool, ashamed of the way I'd acted, especially with the prayer.

Aubrey needed to believe that everything was going to be okay, and that if it wasn't, I would be beside her to support her with everything I had. I abandoned her once, and that had been the worst mistake of my life. I put other priorities ahead of her, and there was no way in space or time I would make that mistake again.

So I decided I would have another drink or two and have a talk with God to see if he could give me any insight on how to handle this. Then I'd finish my cigar and stumble my way back home. I'd go into our bedroom, lie down beside Aubrey, hold her close to me, and find the courage to take a leap of faith.

CHAPTER NINE

I woke up barely perched on the edge of my side of our king-sized bed. Aubrey had her arms and legs splayed around me like an octopus. I couldn't roll over if I tried, and if I'd had to sneeze, we would have both fallen off the bed. But I smiled, knowing that whatever I'd said or done the night before must have been good or she wouldn't be wrapped around me like a pretzel. Instead, she'd be half a mile away on the other side of the bed.

I could hear the dogs outside the bedroom door whining to be let out and fed. I was ready to get up and start the coffee, but I was caught in a web of limbs and not exactly sure where we stood, so I didn't make a move.

After a few minutes, the dogs whined even louder, this time stirring Aubrey, who unwound herself from me and rolled over. Slowly, I adjusted my weight and eased off the bed, grabbing my robe and sneaking quietly to the door. Silently, I cracked it open, eased out of the room, and shuffled the dogs into the kitchen. I wanted to scold them for being noisy, but instead I gave them treats and let them out.

I made a pot of coffee, poured myself a cup, and stepped outside to the porch to enjoy the spring morning. Other than a slight headache and the stale taste of cigar, I was feeling good; it was a perfect day with just enough chill in the air for me to see my breath. I'd been sitting a few minutes when I heard a turkey gobbling somewhere near the pond. He was trying, I imagined, to convince a hen to come his way for a little morning romance. It was spring and mating season. Love was in the air—at least for the turkeys. After the night before, I didn't think a gobble or anything else would be an easy fix for my situation. Even though I'd woken up with Aubrey wrapped around me, that didn't mean I was out of the woods.

The latch opening on the front door let me know I was about to find out just how deep in the doghouse I was. Aubrey walked over and sat in the rocking chair beside me. She was wearing a worn pink robe that I think had been her grandmother's, cradling her cup of coffee to stay warm. Aubrey would be cold in the desert.

"Good morning," she said sleepily but cheerfully, which was a good sign.

"Good morning," I replied, feeling hopeful.

"Someone tied one on last night," she said with a little laugh, taking a sip of coffee.

"Someone did," I cautiously replied, still not sure where someone stood.

Aubrey stared out into the woods before she spoke. "Although I doubt you remember much of it, everything you said last night when you came back from the pond was really sweet and thoughtful. I shouldn't have been so hard on you, and I'm sorry. After you left, I lay in bed, and when I calmed down, I made myself think about our pregnancy from your perspective. I know how you think, and it's just in your nature to be cautious and analytical. You have every right to ask questions and be concerned. You also have every right to have mixed emotions about the news that you're going to be a parent. I know you were looking forward to getting back to a normal life and enjoying your retirement. You saw the next years of your life as a time to fly and teach, and you weren't expecting the curveball of all curveballs." She then turned to face me.

"You've been living alone for almost your entire adult life," she said, "and now in the span of a single year, you're married and have a baby on the way at the age of forty-seven. So what you said last night meant a lot—that this was a blessing, to be given the privilege of having a child with the love of your life." With tears in her eyes, she reached over and squeezed my hand. We sat silently for a few moments.

"Also, I got a reminder from Frank that Dr. Bradley can fit us in this week," she said. "Do you think you can be available?" She knew the answer was yes that there was nothing in our lives more important than the baby.

"Yes, I will definitely make that appointment and any others you schedule. And I do remember what I told you last night, and I meant every word. You were right to send me off to get my mind straight. I promise to focus on nothing else but being positive." I was pretty sure I'd just gobbled myself out of the woods and back into her good graces.

She laughed and rolled her eyes. She knew I didn't remember a single word of that little speech, but she did know it had come from my heart.

We left the porch and planned our day much as usual. We were entering the last week of the first trimester, and things for Aubrey had yet to change. She had not been sick or had any issues, so until we could see the obstetrician, it was business as usual. There was no need for me to stay home and obsess over every little detail and be useless. So, after kissing my bride and scratching the dogs behind the ears, I grabbed the dreaded lunch cooler and headed to the airport.

The Mario Brothers, as I would now call them after my clever joke from the day before, had a lesson at ten a.m. If they were going to stay on their training schedule, they would need to start showing some vast improvements. But sometimes a student's worst flight is followed by their best. I knew this from my own experience.

After a dismal instrument flight well into my training, my brain was overloaded with new information, and I was feeling overwhelmed. I failed every task I was given. My cocky little Italian flight instructor didn't help with his lack of encouragement, telling me I might just not have what it took to become a professional pilot. I went home dejected and thought about giving up. But it was his smirk that made me determined to succeed. And the next day I nailed every approach and mastered every situation he put me through. It took me becoming a flight instructor myself to understand what he had been up to.

When student pilots are introduced to new technical inputs and methods of calculation while they are also having to fly, their brains may become overloaded and unable to process the new information and keep up. Their minds need to absorb the new information, and usually that happens on their way home or while they're lying in bed, trying to go to sleep. I hoped that would be the case with Alan and Mitch.

Arriving at the airport well before anyone else, I opened the hangar and began preparing for the day's flight lessons. Looking down the runway, I saw that it was covered with the typical morning ground fog. With the airport being a large mass of heat-attracting asphalt, there were always some meteorological phenomena, like thunderstorms or low clouds in the area. And most of the time, these were not conducive for flying.

With an hour before the boys showed up for their lessons, I decided that after the previous night's escapade with the Scotch, I might need a couple more cups of coffee to clear my head. I grabbed a partially clean mug from the counter and poured some steaming-hot coffee from my thermos. I plopped down on the couch, reached for a flying magazine from the table, and there it was—the envelope.

After finding the positive pregnancy stick staring at me from the muffin, I had forgotten all about the mysterious delivery. I picked up the envelope and noticed how someone had taken extra time and care to write my full name in calligraphy-style letters.

Before opening it, I turned it over in my hands, inspecting it for any clues about the contents. It had no return address and wasn't very heavy. I felt a sudden wave of nervousness. My instincts shouted that whatever I was about to learn was not going to be good. I broke the seal and pulled out a letter.

Dear Colby,

I have started this letter many times over the years, and every time I have fallen short in trying to come up with the right words to complete it. Maybe I knew if I finished it, I might not have the courage to send it. I am at the point in my life where time is short, and I have spent most of the last few weeks reflecting on choices I have made and how they have impacted others—especially you.

My name is Jack Windham, and I want to first apologize for any hurt or confusion this letter might bring you, but sending it is something I must do. I hope that after reading it, you will forgive me. I will start at the beginning.

I was born in Houston, Texas, and lived there most of my life. When I was a young man, just starting my career, I bought my first house in Stafford, a little community a few miles southwest of Houston. It was there that I met the most beautiful, caring, loving person who would ever come into my life. She lived in the house next door, and after months of casual conversation in our yards, we became friends.

Over time our friendship grew, and we would spend a couple of mornings a week having coffee and talking. She was so full of life, and I had never met anyone like her. It was not long before I fell in love with her. One morning we opened up and shared our feelings, and I found out they were mutual.

But she was married and had a young family. Her husband traveled for work and was seldom home. We knew that acting on our feelings would only bring trouble and heartache, so we agreed to stop having coffee and visiting. I made a point of traveling and working out of town as much as I could, but she was always on my mind.

As the weeks went by, I would see her in the yard, and my heart would beat wildly. I just couldn't take it. I was in love with her, and I had to see her and be with her, no matter what.

Colby, I want you to know that I tried everything to reject those feelings, but for both of us, they were just too powerful. In another place and time, I have no doubt, we would have had a loving, vibrant life together—but this was not our time.

Things escalated over the next few months, and I am ashamed to say we acted on our love in ways we shouldn't have. Your father was a fine man, and I regret to this day how we betrayed him.

When our guilt got to the point that we were both miserable, I put my house up for sale and planned to move, but it was too late. Your mother by then was pregnant, and there was no doubt I was responsible.

We met several times in Houston to discuss our options. There were several we considered, but they would have destroyed innocent lives, and we were not going to do that. In the end, there was only one right choice. She would have the child, and it would be your father's. It may not matter to you, especially coming to you like this in a letter, but I would have done anything to have changed that outcome had it been under different circumstances.

Not long after you were born, your father got transferred to Atlanta, and it was all over. I did get to go to the hospital one morning while your dad was at work, and I got to hold you—for just a moment. I am not a man of many emotions, but on that day I held you, I sobbed uncontrollably, knowing I might never see you again. I have carried that moment with me my entire life.

As the years have gone by, you have never been far from my mind, and I have loved you from afar. Your mom and I stayed in touch, and I have discreetly followed your life.

She would send me pictures and newspaper articles with details of your accomplishments. I know this may be too much to hear, but on a few occasions, I traveled to Atlanta to attend some of your high school baseball games. I stood in the back of the stands; your mom or dad never knew I was there. You looked just like me at that age, and I wanted so badly to give you a hug or shake your hand. Instead, I watched as your family hugged you and congratulated you on a good game.

I also watched you graduate from the University of Georgia. I was so proud of you and will never forget your smile when you walked across the stage to receive your diploma. The flights back to Houston were spent deep in thought about how things might have been different. It was tough, but I deserved it. As far as I know, your father never knew of the circumstances, and I pray that was the case.

Colby, I am eighty-one years old, and I don't have much time left in this life. I have been fighting cancer for several years, and from what the doctors tell me, it will win the battle in less than a year. I know this is a lot to ask, but if you are willing, it is my sole desire to meet you again before I pass *from this life. I am aware of your father's passing, and I would never have put you in this position if that were not the case.*

I am currently residing on Chub Cay in the Bahamas. Like you, I am a pilot and would fly to pick you up if I could. Instead, I could send my jet for you, or maybe you would like to fly your new Cessna 310 to the island. I know all about what happened in Haiti and would love to hear the story.

What I have told you is a lot, and I know I've just turned your world upside down to say the least. I will understand if you do not want any part of this. I have asked myself what I would do in your situation, and I am not sure.

If you find it in your heart to forgive me and are willing to give this old man his dying wish to see you, I would be forever grateful. I will be here on Chub Cay until my health requires me to return home to Texas.

Yours now and always,

Jack

Chapter Ten

I finished the letter, and he was right; my world had just been turned upside down. A million thoughts went through my head as I tried to process what I had just read. According to the letter, my whole life—all the things I thought I knew to be true—were suddenly *not* true.

I tossed the letter on the table, engulfed with feelings of betrayal, and fought back tears, heartbroken. I thought about my father and how much he had sacrificed, the long hours he had worked, saving to help me buy my first car and pay for me to go to college. He had dreamed the two of us could build a dirt-track race car and race it all over the Southeast. But with three kids to raise, he never had the extra money. He gave up so much to provide for his family, and he was as much a victim of the deception as I was. That weighed heavy on my heart and mind, and I could only pray that he never knew.

Looking back, it all made sense. I thought about my teenage years when I shot up taller than anyone had ever been on either side of my family. I remember friends of my parents teasing them about me being the mailman's kid or that the hospital had messed up and sent them home with the wrong baby. It was always just a joke, and I laughed with them, assured by my mother that I got my height from a distant great-uncle on her side. But now I knew I got my height from the bachelor next door.

I then thought about my mother, and I wondered how she could have done this to my dad. My memories of their marriage and our family life were happy. We laughed and played a lot, and my father was always taking us on some adventure. My sisters and mom loved the beach, and every year we would pack up the car and head to Florida. We always stopped at the same roadside pull-off and enjoyed a lunch my mother had prepared.

Other memories involved my dad's Polaroid camera, a source of fun for all of us. He was constantly taking pictures of us, and we would gather around him as he pulled off the paper and waited for the pictures to develop.

My mother seemed to enjoy herself during family time, and I don't ever remember a cross word between her and my dad. From my perspective back then, we had the perfect family, and my parents had seemed happy with their life together.

But the truth is, the mind of a child is incapable of understanding the longings of an adult. Maybe she was just lonely, and with Dad traveling for work, she might not have been getting the attention that she needed. But that did not make it right for her to get her "fix" by walking a few steps to the neighbor's house.

If she were not suffering from dementia, I would have driven to her house and asked her what had been going through her mind back then. Why had she done that to my dad? Had she loved this man, Jack? And what had been so bad about her life that she had to almost destroy our family?

The things described in the letter almost seemed unreal. We hold our parents high on a moral pedestal, and the confessions in the letter were hard for me to absorb.

After my father passed, my mother and I would sometimes talk about the past. We even talked about Stafford and the people she had known from the old neighborhood, but she had never mentioned the name of my correspondent. Guilt, though, is like rust, slowly eating away at your very being. I was sure she must have told *someone,* and I suddenly had a sick feeling, wondering if I was the only one in the family who hadn't known. What if I had just discovered "the" big family secret that everybody knew and was told never to tell me?

I had to get up and move. I needed to find a little fresh air to clear my mind. The best way I knew to do that was to head up to the skies.

I first sent the boys a text that I would not be available today for our flight lesson, and then I pulled the Cessna 182 from the hangar. After a preflight inspection, I taxied to the runway and lined the plane up for takeoff. Full throttle to the firewall, and I was speeding down the runway. About halfway down, with a slight tug of the yoke, I was airborne.

For almost thirty years, I'd come to the sky and been able to leave my problems on the ground. But not this time. This time, my problems took the flight with me.

I flew to the farm and made a low pass around the cabin. If Aubrey and the dogs were in the cabin—and she was not using a power tool or had her music up too loud—she would run out on the porch and wave, the dogs rushing around her in excitement. On my second pass, I saw her leaning over the railing, waving, and I could see the dogs were with her.

It made me smile to see her. I thought about how I was going to break the news about the letter. She had known and loved my dad, and I knew the news would hurt and confuse her.

As I left the pond and flew down the power line that borders the edge of the property, I could see all the ground hunting blinds that Dad had built, spaced out every couple of hundred yards. After the hunting club in Jewell lost the lease for the land, he bought the property to retire on and hunt. It reminded me of our last night together.

We had planned to have dinner that night, and when I arrived around seven o'clock, his house was dark. There was a winter storm in progress with sleet and freezing rain and temperatures in the low twenties. It was well past the time he should have been back unless he had gotten a deer. Thinking that might be the case and that he might need help tracking it, I jumped on his four-wheeler and headed for the power lines.

And that is where I found him, slumped over in a chair in one of the ground blinds. He was wet and shivering, and when I raised his head, his face was pale, his eyes weak and glassy. I pulled him out of the stand, reassuring him everything would be okay.

I lifted him up and onto the seat of the four-wheeler and put his hands on the handlebars. But the effort was too much for him, and he fell forward. I then put my arms around him and drove us back to the house through the mix of sleet and rain. I carried him inside and put him on the couch, elevating his legs with several cushions. He was still breathing, so we still had a chance. I called 911 and gave the dispatcher directions to the house.

It seemed like forever, but they finally arrived and quickly took him to the Washington County hospital. The doctors informed me that he'd had a severe heart attack and they were calling a helicopter to take him to Augusta.

As I stood by his bed, he told me, in his weakened state, how proud he was to have me as his son. He apologized for not being around as much as he should have because of work, and he said he hoped I understood. I told him that I did. He also said the biggest joy of his life was being a father to me and my sisters. His hope for me was that I would find love and one day become a father too. He said he knew I would be a great one. He told me to be happy in life and that he loved me. With one last squeeze of my hand, he smiled and closed his eyes.

Dad left us that cold winter night, but the warmth of his soft, encouraging voice and his kindness and forgiving nature have never left my heart. As I thought back on that night, tears came to my eyes. It was all too much, flying over the memories below. I was in no shape to be flying, so I headed back to the airport.

At the hangar, I pulled a bottle of Scotch from the desk drawer and poured a few fingers into a coffee mug. I sat on the couch and picked up the life-changing letter and read it once again. When I finished, I leaned back and took a deep breath. In summary, a guy named Jack Windham from Stafford, Texas, now living in the Bahamas, met my mother decades ago and not being able to control himself, had an affair with her, produced a child, and is now dying and wants to meet his biological son.

I wanted to hate this guy, but his letter was so forthright and honest that I needed to think more about where he was coming from. Temptation is powerful, and it comes in many forms. We have all succumbed to it, and I wondered if I was rushing to judgment in labeling him as weak. He did have the fortitude to remove himself from the situation, but it was just too late. And my mother had been just as complicit.

Only the day before, my life had been as normal as any other guy's. My biggest challenge then was getting the Mario Brothers to understand the complexities of flying a multi-engine airplane. Then in the course of one day, I had learned that I, at forty-seven, had a baby on the way *and* a supposed biological father living in the Bahamas and hoping to meet me.

I gathered my flight bag and cooler, closed the hangar, and headed home. On the way, I would think about the best way to tell Aubrey about Jack Windham and the letter. She had enough on her mind and didn't need anything else to worry about. I had a lot to think about, and it was looking like another night on the dock, searching the heavens for the answers.

Chapter Eleven

I didn't end up going to the dock after all. Instead, I found my comfort by having Aubrey nearby. I would normally seek solitude to analyze my problems and consider the next steps. But that night, I just wanted to stay close to the love I knew to be real and true.

We took the dogs for a walk around the pond and listened to the chorus of the frogs as they prepared for their nightly courting. The geese were in situ as they honked and flew over the pond in a chevron pattern. I could always count on the geese.

Nature, in its splendor, can be harsh and unforgiving, but it will never lie to you. I thought of ravaging hurricanes, torrential floods, and powerful sunsets over the ocean. I thought of the green flash that comes at the last second before the sun sinks for the night, witnessed by a lucky few. Nature was pure and true, and I could always count on that.

We stopped by the cabin to pick up some drawings of a project Aubrey was working on, and then made the loop back to the house. I pulled a few things out of the refrigerator and put together a haphazard supper. We ate quietly in front of the TV and watched a couple of reruns of Joanna and Chip redoing a couple of houses in Texas. One of them was in Houston, which made me think about Jack Windham. I thought it might be a good time to bring up the letter, but I was tired and didn't have it in me. We were both subdued and quiet, and I was sure Aubrey assumed that I, like her, was preoccupied with the pregnancy. We finished supper, put the dogs out, and settled into bed.

Around three in the morning, I was startled awake. In the glow of the clock, I could see Aubrey sitting up and crying as quietly as she could. As I put my arms around her and she leaned against me, I didn't have to wonder what was on her mind. Our appointment with Dr. Bradley was scheduled for that morning.

She'd told me when we got in bed that she had been experiencing some uncomfortable sensations and was worried. She had called Frank, and he'd asked her the normal questions, like whether she was bleeding or feeling any cramping or dull aches. She told him no, that it was just an uncomfortable feeling she couldn't really describe. He told her it was totally natural to have those feelings and that it was probably a bit of anxiety leading up to her appointment with the obstetrician.

I wanted to ask her if she told him about the thousands of websites she had been poring over, studying the risks of pregnancies late in life. That in itself was enough to cause anxiety. But I was learning that sometimes the best quality in a husband is knowing when to be silent. I held her until she fell asleep and then eased her back underneath the sheets with her head on her pillow.

Morning came, and I woke to sounds in the kitchen. A glance at the clock showed it was six a.m. Aubrey, for the first time since I'd known her, was out of bed before me. I could hear her talking to the dogs, but in a more wistful and melancholic tone than her normal cheerful voice. I had a feeling it was going to be a long, emotional day.

Still groggy from lack of sleep and not ready to have a conversation, I slipped out of bed and into the shower. It's amazing how water can cleanse the mind of negativity and scary thoughts.

Because of its biological connection to us, it seems natural for its touch to offer comfort and forgiveness. As I closed my eyes, allowing the warm water to cascade over my head and shoulders, I could feel the stress leave my body—and then I felt a gentle arm reach around me.

Resting her head on my shoulder, Aubrey spoke so softly I could barely hear her words over the water. "Thank you for holding me last night." She paused. "And for loving me."

I turned and stared down into the eyes that meant life to me, paused so she would understand, and kissed her. It was a kiss that said, "No matter what happens, I will love you forever."

The expression in her eyes let me know she understood. She broke from the embrace and left the shower as silently as she had slipped in.

After we dressed and took care of the dogs, we left the house for our appointment in Augusta. We didn't talk much; we just held hands and remained in our own thoughts.

At Dr. Bradley's office, we filled out the necessary paperwork and took seats in the waiting room. I looked around at all the mothers and wondered what their situations were. From what I had been reading from my secret internet searches, no two pregnancies were alike, and very few—especially at our age—progressed worry-free. But every mother there seemed to be a fraction of our age, and they all were watching Aubrey. We both grabbed magazines and kept our heads down as we waited for our turn.

It was not long before a nurse or aide came out, chart in hand, and called Aubrey's name. After we followed her to a designated room, she placed the chart on a table and said a nurse would see us shortly. As Aubrey sat in a chair and stared out the window, I walked around the room, reading the diplomas to make sure they weren't from some online medical school.

After a long ten minutes, an older lady with gray hair pulled into a bun came in and cheerfully introduced herself. "Good morning.

I'm Samantha, Dr. Bradley's nurse. Welcome to your first visit. Today, we will be doing an ultrasound to check the baby's progress and, if you want, find out if you're having a boy or girl. Do you want to know, or shall we keep it a surprise?"

We had not had the discussion, and Aubrey looked at me for an answer.

"I think it would be nice to know," I said. "What do you think?" She nodded in agreement.

The nurse then instructed her to move onto the table, lie down, and pull up her gown. Looking at her profile, I was surprised that she had put on a little weight. I had a wave of panic that there might be more than one of them in there.

The nurse pulled the cart over to the table and began preparing the ultrasound machine. In front of the table was a video monitor that was presumably connected to the ultrasound. The nurse opened a pack of gel and rubbed it over Aubrey's abdomen. Then she took the wand connected to the machine and moved it over the baby. She started doing measurements at the baby's feet and then moved up his or her little body.

"Everything looks good so far, and it looks like you're going to have a little girl."

Aubrey was holding my hand and gave it a little squeeze.

"That means I get to make little dresses and host tea parties," she said.

"And it means that I will be flying less and spending more time at the mall," I said.

They both laughed at my reply.

The nurse was humming a song with a content look on her face and continued to move the wand further up the baby's body. To get a better look at the baby's head, she had Aubrey move onto her side and then tapped a few buttons on the machine to enlarge the area.

When the screen changed, the nurse stopped humming and her smile faded. Before she could pull the wand away, we both saw the reason for her concern. In the middle of our little girl's brain was a large, dark void.

Aubrey, with panic in her voice, asked the nurse what it was.

As professionally as she could, without making eye contact, the nurse moved the ultrasound table away from the bed and said the doctor would be in to see us shortly. She made her best attempt at giving us a smile, but she quickly lowered her head and slipped out of the room.

CHAPTER TWELVE

We'd barely had time to talk about what we thought we'd seen when the door swung open.

A tall, tanned, lean, angular man with a shock of gray hair walked into the room. He was dressed in all black, including his Converse shoes. He studied the chart for a few seconds and then walked toward us.

"Good morning, Mrs. and Mr. Cameron. I'm Davis Bradley," he said as he shook Aubrey's hand, then mine.

"If you don't mind, Mrs. Cameron, please lie back and let's have a look," he instructed as he wheeled the ultrasound machine back toward the bed.

With the wand in hand, he moved it directly to our daughter's head and enlarged the image. Again, we saw the large, dark void that took up most of the space. He took a deep breath, removed the wand, and rolled the machine away from the examination table. I could see the concern in his expression, but I also sensed the calmness of a professional. This kind of situation would not be new to him. He clasped his hands together as if searching for the right words. It took him a few seconds, and then he bluntly said, "Your daughter's brain is not developing as we would hope at thirteen weeks. The dark spot you see is abnormal and is sometimes—but not always—a matter for concern," he said, folding his arms.

His body language told me it was definitely a concern.

He took a seat. "This could be—and I think that it is—a benign cyst. We do see these occasionally, but usually not this early and usually not this large," he said, rolling the chair a few feet further from us. Another retreat. "Or it could be a genetic birth defect, but I don't think that it is."

Aubrey sat up on the table. The shocked and frightened look on her face made my heart stop for a moment. For a few seconds, there was only silence. Someone had to say something, so I asked, "What kind of birth defect, and what would the outlook be if that's what it is?"

The doctor leaned toward us in his seat. "The birth defect is called trisomy 13. It's a chromosome disorder in which there are three copies of the chromosome 13 in the baby's cells instead of two. It is also called Patau syndrome. There are fewer than twenty thousand cases a year, which breaks down to one in about every sixty-five hundred births."

That basically meant . . . nothing.

"Is trisomy 13 fatal, or can it be cured?" I asked. "What exactly would it mean if our daughter has it?"

"What we would be seeing is what is called alobar holoprosencephaly. That occurs when there is a complete failure of the brain to divide into right and left hemispheres, which results in the loss of the midline structures in the brain. With the brain not physically developing like it should, there are all kinds of issues that affect the whole body." He paused, taking a breath and getting to the rub.

"Most fetuses with trisomy 13 die in utero or are stillborn. The twenty percent that do survive birth will only live for a month or two, and the five percent who survive six months are severely mentally and physically handicapped." He kept his eyes down on the floor.

Aubrey put her head in her hands and started to cry. I put my arm around her and pulled her toward me. She looked up at the doctor in tears and said, "This is all my fault. I shouldn't have become pregnant at my age, and now my baby will have to suffer a horrible, short life." She put her hands back over her face and sobbed.

Dr. Bradley sprang into action and moved to Aubrey. He pulled her hands from her face so she could see him. "Aubrey, I can assure you this is not your fault. Contrarily, most of the cases are with women much younger than you. This has nothing to do with your age. Let's remember that this is most likely just a cyst. Your daughter does not have any of the other physical attributes we would expect to see with this defect," he said, still holding her hands.

"We will do another ultrasound in six weeks and pray that the cyst will be gone and we see a normal, healthy brain. If it wasn't my responsibility to report all potential diagnoses, I might not have even told you about the birth defect. I think the chances of it being something bad are slim. I truly believe it is a cyst." He then backed away from the table, and I knew that meant the appointment was over.

I reached out and shook his hand and thanked him for being so honest and candid.

He nodded and then leaned forward and put his hand on Aubrey's shoulder. "If you feel anything that doesn't seem normal or if you have any questions, you can call at any time. I'll give you both the number for my cell. We will get through this together, and I will keep you and the baby in my prayers." He gave us a humble smile before he exited, gently closing the door.

CHAPTER THIRTEEN

With heavy hearts and broken spirits, we headed home. We had planned on making it a full day with some shopping in Augusta. Aubrey wanted to go by the baby superstore to pick out some clothes and look at bassinets, but after our appointment, neither of us was up for that.

The sober mood and silence in the car were just too much, so as a distraction, I turned on the radio. Aubrey recognized the song immediately and slumped down in her seat. It was "My Little Girl" by Tim McGraw, a song about a dad having to let his little girl go as she moves out into the world to chase her dreams. Still in shock after the appointment, we listened to him sing about a daughter who'd had her father wrapped around her little finger since she was very small. Aubrey turned her head and stared out the window. I felt my eyes turn misty and switched off the radio.

Aubrey fell asleep soon after that, and I spent the rest of the drive home thinking about the song. I could picture myself checking in on my little girl as she slept, whispering to her how much I loved her and promising to protect her always. Tears ran down my face, and I said a prayer that we would have the courage to face whatever fate might have in store for us.

After what seemed like hours, we finally made it home. Aubrey woke with swollen eyes and gave me a weak smile. Without any words, we walked to the house, giving half-hearted rubs to the enthusiastic dogs, who were thrilled to see us. Once inside, Aubrey headed straight to the bedroom and shut the door. I completely understood her need to be alone and thought that some alone time might be good for me as well.

When I had things on my mind, I either took to the air or got on my tractor. Working the roads and trails was always a good way for me to relieve stress, and today I had an abundance of stress to relieve. I put on my Carhartt overalls, pulled a cigar from the humidor, and headed to the barn with the dogs. They knew when I lit the cigar, it was tractor time, and they never missed it. They always got excited when I hooked up the plow and headed for the fields. Following behind the tractor, they loved to hunt the mice and moles the disc would turn up from the soil. But today I didn't have the energy to plow, so I just scraped the roads for an hour and then put the tractor up and took a walk to the pond.

On the bluff overlooking the pond, I thought about all the times over the past couple of years that Aubrey and I had played and pushed each other off the dock and even made love there. It was our safe place, where we could talk about anything. It was where we had finally been honest with each other about what had happened when I made the decision to start college early and give up on us. It was where we chose to love each other again for the rest of our lives—and it was there I wanted to tell her about Jack Windham. Maybe it was not the best time, but maybe it was. After the news about the baby, it could be a distraction.

I walked back home and could see all the lights in the house were lit. I opened the door and found Aubrey in the kitchen preparing supper. That gave me an idea. I walked to the pantry, pulled out a picnic basket, and set it on the counter.

She gave me a curious look. "What is that for?"

"Well, it's a mild evening, and I was thinking maybe we could have dinner at the dock."

She brightened up and agreed it was a good idea.

We finished cooking and placed the covered plates of baked salmon, sweet potatoes, and rice in the basket. I put some raspberry tea in a soft cooler while she got the blankets. Under the scrutiny of the dogs, we loaded it all into the Ranger. I think they sensed they would not be part of the adventure. We fed them and left them into the house to watch a recorded rerun of the Westminster dog show, one of their favorites.

With everything ready, we headed to the pond. On the way, Aubrey reached over and ran her hand through my hair. I could see a slight smile on her face, and it warmed my heart. It had been an emotional day and I was glad to see her in better spirits.

We pulled up to the dock and began unloading. She threw a tablecloth over the table, and I spread out the contents of the basket. She lit a few candles, I poured some tea into two wine glasses, and our romantic evening on the dock began.

The sun had begun to dip below the trees, and we turned our chairs to face west, watching the brilliant colors filter through the clouds. I was lost in thought about how to bring up the topic of Jack Windham, so I didn't hear her when she spoke.

She gave me a nudge, a question in her eye. "Where are you? I just asked you twice if you were ready to have supper."

"Just looking at the clouds and thinking," I replied, taking a sip of my tea. We were silent for a minute, but I knew Aubrey's mind was working. She didn't miss a thing.

"I'm beginning to think this 'romantic' evening on the dock might not be about romance," she said. "You have something on your mind you want to talk about?" She seemed curious, not stressed, and I sensed she knew this was not about the pregnancy. I couldn't have asked for a better segue. I had wanted to save the talk for after dinner, but the opportunity was now, and I had to take it.

I turned my chair to face her and saw the concerned expression on the gorgeous face I loved.

She knew I was stalling. "Just tell me what's on your mind. We can have supper later." She pulled her knees up in the chair, spread a blanket over her legs, and waited.

So, I started at the beginning. I told her about the strange man and our encounter at the airport.

"Don't tell me it was another one of the government agencies wanting to ask questions about Haiti."

"That is exactly what I thought, and I was ready to send him on his way when he assured me it wasn't about that. Then he pulled out an envelope from his briefcase, and it had my name handwritten on the front."

Easing forward in her seat, she asked, "What was in the envelope?"

I paused before I answered, knowing that after I told her, things would never be the same. Not that our lives would really change, but this was about my heritage, which suddenly looked different because of a stranger's words.

"It's a letter, a very personal letter," I replied, expecting the question that would, of course, come next.

"Who was it from?"

"I think it would be better if you read it. I should have brought it with me, but I'm not thinking too clearly today. Let's have supper, and you can read it when we get back to the house."

With the secrets of the letter waiting for her, our supper did not turn out to be in any way romantic. We ate quickly without much conversation, and after about thirty minutes, we packed up everything and made our way back to the house.

Instead of unpacking the Ranger all the way, we just grabbed the leftover food and cooler. Then we opened the door to three attentive dogs lined up on the couch, still watching the dog show. On any other occasion, it would have been a picture-worthy moment and made for a good laugh.

While Aubrey put away the plates, I went to my office and retrieved the letter. Then I went back to the kitchen and poured myself a Scotch and her a glass of wine. The things we had been through that day—and the things she was about to read—called for a glass of her favorite chardonnay. She took a seat at the table, and I put the glass of wine and the letter, still in the envelope, in front of her. I chose my words carefully.

"What you are about to read will change my life and possibly *our* life. I'm not quite sure how, but I suspect it will. I was going to share it with you the day I read the letter, but with the pregnancy, I didn't think it was the right time. I'm going to sit out on the porch while you read it. I want you to process it and collect your thoughts before we discuss it. Come get me when you're finished."

I found myself getting a little emotional. With the news about the baby, I had not had time to really process all of it myself. Now that I was about to share it with her—someone who knew and loved my dad—it suddenly was real.

She could see the hurt in my expression and was about to get up and comfort me, but I shook my head. I didn't want consoling. I wanted her to read the letter so we could discuss it. I gave her a peck on the cheek and left her with the letter.

Outside, I sat in a rocking chair just out of her view and watched her as she read it. When she finished the second page, and the reality of what was happening became apparent, she looked up toward the door, unsure what to do. She took a sip of her wine and continued reading.

About page three, I could see her wiping her eyes. She drank some more of her wine and stared up at the ceiling. I could only imagine what was going through her mind. She read the rest of the letter, and when she was finished, she slowly shook her head. I was about to go back inside when she got up and walked toward the door. She slowly opened it, and looking at me with teary eyes, she said, "I am so sorry." She knew how much I loved Robert Cameron and how this letter must have affected me.

In that moment, my heart was filled with sorrow, and yet it was filled with peace as well. I had to face the fact that my dad might not be my biological father. My aunts, uncles, and cousins might not be a part of my real heritage when it came to the ties of blood. But having Aubrey in my life, loving me unconditionally, eased the disquiet that I felt. What we had was unchanging; what we had was real.

She reached for my hand and laid her head on my shoulder. I took a deep breath and stared into the sky. Here it came: the conversation about meeting the man who claimed to be my father. I knew I could not leave Aubrey now, when we were going through the most important struggle of our lives. Timelines were conflicting in a way that would make it hard to arrange a meeting. With the baby due in six months, we would be preparing for a new life while Jack Windham's life drew to a close; he didn't seem to have much time.

I could possibly ask him to come to Sandersville and meet him at the airport, but I wasn't sure I even *wanted* to meet him. I was feeling exasperated and unsure when Aubrey wrapped her arms around me and held on to me tight. I was brought to tears by the way she fit herself against me, getting as close to me as she could to demonstrate her love.

"Do you want to meet him?" she asked softly.

"I don't know. Part of me would like to sit face to face with the man who, if what he says is true, has stolen the legitimacy of my family from me. He has ripped away the idea of a biological connection to the man I loved more than I can describe. Part of me would love to tell him how much I detest him and how I wish he had just died and never tried to get in touch with me."

I took a breath. "And part of me would like to give the man the chance to tell his story. He was not alone in this, and there are two sides to every story. And it's too late to ask my mother what happened all those years ago." A feeling of resignation overtook me. "What do you think I should do?"

Before she replied, I watched her subconsciously rub the spot on her midsection where a new life was forming. The compassion and love that filled her eyes let me know before she spoke what she was about to say. I wanted to stop her, but I didn't.

"That letter wasn't from a man who just had a fling with your mom. He truly loved her, Colby, and he made the choice, a painful choice, not to disrupt her life. I know what he did was wrong, but as much as he wanted to be a part of your life, he knew it would destroy your parents' marriage. He made the right decision." A sadness filled her eyes. "And think about the way he kept up with you and everything you did. Can you imagine how hard it must have been for him to be at one of your baseball games and then . . . just to leave? He sounds like a good man who's had to live with the sadness of never getting to know his son."

She reached up to touch my arm. "Nothing will ever take away or replace the bond and the love you shared with your dad. But I think there would be nothing wrong with meeting the man whose genes are, after all, a part of you. It takes nothing away from the relationship you had with your dad or that you have with your family. If you don't meet him, Colby, I think you might regret it."

"So, you think I should meet him?" I figured she would say that only I could make that decision.

"Yes, I think you should. You should fly to wherever Chub Cay is and meet him. And I think you should do it now. We have six weeks before our next appointment, and there is absolutely nothing we can do between now and then about our situation. And I also think I could use some time alone to finish all my projects and relax."

I had not expected that reaction, but she had made a convincing argument. I had one shot at this, and if I was going to do it, it had to be now. If I waited until the ultrasound and we got bad news, wild horses could not separate me from her, and he would die without us meeting. I decided to sleep on it and make my decision the next day.

CHAPTER FOURTEEN

The morning sun snuck through the pines and into the windows of our bedroom. I looked over at Aubrey, and she was curled up, fast asleep. I stared at the ceiling and thought about the dream I'd had. Usually, I don't remember what I dream, and if I do, the memories are hazy. But this dream had been different.

Maybe it was the torrent of emotions that had hit me the night before. Maybe it was because my father's final words to me had been on my mind—that he hoped I would someday be a father too. For whatever reason, this dream was as clear and vivid as the memory of a real event.

We were at Aubrey's parents' house in Jewell, and it felt like early spring on a Sunday afternoon. Her parents were there, along with my parents, my two sisters, and their husbands. Mr. Reese and my dad were grilling on the porch, and the smell of charcoal filled the air. The ladies were sitting at a table across the porch, enjoying white wine in tall crystal glasses. They were laughing about something my mom had said, and it was odd seeing her so sharp, bright-eyed, and full of life. Perhaps, I thought, the doctors had been wrong, and she didn't have dementia. Aubrey was sitting next to me on a couch, wearing a floral dress, with her hand in my lap. She was smiling, watching our moms and my sisters.

What struck me now as strange was the time frame of the dream. The house and porch were exactly as they had been in the early eighties when Aubrey and I were sixteen and falling in love. But in the dream we were adults, and although my father had been gone for years by the time we got back together, there he was, locked into a serious conversation with Mr. Reese.

In the dream, a loud commotion in the yard got everyone's attention. We all stopped and looked as several kids with wet hair and wet clothes ambled onto the porch. My nieces walked over to my sister to show her something they'd found at the river. The third child came over and stood next to us. She was about thirteen years old and had the same auburn hair as Aubrey. Aubrey got up and wrapped a towel around her. Then she sat back down, patting the seat next to her. The girl sat and, with the most peaceful and contented smile, leaned up against her mother.

Sitting there, watching those events unfold, I knew the scene before me could not possibly be real. I considered that I might be in a dream, but I soon dismissed that idea, wanting to believe that my dad was still alive and my mother healthy.

But it was not to be. The last thing I remembered was looking into my daughter's eyes and thinking how much they looked like mine. She gave me a smile, and then I woke up. The dream had been so real I almost wanted to walk down the hall to see if our daughter was asleep in her room. That's when a sudden chill came over me. I could feel goose bumps on my arm, and my heart began to race. Call it a premonition or a nod from God, but I knew in that moment that Aubrey would give birth to a healthy daughter. I could even remember hearing Aubrey say her name when she patted the seat beside her on the couch.

Aubrey must have sensed that I was awake and rolled over and curled up next to me. "What are you still doing in bed, and why are you staring at the ceiling?" she asked me.

"Well, I was thinking that if I lie here long enough, you might wake up and want to show your husband how much you desire him." I was not sure I wanted to tell her about the dream, and any mention of sex would stop any further questions and get me kicked out of bed.

To my surprise, I was wrong.

Wordlessly, she pulled me on top of her and positioned me in a way that felt just right. I leaned into her, and we fell into a soft, heated rhythm. It was making love more than having sex. There was certainly a difference, and there was a time and place for each. This was more of an affirmation of the bond between us, an expression of the fact that we were joined in every way—mind, body, and spirit. It was a way to show each other we would face together whatever challenges might be ahead for us. Not only now, but for the rest of our lives.

Afterward, though, and as meaningful as our time together was, I was itching to get out of bed. Aubrey, on the other hand, wanted us to hug and kiss and rub on each other. I half-heartedly indulged her for as long as I could—maybe for five minutes—then said I needed to let the dogs out and get the coffee going. She tried to pull me back, but I resisted.

"Now you know why I don't let you have your way with me in the mornings," she said. "You are always too quick to jump out of bed and leave me. If you want more of this, you'd better learn how to give me more snuggle time." She stretched out across the bed, giving me an alluring view of her long, naked body.

Since I was no fool, I got back in bed and gave her the massage of a lifetime.

Afterward, she rolled over and purred, "I think you just figured it out. That was amazing. You keep that up, and there may be more of this in your future." She gave me a kiss, rolling out of bed and making her way to the bathroom.

I headed to the kitchen to make coffee. It was almost nine, and I could never remember staying in bed that long. But I could get used to it.

I fed the dogs, let them out, and poured us some coffee. Instead of having coffee on the porch, I decided it would be a nice change to sit by the pool. I'd spent most of the previous weekend trying to turn the green water blue, and it looked like my efforts had paid off. Aubrey, with a wet head, soon joined me, and it didn't take her long to bring up the subject.

"Quite an evening of conversation." She took a sip of coffee, glancing at me. "I want to talk with you about it but was thinking we might wait till this evening. I have a few projects to get started on, and I know you are flying with the boys today. Can we discuss the possibility of you going to meet Jack Windham later?"

"We can," was my reply. After our earlier conversation, I was leaning toward going to Chub Cay. I agreed with her that if I didn't take the opportunity, I might regret it. There were so many questions the letter had stirred up, and I knew I would never get the answers from my mom. Maybe he could tell me if my aunts and uncles knew.

We finished our coffee and went inside to get ready for the day. I had a busy morning trying to get the Mario Brothers to understand how to fly an instrument approach in the multi-engine Cessna. Aubrey was starting a project for our friends DeDe and Doug Keir. They'd built a house in Wyoming a few years before and wanted Aubrey to build them a table from a slab of Aspen wood they'd harvested from their property. They wanted it to blend with their décor, and Aubrey was having a tough time deciding what to do. I suggested that to do a proper and professional job, she needed about a week in Wyoming to make an assessment. I told her I would fly her out there and could probably find something to do—trout fishing or maybe hiking—to kill time while she worked. I also told her that since she was the artist in need of inspiration, she should be the one to ask them for a week at their house. I promptly got the eye roll I was expecting.

I gave my bride a kiss and left the house for the airport. With all that had happened in the past few days, I hadn't had a chance to catch up with my internet pilots and needed to check their progress. They seemed to be doing fine on the flight simulator but were intimidated by attempting the same maneuver in the airplane. If they were going to be professional pilots, they needed to get over whatever was holding them back.

Pulling up at the airport, I could see they already had the airplane out of the hangar and pointed toward the taxiway. I had told them to always have the preflight inspection completed before I arrived. But they had been slacking on their thoroughness with that and didn't take me seriously when I told them that being an accomplished pilot was not just about the ability to pilot the aircraft, but about knowing every mechanical, electrical, avionic, and navigational aspect of the airplane. If there were to be an emergency during any phase of flight, the pilot would have little time to figure out the problem. He or she had to be armed with knowledge about the complexities of their airplane.

"Have you boys done a complete preflight inspection?" I asked, walking up to the airplane.

"Yes sir. We've gone over every inch, and the airplane is flight-worthy," Mitch replied with confidence. Little did they know the last time I was at the airport, I'd made a minor alteration to the airplane just before I left.

"Okay, since everything checks out, let's go flying," I said, knowing that I had them. I'd pulled the fuse that lowers the landing gear, but I had the fuse with me and could easily replace it while we were in flight. They had not been checking the fuses, and this would teach them a lesson.

"So, who is flying first today?"

They both looked at their feet, which meant it would be my decision.

"Mitch, get in the left seat. Alan, get in the right. I'm riding in the back today." This would be the first time I let them take both pilot seats. I was curious to see how they would do, especially on landing.

We taxied to runway three-zero, and they did all the proper run-ups of the engines and announced our departure from the airfield. After we cleared the runway, I had them turn to a heading of one-three-zero and stay in the traffic pattern for landing. We had a lot of training to do, so I wanted to get the failed-landing-gear lesson out of the way.

"Mitch, line up for three-zero and do a touch and go, then maintain runway heading," I instructed over the headset.

"Touch and go, three-zero, maintain runway heading," he replied.

"Read-back correct," I reported.

They pulled out the pre-landing checklist and began going over the procedures for landing. When they made the turn to final and had the runway, Mitch instructed Alan to lower the landing gear. I sat up in my seat so I could get the full view. I had the fuse in my hand and was ready.

To my surprise, all three green lights lit up, signaling that the three gears had retracted. My students did the touch and go and maintained runway heading as instructed. I leaned back in my seat and was glad they could not see my reaction.

"What now, boss?" Mitch asked over the intercom.

All I could do was laugh. I handed the fuse to Alan. "Well done. You both have proved you understand the importance of the preflight inspection. Most emergencies that happen in the air are from things that were overlooked on the ground. Now, let's see what you've learned since the last time we flew. Mitch, line us back up on three-zero and pull your left engine a half-mile out and show me what you've got."

Mitch lined up on three-zero and reluctantly pulled the power from the left engine. The airplane immediately yawed and lost altitude. While trying to stay on the runway heading and get his altitude back, Mitch dangerously lost airspeed. I quickly instructed him to power up the engine and abandon the approach. We tried it one more time, and it was only marginally better. I had him land, and we silently taxied back to the hangar. I told them to take care of the airplane and then I wanted to see them in my office.

Not long after that, they entered the space that I called my office, and I had them take a seat in the two chairs in front of my desk.

"This isn't going well," I said. "You both did so well with the single-engine training, and I know you understand instrument flying really well, so what is the problem?" I raised my voice in frustration and threw my arms up in the air.

They both remained silent and looked at the floor.

"I know both of you have spent hours upon hours on the flight simulator doing exactly what you failed to do in the airplane. Alan, you didn't get to fly today, but I don't expect it would have been any better if you'd been in Mitch's place. Please explain to me why you can't perform in the air like you can on the computer." The irritation in my voice was growing.

They remained frozen in their chairs, still staring at the floor.

I began pacing around the office, trying to understand why they could not perform. Then I caught sight of a trophy on top of my file cabinet—and I finally got it. I knew what it would take to get these guys in shape.

The trophy made me think about a similar situation I was in a few years before. I had just moved back to Georgia and wanted to get familiar with the racetracks in the area. I'd done a bit of short-track racing while I was in Winnipeg but never on a road course. I'd wanted a Porsche 911 since high school and now had the means to buy one. So I did some research, and I found a car builder in the Braselton area, near the famous Road Atlanta racetrack. It turned out that the builder I hired was also a skilled driver who'd won races, and he offered to teach me after the car was built.

A month after my car was finished, I trailered it to the racetrack with my new instructor, Kerry. It did not take me long to get used to the car and learn the lines and nuances of the track. After two days of instruction and practice, I was happy with my progress—but Kerry was not. He looked at my lap times and told me I had a long way to go before I could be competitive in a race. He said I needed to shave off at least three seconds if I wanted to be in the top ten. More if I wanted to win.

Three seconds is an eternity on a racetrack. I was already pushing the edge and saw no way I could get fast enough to compete. Filled with disappointment, I told Kerry I didn't think my car was capable of shaving off that much time. He said *the car* couldn't and told me to get back into the driver's seat. Sitting in the passenger's seat, he observed me drive a few laps and then told me over the headset to listen carefully to his instructions and do exactly what he said. I agreed.

We were approaching the end of the long backstretch and had gained a significant amount of speed when he told me to hold the throttle pedal to the floor and to not let up. But as we entered the sweeping downhill turn, I couldn't do it. If I had held the pedal down, there was no way we would have made the turn. We would have gone sliding into the concrete barrier that bordered the track. Kerry didn't comment on my failure to follow his instructions.

During the next lap, leading up toward the backstretch, he came over the radio, saying simply, "Trust me."

We again approached the sweeping turn, and again I went to lift my foot off the accelerator. This time, with as much force as he could, he put both arms on my leg and held it down. I tried to resist, but I couldn't raise my leg. I went full throttle, and with a calculated slide across the track, I made the turn. With Kerry still pushing down my leg, we continued down the hill into the brake zone, heading toward the next turn. I didn't know how we would make it, but I trusted him that time and didn't try to lift my leg.

Suddenly, he let up off my leg and yelled for me to "Brake now!"

I stood on those brakes with my right foot, and the car sunk down into the track.

"Turn!" yelled my instructor.

As I turned in, the g-forces pinned me into the safety harness, but I made the turn. We did a few more laps, and I began to feel more comfortable in the car. We pulled into the pits, and he pulled the lap timer from the car. In just that single session, I had shaved two seconds off my time.

He looked at me and said, "Sometimes, to believe something is possible, you just have to see it for yourself. You have the skills to drive this car, or I would have never put either of us in that position. Go out there and do that on the other twelve turns and brake zones, and you will have what it takes to win races."

I took his advice and won several races that year and the Southeast championship the year after that. Now, I was about to teach that lesson to the boys.

"Back in the airplane, boys. I want you both in the back seats," I said, walking ahead of them to the airplane. I jumped in the left seat, and after an abbreviated preflight run-up, I taxied to runway three-zero and pushed full power to only the left engine. With full pressure on the brakes and rudder, I revved up that engine until I had maximum power and then let go. The plane tried to shoot to the left, but I held the opposite rudder to the floor, and, pointing sideways, it slugged down the runway until it was airborne. I flew the airplane all over Washington County with just one engine. I did extreme turning and climbing maneuvers that would have been difficult with *both* engines.

Back at the airport and on final approach, I had the boys open every window and even the luggage hatch door. Then about a quarter of a mile out, with deafening wind noise and the air wildly flowing through the cabin, I shut down the remaining engine. I jammed the nose forward toward the runway and kept the airspeed a few knots above the stall speed. I knew what I was doing, because under different circumstances, I had done it before.

Without any power to either engine, I sat the Cessna down on the runway like the landing was a Sunday-morning walk in the park. I restored the power and taxied back to the hangar, where we went inside for our second briefing. We sat on the couch, and I gave it a little time before saying anything.

"Remember when you boys showed up here with your arms folded smugly across your chest, asking me about the things that happened on my flight in Haiti?" I began. "Well, what you saw just now did not include the bullets screaming through the fuselage and blowing out the windows. Back then, a friend with a bullet in his chest was bleeding to death on the floorboard. Panicked passengers were yelling; there were no avionics because the whole front panel had been shot out. I was flying the plane at night with just one engine—and that one was on fire—trying to find a canopy of trees to land in before my airspeed ran out and all of us were killed. What you just experienced wasn't even close to how I had to fly that airplane that night to save our lives." After I calmly finished with that statement, I paused for a few seconds to let my words sink in.

"Did I have the experience to react to a situation like that? No, I did not. I don't think anyone, with the exception of combat military pilots, has the experience for that kind of situation. But I had put a lot of time and tireless effort into doing single-engine approaches without the use of the instruments. I didn't think I would ever have to put those skills to use, but I knew they would make me a better pilot and increase my confidence in my airplane.

In the words of a friend who had to teach *me* that very lesson, sometimes to believe something is possible, you need to just see it for yourself. You just saw the limits of that airplane, and neither of you has come close to them. I think you are more worried about the capabilities of the aircraft than about your ability to execute the approach. Don't be afraid of the airplane. As you saw, it can handle it."

I took a breath then looked each of them in the eye. "For the next week, I want you both flying approaches and unusual attitudes with only one engine until you master that. If you can accomplish that, you both will be headed for piloting careers. If you can't, you will never have what it takes to safely fly passengers on commercial airlines.

I'm going to take about a week off for some personal business, so you will be on your own. Work together to keep each other safe, and when I get back, my airplane better be in the condition I left it in—and you two had better be ready to take your multi-engine check rides. Do you understand?" I asked them sternly.

"Yes sir," they answered in unison.

CHAPTER FIFTEEN

Feeling like I'd made my point, I left the boys to think about what I'd said. Hopefully, they would steal a couple of beers from the refrigerator and have a heart-to-heart about what they'd been doing wrong and how to correct it. They had the skills and talent; they just needed the confidence.

On the way home, just as I was rolling through our little hamlet of Warthen, I realized that while I had stomped around the hangar, beating them up over not being able to perform, and setting them up with a challenge, I had given up my airplane in the heat of my discourse. My plan had been to fly the Cessna 310 to the Bahamas via Fort Lauderdale then on to Chub Cay. It was about an hour-and-a-half flight over water, and it would have been nice to have had an extra engine in case of trouble. In a single-engine, there was no gliding to land; it would be ditching and praying.

But there was no way I could change plans now as far as Mitch and Alan were concerned. This was a pivotal time for the boys to take the lesson I had given them and put it into practice. They needed to immediately get back in the air. The lesson they'd just had in flight wouldn't mean as much if I let a week go by.

Although I would have preferred to have the 310 to fly over the Atlantic, I had full faith and trust in my single-engine Cessna 182. It would not be nearly as fast—taking an extra forty-five minutes to get there—but with a few extra empty Gatorade bottles, the flight would be fine.

When I drove up to the house, the dogs greeted me at the truck. As was my daily routine, I tossed them each a treat from a bag I kept in the side of the door. I grabbed my flight bag and was walking up the sidewalk toward the house when I saw the door swing open. I walked a few more steps, and when no one came out, I stopped, thinking something wasn't right. That is when I saw a long bare leg appear, moving suggestively as if it belonged to a dancer in a cabaret. Then the leg was hooked around the frame of the door, sliding seductively up and down.

For the life of me—as much as I try to get Aubrey to do more things like that—I don't know why I opened my mouth and said what I said next. I knew I was about to blow any chance of a romantic evening, but there was nothing I could do about it. It was part of my DNA to be a smart-ass when the opportunity arose.

"Ms. Myrtle, is that you?" I yelled toward the door. Ms. Myrtle was sneaking up on eighty and had been my housekeeper before Aubrey and I got married. Aubrey knew Ms. Myrtle and loved her. She was the sweetest elderly lady and loved to take care of me.

The leg immediately shot back inside the door, and a second later, a hand with an extended middle finger took its place. I started laughing so hard I fell to the sidewalk on my knee. When Aubrey called me a name I won't repeat and then slammed the door, I had to sit down because I couldn't breathe. I thought I was going to hyperventilate. With all the stress from the week, a good laugh was exactly what I needed.

I finally picked myself up and walked to the house. But when I reached the door, it was locked. Knowing I should stop, I continued with my fun while banging on the door.

"Please let me in, Ms. Myrtle. Please!" I got so tickled at myself I had to lean against the door.

Aubrey flung the door open and tried to give me her best angry look, but it only lasted for a second. Then she was laughing so hard I think she peed in her pants. We were both in tears, and it was the medicine we needed.

"I'll have to admit that was a good one," said Aubrey, "and I hope it was worth it, because there is no way I can do what I had planned while thinking about Ms. Myrtle."

As we walked into the house, I dumped my flight bag on the couch. Then I pulled her close, and she gave me a quick kiss on the lips. I pulled her even closer, hoping I might still salvage the romantic interlude I'd blown.

But she leaned back and shook her head. "You smell like an airplane, and Ms. Myrtle has supper to prepare. Go take a shower," she said, pushing me toward the bedroom.

When I was finished with my shower and walked into the kitchen, the aroma took me back to a time years before. My mother, who was one of ten children, grew up during the depression, just on the edge of poverty. Her family could not afford to buy vegetables at the market and had to get by on whatever they could grow and find.

One of the leafy vegetables they ate was a wild plant called pokeweed. It grew mostly on fence lines and on the sides of roads. Although my mother claimed it had high nutritional value and swore it was why none of the family ever got sick, she insisted it had to be boiled three times or it could make whoever ate it deathly ill. I always wondered who, after the first person got sick from eating it and almost died, said, "Let's just boil it more and try again."

Maybe it was the intrigue of the story, but I always looked forward to the spring, when it would grow in the empty lot across the street from our house. I would pick as much as I could, and, together with my mother, I would boil it the required three times.

She always made me be the tester, and she would have fun with that, grabbing the phone playfully, as if to be ready at a moment's notice to call an ambulance. Whenever I came home from college, I could count on seeing pokeweed on the supper table.

She and I were not that close—my two dramatic sisters took up most of her time—but we did have our special kitchen time bonding over our pokeweed.

It was abundant around the farm, and I had been cooking it since my return to Georgia. I had explained to Aubrey that it tasted like spinach, but she would never try it. Her reply was always, "Why not just cook spinach and not take a chance on dying?" It was hard to argue with that, but she knew how much I liked my pokeweed and learned to make it for me.

"Poke salad night, I see." I walked over to the stove and lifted the lid off the pot.

"Yep. Also making chicken and rice, another of your favorites."

"So, you did boil it three times, didn't you?" I teased her with a suspicious look.

"Now, why would you think I wouldn't? You haven't done anything to make me want to get even with you, have you?" She slowly stirred the greens and gave me a sly grin.

"No, no. As far as I know, I'm still the same loving, faithful husband, and if I were to get sick, I could probably no longer give you the long massages that you love. That sure would be a shame." I stretched out my hands and flexed my fingers.

"I actually boiled them an extra time to make sure, so get those hands ready," she said, pointing the spoon at me.

It was Friday evening and date night. I set us up on the coffee table she'd made from the wood of a turn-of-the-century dairy that had fallen into disrepair on the property next to us. It was my turn to pick the movie, and as I was going through the choices, she looked at me with a pinched face. "Is it your week to pick a movie? I thought it was mine."

"Nope, it's my week," I replied smugly, and she shook her head. I was the sappy one in the family and loved a good romance or romantic comedy. If it were left up to her, we would be watching *Die Hard* or *Terminator* or some kind of action-packed movie every week.

But it was my night, and I went with *The Lucky One*, based on a book by Nicholas Sparks.

Settled in on the couch, I sipped on a pinot noir my friend Eric had sent me, and Aubrey drank something called "Vitamin water." We enjoyed our supper and the movie, and then, taking advantage of the cool evening, we ventured out to the deck to have the discussion about me going to Chub Cay to meet Jack Windham.

Underneath a clear sky with millions of stars, we made small talk about the progress of the boys and how I must have gotten something in my eyes toward the end of the movie.

Then she brought up the subject. "Have you made up your mind? Are you going?"

"I think I am. I told Alan and Mitch today I'd be gone for a week, and looking at the weather forecast, it appears the route to the Bahamas will be clear for the next ten days or so."

"So, when do you think you'll leave?"

"I'm thinking this Sunday. It would give me tomorrow to complete the permits and declarations I need to fly to the Bahamas. Is that too soon?"

"No, I kind of figured if you made the decision to go, you wouldn't wait. Do you plan on contacting Jack to let him know you are coming?"

"I'm not sure. It would probably be best, but since that message from him just came out of nowhere, with that guy flying into Sandersville and catching me off guard, I'm thinking I will do the same."

"But what if he's not there? He may have gone back home or taken a trip somewhere."

"Oh, he is there all right, or at least his airplane is. It hasn't been flown in the last five days. I think the last flight, in fact, was when he had his man bring me the letter."

"How do you know that? I didn't know there was a way to track the history of an airplane."

"Well, for the general public, there isn't. There are apps to track an active flight once a flight plan has been filed and the aircraft is in flight, but the FAA does not report information on an aircraft not currently in flight. On the other hand, . . ." I gave her a sly grin.

"So, how do you know?"

I was pretty sure she already knew the answer. "I'll give you one guess," I said.

"Nathan."

"Yep, good ol' Nathan, your former co-conspirator. He checked the FAA records and had the station chief in Nassau check the records in the Bahamas. The airplane hasn't left Chub Cay since it returned from Sandersville. I'm all set for a surprise visit."

"Are you nervous? Have you thought about what you're going to say when you meet him? Also, have you thought about his considerable wealth and how that might come into play? If he only has a short time to live, you know what that might mean. Does he have any other children?"

I had been so preoccupied with the news of the pregnancy, the doctor's visit, and everything else that had been happening, I had not taken the time to do a thorough search on the internet. So far, I had found little info on Jack Windham and not a single picture. I'd also found nothing about him having any children. He must live a very private life, I thought— or know how to keep information off the internet.

"No, I'm not really nervous," I told Aubrey. "I don't have any expectations about how the visit will turn out, and I think *he's* the one who should be nervous, really. He hasn't seen me in thirty years, and this is his one and only chance to reconnect and make things right. He has a lot of explaining to do," I said, taking a sip of wine and staring up into the sky.

"And as for the wealth, I'm not even allowing myself to think about that. I don't want any part of it, and I'm sure he has already made plans to settle his estate. For all I know, he has ten kids out there who are set up to inherit everything."

"Maybe so, but estates and wills can be changed in a quick minute, and I would be surprised if you're not in the will. He's followed you your whole life, so it would only make sense that you would be included." She paused to look me in the eye. "You'd better be prepared for something like that, Colby. Whether it would be a good thing or a bad thing, it is certainly a possibility," she said.

"All I want is to meet him and have a conversation, nothing more. I may do that and only stay for a day or so," I replied, getting up from my chair. "As for now, why don't we go home and call it a night? I'm thinking after watching that movie tonight, *you* might be the lucky one." I gave her a wink, and she gave me an eye roll—but she did not give me a no.

Chapter Sixteen

After planning my flight to the Bahamas on Saturday, I got up early Sunday morning and was ready to head to the airport for the flight to Chub Cay. I didn't want to wake Aubrey, but I knew she would be mad as hell if I left without saying goodbye. I made a full pot of coffee and poured it into the thermos I had borrowed from the Cayman Islands hotel on our honeymoon. Aubrey claims I stole it, but I have good intentions of one day returning it.

I went to our bedroom and rubbed on her until she stirred. "It's time to leave. I'll call you as soon as I get to Fort Lauderdale. Are you sure you'll be okay?" I whispered, trying not to wake her up all the way.

"What time is it?" she asked in a sleepy voice.

"It's five o'clock. Give me a kiss and go back to sleep." I leaned down and kissed her.

She kissed me back sleepily and said, "I'll be fine. Call me before you leave Florida, and please be careful, Colby."

"I will." I gave her another kiss and slipped out of the room.

I spoke to the dogs on the way out, but it was too early for them, and they didn't move or bother to reply.

Shortly after that, I arrived at the airport and parked my truck next to the hangar. It was still dark, and the illuminated runway and taxi lights gave the airport an air of mystery. I opened the hangar, turned on the lights, and hit the button to raise the large hangar door. Then I carefully eased the Cessna 182 around the 310 and out of the hangar. I pointed it toward the taxiway, and, after loading my suitcase and flight bag, I was ready to go.

Before climbing into the airplane, I had one last thing to do. I strapped into the back seat of the 310 an eight-by-ten framed picture of me standing in front of the airplane. Aubrey had taken it the day we bought the airplane. I left a note saying, "I will be watching you two."

After closing and locking everything up, I did a preflight inspection of the exterior and then jumped in and thoroughly went through the checklist. I wanted to make sure everything checked out. Especially since I would be flying over the Everglades and then a couple hours over the Atlantic.

With everything in proper order, I did an engine run-up then taxied to runway thirteen. Lined up on the centerline, I announced my departure and gave it full throttle. The 182 did not launch like the 310 with its two engines, but I was airborne by midfield.

Climbing to two thousand feet, I checked all the gauges and my airspeed. I then turned to a heading of 140 degrees and climbed to seventy-five hundred feet. I was thinking I could probably make it all the way to Fort Lauderdale, but if I were to have an emergency, I might be cutting it too close with fuel. I decided it would be best to land and refuel in Daytona Beach. It was a three-hour flight to Daytona, and I had a little over four hours of fuel.

With everything set, I settled back in the seat, poured a cup of coffee from the pilfered thermos, and set the XM radio to a soft jazz station.

Looking outside, I could see golden rays of sun just rising over the horizon. As I made my way farther south, across Georgia and into Florida, rivers meandered through the scene below me, carving their way through the landscape from their distant beginnings in the mountains in search of the ocean.

As I settled in, an expanse of swamps, marshes, came into view. Although man has tried to drain and develop portions of it, its daunting size and harsh environment make it mostly uninhabitable, and hopefully that will keep it safe for centuries to come.

With the winds in my favor, I made it to Daytona in a little less than three hours. I probably had enough fuel to make Fort Lauderdale, but with my Gatorade bottles full, it was probably prudent that I stop.

The tower announced that I was clear to land, so I lined up on runway seven–left and began descending. About a hundred feet from the ground, a strong gust of wind pushed the airplane up and sideways. The stall-warning alarm blared, signaling the airplane was going too slow to continue flying. Suddenly, instead of looking down the runway, I was seeing the control tower through my side windshield.

As they should have, my instincts kicked in, and I quickly pushed the yoke forward and added power to break the stall. With my rudder pedals, I crabbed the nose sideways about twenty degrees to align the airplane back on the runway. Within seconds, the airplane made contact with the runway. As I had been trying to explain to Alan and Mitch, that is how quickly things can go wrong.

Safe on the ground, I taxied to a small, private FBO at the end of the field and was met by the fuel truck. The attendant waved flags to direct me to the parking area. When he had me where he wanted, he raised and crossed the flags, holding them in place until I had safely shut the engine down. I then turned off the switches and stepped out of the airplane. The attendant was about my age and was dressed more like a flight instructor than a fuel worker.

As happened at my airport, the aircraft owners and instructors, it would seem, helped with those kinds of duties.

"Top it off?" he asked. I had not requested fuel from the FBO, but I guessed the way to sell it was to approach all incoming aircraft with the offer.

"Yes, fill it up. It should be close to empty."

As he was preparing to fuel, he noticed the newly dated permits adhered to the side of the window. "Headed to the Bahamas?"

I replied that I was. I told him it was my first trip there and asked him for any advice he could give.

"Keep your altitude at fifty-five hundred feet or lower. As the day warms up, the winds can get wicked above that. And, of course, as I'm sure you know, your route is notorious for the sudden appearance of thunderstorms, so keep an eye out for them." He rolled up the fuel hose.

"I will. Thanks for the advice."

After settling my fuel bill and taking a much-needed trip to the bathroom, I was back in the air and set my compass and GPS for Fort Lauderdale.

It was a short hour to my destination as I took in views of the ocean. Just before arriving, I contacted approach control, gave them my position, and requested permission to land. They issued me a squawk code, allowing them to locate my aircraft on their radar, and then gave me a directional heading for the final approach to the runway.

That landing, thankfully, was a little less dramatic than Daytona. The winds were straight down the runway, and after a smooth, uneventful set-down, I taxied to my prearranged spot at Signature Aviation. Just as in Daytona, the attendant guided me to my parking spot and signaled me to shut down the engine. The fuel truck was pulling up as I stepped out of the airplane; the driver would be disappointed I just needed topping off.

Inside the FBO, I found the flight-planning room, where I could check the weather and file a flight plan to Chub Cay. I pulled up the weather along my route, and, just as the flight instructor in Daytona had warned, there was an AIRMET issued for moderate to severe turbulence at about seven thousand feet and thunderstorms along my route. I could feel a little tightness in my stomach at the thought of what might lie ahead—possible inclement weather over the ocean in a single-engine airplane. If I had taken the 310, I could have made the flight in half the time and had the speed to avoid the possible bad weather.

I chose a lower altitude and a path that currently seemed to be clear of the convective activity. My flight plan would take me directly to Chub Cay, but I would be flying over Nassau and could make a landing there if needed due to weather. Plus, I had a raft and all the safety equipment I would need if I had to ditch the airplane.

With everything in order, I could feel my stomach grumbling, and it was time for a late breakfast or an early lunch, depending on what the airport café was serving. On the other side of the wall was the café, and for some reason—probably some bureaucratic nonsense having to do with codes—they did not have a door connecting the FBO and café. So, I left the FBO, walked twenty feet to my right, and entered the café. There did not appear to be any waitstaff, so I placed my order for a double cheeseburger, French fries, and a Coke at the counter. A pleasant lady handed me a cup for the Coke and said she would bring my order to my table when it was ready. While I was sitting at the table, watching the activities on the tarmac, my phone rang; it was Aubrey.

"I see you are at the airport café," she said when I answered. "I hope you are not eating from the vending machine or having anything that's fried." Her tone was accusatory.

I looked around the room for cameras but didn't see any. I was about to ask her how she knew I was at the café, but then I remembered we had Google location sharing.

"So, you're spying on me, huh? Well, if you must know, you are interrupting my lunch, which consists of a dressing-free tofu salad with extra sprigs and stems and gluten-free crackers. And I'm drinking one of those Vitamin waters. Aren't you proud of me?" I asked as the lady approached the table with my order. The grease had already soaked through the wrapper of the double cheeseburger.

"You're so full of it. I know you are having a cheeseburger, fries, and a Coke. Liar!" she replied.

Once again, I looked for cameras. "I am hurt that you would think I would lie to you. It's that kind of accusation that would make me seek the solace of the double cheeseburger, fries, and large Coke that you speak of. You have brought this upon yourself." I worked some hurt into my voice.

I heard her try to stifle a laugh. "You are such a child! When are you leaving Fort Lauderdale? How is the weather?"

"I'm all fueled up and should be wheels-up in about half an hour. The weather is about what you would expect between here and the Bahamas. I think I've picked a route that will keep me clear of the thunderstorms. What are you up to?"

"The dogs and I are at the shop, and I'm thinking about driving to Augusta to spend a few days with my mom. Dad is at the river house doing repairs, and you know how she can't stand to be alone."

"I know. I'm sure she'd love having you around. Maybe you can tell her about the letter and why I'm flying to the Bahamas. Depending on how things go, we'll have to tell everyone, I guess. We might as well start with her."

"Speaking of telling everyone, your sister called and asked me to do a project for their cabin remodel. She asked where you were, and before I thought about it, I told her you were flying to the Bahamas. And of course, she asked why. I told her you were meeting some friends for a fishing trip. I hated not telling her the truth. I think as soon as you get back, you need to tell them."

"I know. I really haven't given it much thought." I looked at my cheeseburger, which was getting cold. I needed to eat and get in the air. "Hey, look, my tofu salad is beginning to wilt, and I need to get airborne soon. I'll call or text you, depending on the service, when I get there. I love you," I said, ready to get off the phone.

"I love you too, and don't forget to call as soon as you land—and be careful."

I had just taken the cheeseburger out of the wrapper and was hungrily going in for a huge bite when the phone rang again.

With a sigh, I put down the cheeseburger and picked up the phone. I saw it was Nathan. Whatever could he want?

"I see you're having lunch in Fort Lauderdale," he said. "I figured you would be in the air by now. I hope you have thoroughly checked the weather; there are some mean-looking thunderstorms in the direction you'll be heading in."

I shook my head and rolled my eyes. He was the last person I'd expect to be checking on my whereabouts. "So, you have nothing better to do on Sunday morning than to check your phone to see where I am," I teased.

He laughed, and I knew Aubrey had probably sent him a text and put him up to it.

"I just wanted to see that you are eating a healthy meal and not waiting too late to get started on your trip," he said.

"I've had enough of you two today. I'll give you the whole rundown when I get back. Stay out of trouble while I'm gone. I know how easy it is for you to get involved in something that I end up having to fix."

"Have a great trip. I can't wait to hear how it goes. Be safe."

"Sure will; take care." I said, hanging up.

My cheeseburger and fries were cold, so I wrapped them up in the tray, deciding I would eat them on the way. I refilled my Coke and headed for the airplane.

Soon, I had cleared customs and departed Fort Lauderdale. Climbing to my initial altitude of one thousand feet, I contacted Miami Center and opened my flight plan. It took about seven minutes to climb to my cruising altitude of fifty-five hundred feet. As I went through the checklist, everything looked good, so I set the autopilot for Chub Cay. Barring any diversions around towering cumulus thunderstorms, I had about an hour and a half to think about what awaited me.

With so much time alone to think, I was hit with second thoughts about surprising Jack Windham with my visit. Yes, he had surprised *me* at the airport in Sandersville; the sudden arrival of the man in the blue suit had brought with it quite a shock. But still, I'd had the choice of reading the letter at my convenience with time to process what I'd read.

And now here I was, showing up unannounced. What if he was having a bad week with his illness and was unable to see me? Or he could be away on a fishing trip or visiting another island. I probably should have listened to Aubrey and contacted him before flying to the island. If he was away, I wasn't sure I'd have an opportunity to return.

Assuming he was there, I wondered what kind of shape I'd find him in. Had his health deteriorated to the point we would have to get acquainted with me by his bedside? I hoped not. I wanted the opportunity to be angry if that was what I felt. I wanted to be able to ask him some tough questions and demand some answers. But if he was sick and feeble, I would not put that on him.

Was this going to be a kind of formal thing? Us meeting in his office with him dressed in a suit at one end of a table and me sitting at the other? Or would we maybe meet at a café, somewhere comfortable, and have the heart-to-heart that I felt we needed. All these questions and more were flooding into my mind when I got a call on the radio: "7175Quebec, Nassau approach."

I looked at my GPS and could not believe that more than an hour had passed. I was only thirty miles from Chub Cay. I could not remember ever looking out the window—and I never did get to that cheeseburger.

"Nassau approach, 7175Quebec," I called back.

"75Quebec, we have you twenty-five miles southwest of Chub Cay. Please announce when you have the airport in sight," instructed the controller.

"Will report field in sight, 75Quebec," I answered. Looking out my window, I could see Andros Island on my right, and just past that were The Exumas. Nassau was tucked in between them and just off my nose.

According to my GPS, I would be arriving in fifteen minutes. I went through my checklist and set up for landing. About five miles out, I could just see Chub Cay on the horizon. About three miles out, I could identify the airport and canceled my flight plan.

Before entering the landing pattern, I circled the airfield to get my bearings. Looking down, I could see the Gulfstream G650 jet. It was the largest aircraft on the field. Knowing he was there made everything suddenly seem real. I could feel the bees swarming in my stomach, thinking that within minutes, I would be on the ground. Soon I would meet the man who claimed to be my biological father.

CHAPTER SEVENTEEN

Aubrey set the phone on the table in her shop and laughed. Colby wouldn't know a tofu salad if it were put in front of him, and he certainly wouldn't eat it.

She poured a cup of coffee and took in her surroundings. The shop was her peaceful place, and Sunday morning was her favorite time of the week. Colby and a few of the older pilots usually met for coffee and talked flying on Sunday mornings, which gave her some time alone. The dogs would join her as she lounged around the shop, lazily working on a project. Or she might just sit on the porch overlooking the pond and drink hot tea or coffee.

Part of her routine was to turn the radio on at eleven o'clock and listen to one of Colby's childhood friends who was the pastor of the Crawfordville Baptist Church. His subject that Sunday morning was acceptance, and he used The Serenity Prayer as part of his message. Written by a theologian in the early twentieth century, the prayer is a petition to God for peace and tranquility in all matters of life. It asks for strength and courage when making decisions, and for acceptance when things are outside our control.

Listening to the message, Aubrey felt tears welling up. She put down her paintbrush and walked to the window. She thought about all the things happening in her life and rubbed her hand across her stomach. She knew things were in motion that she couldn't change. She thought back at the anger she had felt when Colby pointed that out in his prayer. But now she understood she might have to put into practice the "acceptance" part of the famous prayer if things didn't go her way. Although she felt in her core that the baby was going to be okay, she wasn't fooling herself that there were not risks.

Wiping her eyes and holding on to the windowsill, she knelt and prayed for the courage and strength to accept whatever the outcome might be. She felt her little girl move inside her, and in those movements, Aubrey sensed a strength and vitality that settled her anxious heart. A peace washed over her as she finished her prayer. Everything would work out the way it was supposed to—and Aubrey and Colby would face that unknown together.

After the emotional morning, it was time to head back to the house with the dogs. She'd promised her mother she would be in Augusta in time for supper, but she still had to finish a few things around the house. Just as she walked inside, her cell phone rang.

It was her mom. "Hey darling, have you left yet? I'm so excited to see you and can't wait until you get here."

"Not yet. I just finished up at the shop and am about to jump in the shower and head that way after I finish up some things. Can I pick up anything?"

"No, just hurry up and get here, but be careful driving. I have a whole evening planned for us, and I'm going to fix your favorite meal tonight."

"Sounds great, and I'll see you in a bit. Also, I have a very interesting story to tell you."

Aubrey showered and after loading up the Jeep with her bags and the three dogs, she was ready to leave for Augusta. She had just left the house when her mom called her back. "Hey, there's been a change of plans. I was just talking to your dad, and he is not happy that you're coming to Augusta while he is in Jewell. He said he didn't know Colby was out of town and that you were coming to see me. Of course, I told him, but he never listens and is now pouting that you and I are getting together without him. Do you mind if we meet in Jewell instead?" Aubrey's parents had moved from Jewell back to Augusta after they retired, but her dad still spent most of his time at the river house.

"Of course not. That will be fine. I know you had the weekend planned for us, but we know how Dad can pout. Also, what I want to tell you Dad needs to hear as well. It's quite a story, and you may want to bring a couple bottles of wine. Are you ready to leave?"

"Yes, most of what I need is there, and I'll be out the door in ten minutes. It shouldn't take me more than an hour."

"Okay. I may stop by Hamburg State Park and let the dogs go for a swim. Drive safe, and don't be in a hurry. I'll see you soon."

"See you in a bit."

It took Aubrey about twenty minutes to get to the park, and when she pulled up, the dogs began to twist and bark. They knew exactly where they were. When Aubrey opened the hatch door, they flew across the grass like they'd been shot out of a cannon. Their favorite thing was to chase the ducks. So far, there had not been a single duck caught, and they probably wouldn't know what to do if they caught one.

Aubrey watched the ducks, who always seemed to enjoy—or at least be amused by—the game. The ducks would lead the dogs out into the lake, swimming in circles just a few feet in front of their pursuers, quacking and teasing them. She laughed, thinking the ducks were having as much fun as the dogs.

After half an hour of swimming, barking, and quacking, it was over. The ducks flew back to the bank, and the dogs followed, out of breath. Aubrey fed them snacks and no longer interested in the ducks, they found some shade underneath a big oak tree.

Giving the dogs time to rest and get dry before she loaded them back up, Aubrey walked over to the pavilion next to the dam and gristmill. Settling into a swing facing the pond, she thought about all the weekends her family had spent at the park fishing, boating, and having picnics. She thought back to when she and Colby were teenagers. Colby's family had come down from Atlanta one weekend to help her mom put on the spring Dogwood Festival at the park. They'd set up a welcome booth at the pavilion, and she and Colby were in charge of selling tickets and handing out information.

After the festival, Colby's family, along with his sisters' boyfriends, all came back to the river house. While the kids spent the afternoon jumping off the rock that hung over the river, the parents sat on the porch and shared stories about their two different worlds, comparing city life to living in the country. It was the only time the two families ever got together, and she smiled at the memory. It had been a magical day and one full of fun, laughter, and innocence.

She thought about the thirty years that separated that bright day and now. She had gotten married right out of college to a guy she'd only dated her senior year. Other than Colby, she had never dated or been with another guy. When he asked her to marry him, life seemed to be falling into place the way it was supposed to—graduation, marriage, family. But in less than a year, it all fell apart. He was offered a job in New York and wanted to take it. Aubrey was just starting her teaching career and wasn't ready to move. In the end, he chose to go, and Aubrey chose to stay. After a heart-to-heart, they both understood they had jumped into the marriage without enough thought and didn't have the same goals and visions for the future.

After the failed marriage, she put her energy into her career as an art teacher at the middle school in Madison, and the next twenty-plus years seemed to go by in a blur. She had a few relationships but nothing serious. Now, she rarely thought about her life before she and Colby reconnected. She couldn't remember the last time she talked to a friend from those days. She didn't like to admit to herself that during all those years, she'd felt something was missing. But maybe—on some subconscious level—she had been waiting for him.

What if they had never reconnected and he had married someone else? What if Colby had never moved back to Madison? How many people go through their lives just hoping someone will come back, someone will change their mind? A lifetime is a long time to carry a love for someone who might never feel the same for you.

Which illustrates the wisdom of The Serenity Prayer, which tells us what we must do: accept the things we cannot change, find the courage to change the things we can, and seek the wisdom to understand the difference.

Aubrey realized she had been at the park for almost an hour, and she figured her mom should already be in Jewell. She loaded up the dogs and made the ten-minute drive to the house.

As she pulled up the driveway, she was greeted with smiles and waves from her parents. When she opened the Jeep door, the dogs piled out, racing to the porch, wiggling for affection. So far it was a perfect day, and the only thing missing was Colby.

Chapter Eighteen

I lined up for runway eleven and announced to the controller I was on final approach. After I canceled my flight plan with Nassau Center, I was turned over to the local frequency that handled communications for the private airfield.

"Welcome to Chub Cay, Mr. Cameron. After landing, please taxi to the FBO, where an attendant will guide you to a parking space and take care of you from there." The pleasant voice coming over the radio had a Caribbean-island accent. I had been flying for almost thirty years, and this was the first time I had ever been personally greeted.

After an uneventful landing, I taxied to the FBO and noticed a long line of private jets. None of the aircraft had propellers other than my airplane and two identical Beechcraft Barons that had decals on the doors and were probably used as an island shuttle service. The jets certainly spoke to the wealth of clientele who were visiting or owned property on the island, but none of the jets compared in size or grandeur to Jack Windham's Gulfstream 650.

When I reached the terminal, three sharply dressed attendants in white uniforms guided me to a parking spot near the 650. My airplane looked like a gnat pulled up next to it. As I shut the airplane down, I noticed a black Suburban parked next to the hangar. I could see the driver had on dark sunglasses and was watching me. Normally, someone watching me from a black Suburban would set off alarms. But I had an idea who was in the vehicle, and it wasn't the government. It was most likely a security detail for the island's resort or Jack Windham.

The smiling attendants met me at the door and were quick to greet me and welcome me to the island. They retrieved my bags from the luggage compartment and led me to the FBO. Once inside the terminal, the first person I saw was the man in the blue suit. Although today he was dressed in a tan linen suit with an open-collar white shirt, still looking as professional as he had at the Sandersville airport.

"Good morning, Mr. Cameron. I hope you had a good flight, and welcome to Chub Cay," he told me warmly.

"I did. Thank you. And why am I not surprised to see you here?"

He gave me a smile and a little laugh. "Mr. Windham has been tracking for active flight plans for both your airplanes since I delivered the letter. He wasn't sure if he would receive a formal reply to his invitation, and he wanted to be prepared if you decided to pay him a visit." With a look of slight amusement, he asked,

"How did you know Mr. Windham would be here? Did you call ahead and inquire with the hotel, or did you just take a chance?"

I could tell by his tone that he knew I had not called the hotel. I suspected if anyone ever called inquiring about Jack Windham's whereabouts, someone from his staff would be immediately informed.

It was time for me to have a little fun and be mysterious myself. "First, so I can stop thinking of you as the man in the blue suit—and now the tan suit—maybe it's time we formally meet."

He approached and offered his hand. "Of course. I apologize for my rudeness. I should have introduced myself when we met in Sandersville, but I was so struck by the resemblance between you and Mr. Windham that I forgot my manners. My name is Charles Westcott."

I shook his hand and continued with my answer. "As for how I knew Mr. Windham would be here, I did not call the hotel or make an inquiry with anyone on the island. Let's just say your boss is not the only one with the ability to keep track of someone." I gave him a slight grin.

He folded his arms, leaned back on the counter, and said, "Touché, Mr. Cameron. Like father, like son."

His comment took me off guard and made me feel a little uncomfortable, since in my mind, Jack Windham was not my father.

I think Westcott sensed that, and he changed the subject. "I know you've had a long flight and would probably like to get settled in and freshen up. Please allow me to show you to your quarters." He motioned toward the door.

I had not given much thought to where I was going to stay. I knew there was a hotel on the island, but I had no way of knowing if there were any vacancies. But I also had an idea, since I had been invited, that if Jack was there, I would have a place to stay.

Outside, parked in front of the FBO was a long red golf cart with shiny chrome wheels. It was fully customized to resemble a limousine. The attendants had already loaded my bags and were waiting with the doors open. Charles motioned for me to sit in the back. It was the first golf cart I had ever seen that had leather seats and air conditioning. Charles took a seat up front and instructed the driver to take us to the resort.

We left the airport and meandered down a pathway on a bed of broken and crushed shells lined with perfectly groomed palm trees. The trip from the airport to the resort was about ten minutes.

Arriving, we pulled up to a courtyard, where a wide circular set of marble steps led to a pair of doors whose wood looked old and weathered. The whole courtyard was surrounded by bougainvillea, palms, and cypress trees along with a myriad of other low-growing tropical plants. There was a slight cool breeze blowing across the grounds, just as one would expect. The three-story resort felt alive.

Before I could take it all in, the attendants had my door open, had already removed my bags, and were gently ushering me to the lobby.

Inside the foyer, the first thing that caught my attention was a large inlaid mineral and stone compass in the marble floor. It symbolized the navigational device that had guided mariners and pilots for as long as men and women had taken to the air and the sea. With points for all four cardinal directions as well as the degrees in between, it was expertly done.

Past the foyer were high ceilings bordered by extensive trim leading to a dining room and bar. The back wall was all windows. Heavy white cotton drapes were pulled open, showcasing a perfect view of the ocean and beach as well as an infinity pool that was connected to an outside bar. It was approaching noon, and I noticed there seemed to be more attendants and waitstaff than guests. The guests in the dining-room bar and pool area were mostly well-dressed ladies and children. Most of the men, I assumed, were fishing.

To my left was the check-in counter, where Charles was quietly talking to a smiling lady who appeared to be a native of the island. When I approached, she welcomed me to the resort and handed me a heavy brass key ring decorated with an image of the compass rose. I took the key and thanked her.

Also on the left, past the check-in counter, was a large ornate spiral staircase, and next to that was the elevator. I was about to move toward the elevator when one of the attendants pointed me toward the door instead. We walked back to the limo golf cart, where the chauffeur was waiting to help me to my seat. I was apparently not staying at the main hotel.

We pulled away and took a cart path through a tunnel of palm trees. After a few turns, we came upon a private cove, where a cabana overlooked the turquoise ocean with sandy beaches spreading out into the distance. It could be—and probably had been—the inspiration for a painting.

The cabana was styled differently than the hotel. It was constructed of stucco and had a really cool cantilevered sloped terracotta roof. It had an intimate covered porch surrounded by tropical plants and trees. The porch was furnished with tasteful white wicker sofas with floral cushions and a swing that faced the ocean.

The chauffeur stopped the cart, and the attendant unloaded my bags and took them into the cabana. This must be, I decided, where Mr. Windham lived. But I soon learned I was wrong.

Charles led me inside, and the interior was just as impressive as the outside. The ceilings were high and vaulted with slow-moving wicker ceiling fans cooling the area below. The walls were cream-colored shiplap, and the floor featured multicolored Mexican tile. Windows took up most of the wall space, allowing expansive views of the ocean, and the living room flowed into the kitchen to make one large open space.

I followed the attendant as he took my bags to the master bedroom, and it was just as amazing as the rest of the cabana. All I could think of was how much Aubrey would enjoy staying there. I thought if all went well, maybe I could return with her for a visit. Maybe a second honeymoon since, thanks to Nathan, the one in the Caymans was cut short.

With the bags put away, we walked back to the den. Charles showed me to the bar and told me to make myself at home. He said Oscar, the chauffeur, would be back at seven fifteen to pick me up for dinner.

Dress would be casual, he said. I was not sure what that meant and didn't want to ask. Casual in my world would be shorts and a

T-shirt. In their world, I imagined it meant slacks, a linen collared shirt, and an ascot. Fortunately, I had brought two of the three. Since no one had mentioned Jack Windham, I assumed Oscar was picking me up to join him for dinner. If the meeting, in fact, was going to be that night, I decided I needed a long nap. I should really be well rested for what could turn out to be an epic evening.

CHAPTER NINETEEN

I woke around six o'clock, well rested but also feeling a bit anxious. I went to the bar and poured a glass of wine. Then I sat in a rocker gazing at the beach and the ocean, thinking how much Aubrey would love the cabana and Chub Cay. That is when I almost spilled my drink, jumping up to run and grab my phone from my flight bag. I had been supposed to call her when I got there.

Pulling my phone out, I saw she had called three times and sent a string of text messages. Taking a deep breath, I took my wine back to the porch and called her. She answered on the first ring.

"Hey, how are you?" I asked in a cheerful voice.

My greeting was met with silence before she finally spoke. "I'm waiting for a story about how you had to land in the middle of the Atlantic and were miraculously saved by a pod of dolphins that *just now* brought you to safety—which is why this call is eight hours late." She did not sound cheerful.

"Oh my God, that is *exactly* what happened! Has it already made the news?" I knew I was digging a bigger hole.

But in the silence that came after, I thought I heard a snicker. "You are such an ass! Why haven't you called me? I've been worried sick."

"Oh, Aubrey, I'm so sorry. I was so exhausted from the flight—and the anticipation—that I lay down for just a minute. Or that was the plan, and I've been out six hours. I just woke up and was about to get in the shower. I'm being picked up in about an hour to meet Jack for dinner, and I'm a bit nervous. Can you forgive me?"

"I am willing to forgive you if you call me first thing in the morning and give me a full account of the evening."

"Deal. I will call and give you every detail. How are things going with your mom? Are you two having fun?"

"Our plans changed, and I'm at the river house with Mom and Dad both. He was upset he wasn't going to get to see his lovely daughter and asked us to come to Jewell," she replied, laughing.

"I think the man is getting soft in his old age. Why would he want to sit around and listen to the two of you gossip and complain? He could be fishing with your cousin Jay or having a beer down at Ms. Jean's."

"Okay, I'm not missing you as much anymore. Go get ready to meet Jack. Don't drink too much, and call me in the morning. I love you—even though you are a nut!"

"Well, I'm your special nut, and I sure wish you were here. This place is amazingly beautiful, and if I get the chance, I want to bring you to this cabana I'm staying in and make up for our honeymoon. And we will promise each other not to tell Nathan where we are this time. Well, I'm headed to the shower, and we'll talk in the morning. I love you, my little artist."

After my shower, I pulled out a pair of blue linen slacks and a mauve button-down shirt. (The mauve had been Aubrey's idea.) I'd also brought a pair of Sperry Top-Siders on the recommendation of a friend who has a boat. Apparently, those were the shoes that boat people wore. I dressed, checked myself out in the mirror, and decided I would at least not look out of place.

Hearing the golf-cart limo arrive, I pulled the letter from my flight bag, thinking for some reason I might need it, and stuffed it in my back pocket.

Oscar was waiting in the golf cart that probably cost more than my truck. There were no attendants this time, so I sat in the back, and Oscar pulled onto a path that seemed to be taking us in the direction of the marina. As we got closer to the harbor, I could see lines of fishing boats and yachts waiting in their berths. Many of the fishing boats had flags hanging high from the lines on their fishing towers, indicating the types of fish that have been caught. I remembered reading years ago that if the fish flag was upside down, the fish had been released. With most of these fishermen being in it for the sport, all the sailfish flags were upside down, and other than a few tuna flags, so were the others.

Oscar stopped at the entrance of the main pier, which was about twenty feet wide and led to the side docks. Now that it was evening, it appeared most of the fishermen were back from a day on the water, and there was a flurry of activity as they washed down the boats, unloaded coolers, and secured the fishing gear for the next day. Soon, I heard a golf cart pull in behind us and turned to see Charles. He told me to wait there for a few minutes as he headed down toward the end of the pier.

Oscar bade me a good evening, said he would pick me up later, and pulled away. I wandered down the pier a bit and found a fisherman who seemed to know how to end a day of fishing. He was sitting in an oversized rocker, pouring vodka into a large Yeti container and then mixing in a pack of something pink. He then pulled a large cigar from a portable humidor. We made eye contact as he lit it.

"Catch anything?" I asked, having noticed there were no flags flying on his boat.

He completed the process of properly lighting his cigar with a device that did not look like a lighter. "We caught a few. We stayed inshore and deep lined for strawberry grouper and flounder. The marlin and sailfish have been a bit finicky, and it's been hit or miss. My captain is up at the grill preparing them. You are welcome to pull up a chair and join us."

I looked up the hill to see several people standing around a community grill. It seemed like a great way of life: fish all day, eat fresh at the boat with your friends, and have a drink and a cigar.

"Thanks for the offer. It sounds like a great evening, but I'm here to meet someone." I looked down the pier for Charles.

"Oh, okay." He took a puff of his cigar and a pull from his Yeti. I could feel the questions coming.

"I'm assuming you flew in, since we know everybody that makes a move in this harbor," he said, laughing with a few of his friends who had joined us. "And you don't look like a fisherman. I don't mean that the wrong way, but you look more like a yachtsman, especially with those shoes." He let out a little chuckle.

I knew then I had guessed wrong on the "island casual," at least with the fishermen. Most of them were wearing Crocs or rubber boots.

"You assume correctly. I did fly in this morning, and I am neither a fisherman nor a yachtsman. But I think I could get used to being either one, especially at the end-of-the-day festivities," I replied, then asked, "Do most of you live here on the island or just stay on your boats?" I wanted to get an idea about whether Jack Windham was a resident or lived on his boat, which I assumed was at the end of the pier.

He laughed again and looked over at his friends, who had pulled up chairs with their own drinks. "Not many people live on the island except for the ones who own it," he replied. "There are, of course, places for the staff to stay, but those are just for them to rent while they're working on the island. You can stay at the resort if there are vacancies, but other than during hurricane season, that rarely happens. Most people make their reservations well in advance, and then it helps to know someone to get one.

We rent berths and stay on our boats as long as they will let us. If a big tournament comes to town and we're not fishing in it, we usually go to Nassau for a few days and then return. This is some of the best marlin and sailfish fishing in the world, and it doesn't come easily or cheap."

He looked around at his friends for confirmation, and they nodded. I wondered if these people had jobs or if they were wealthy and just fished all the time. I had no idea the price of any of the boats in the marina, but I could only imagine they started at somewhere around a million.

"Who did you say you were here to see?" my new friend in the rocker asked.

I saw no reason not to tell him. "Jack Windham."

One of the fishermen let out a long whistle.

"Well, now I know why you're dressed the way you are. Jack Windham is one of the few people who can do what he wants—when he wants—on this island. In case you didn't know, about thirty years ago, Chub had only one small inn and limited amenities for those who came to fish. It was still the place to be because of its access to the fishing lanes. Nassau, though, was becoming more commercial and was trying to pull all the wealthy people with yachts and big fishing boats from Chub."

He paused for a sip of vodka. "After a while, the island became almost abandoned," he continued. "I'm not sure how Mr. Windham got involved, but he and a few of his oil friends from Texas acted pretty quickly. They built the resort, and they built the airport. They expanded the harbor, too, and they built these piers and docks. They brought in the best chefs and staff, and it didn't take long for the wealthy to come back. They were looking for more privacy and less congestion than they got on the cruise lines. Now, it's the most exclusive private island in the Bahamas." He tilted his head to study me. "How do you know Mr. Windham?" He had barely taken a breath during his unsolicited Chub Cay history lesson.

I wasn't prepared to answer his question, so I simply said, "I'm here on business for a few days" then quickly changed the subject. "I apologize, but I don't believe I got your name."

It took him a minute, but he pulled himself up from the depths of his chair and stuck out his hand.

"Toby Cantrell, but my friends call me T. C. If you're going to be here for a few days, you should come out with us one evening. There's a local bar that has live music, and every now and then, it's actually good," he said.

" I'm Colby Cameron and thank you for the offer. If I have time, I may take you up on that," I said just as Charles was walking up.

He nodded at T. C. and his friends and asked me if I was ready. "I see you have met the head of information for the island. Not much gets by T. C. He makes it his job to know about everyone who comes or goes at the marina. If we want to know about anyone, we ask T. C."

CHAPTER TWENTY

T. C. watched as Charles and Colby walked down the pier toward Jack Windham's yacht. He looked at his friends and said,

"If I'm not mistaken, and I never am, Colby Cameron is the spitting image of a young Jack Windham. The picture hanging in the lobby of a younger Jack could be Colby's portrait. Hunter is the only son I've ever met or heard of, and I've known the Windham's for years. I don't think Colby Cameron is meeting Jack for business—unless the business is cashing in on the family fortune. He must have found out the old man is about to die, and now he wants his share." He took a satisfied pull from his cigar.

In a fishing boat a few berths away, Jack Windham's captain was down in the engine bay of his boss's fishing boat. He had some repairs to see to after a fuel leak during an earlier fishing trip. No one knew he was there, and he couldn't help but overhear T. C.'s conversation with this Colby Cameron. He also overheard T. C.'s observations after this newcomer left with Westcott. What he heard disturbed him, and now he couldn't focus on the job.

After a few minutes, he slung down the tools and slipped up top. Looking over the bow, he could see that T. C. and his group had left the dock and were walking toward the grilling pavilion. He waited until they were out of sight before he left the boat. He needed to find out more about this Cameron person.

CHAPTER TWENTY-ONE

After leaving T. C. and his entourage, we walked to the end of the pier, where the largest yacht in the harbor was backed up into probably the best berth at the marina. While all the other boats had to meander through canals to depart the harbor, Jack's boat had a straight shot to the inlet that led to the ocean. One would expect nothing less for the man who, according to T. C., had saved Chub Cay.

About six feet from the yacht, there were candlelit lanterns lined across the pier, blocking anyone from coming any further than the yacht docked next to Jack Windham's. I wondered if he always kept access to his boat blocked, or maybe it was to maintain privacy for this evening only.

Charles instructed me to wait while he let Mr. Windham know I had arrived. While he was gone, I stood back and admired the boat. Not knowing the first thing about boats or yachts, I estimated the "Centauri" to be about a hundred and fifty feet long. But as big as it was, it was sleek and unobtrusive. It had four descending levels or decks, all of them with private balconies that I assumed led to bedroom suites. All the glass was tinted heavily in black, contrasting against the white hull. From my angle on the dock, I could not quite tell, but there appeared to be a helicopter pad two levels above the bow. There wasn't a helicopter parked there, but the tall orange windsock above the area could have no other purpose. The back of the yacht was halfway covered by the second level. Underneath was a full bar, a kitchen prep area, and a large lounge with couches, chairs, and tables extending out to the rear of the yacht. I could imagine sitting there while out to sea, having dinner, drinking wine, and listening to jazz or maybe big band music while gazing at the heavens. Or catching the last glimpse of a sunset with a cool ocean breeze blowing across the stern.

Charles returned and welcomed me to board the yacht. He said to have a seat anywhere and that Mr. Windham would be out to join me shortly. I was sure he could see my nervousness, and, after a brief pause, he smiled and nodded, as if to assure me everything would be all right. Then he left the boat. And I found a seat that faced the double doors that Jack Windham would soon be walking through.

Waiting, I surveyed the luxury and opulence around me. How surreal it was to be standing in that place. There I was, a guy with a middle-class upbringing on a super yacht of the one-percent variety. Waiting, no less, to meet the man who owned it—and who claimed to be my father.

Then suddenly, the tinted glass doors opened, and my stomach made a quick three loops.

The man who walked out appeared to be of Spanish descent. He was of average height and dressed in a uniform. Introducing himself as Miquel, the bartender, he moved behind the bar and got to work. After a few minutes, he presented me with a drink and said he hoped it met my approval. I took a sip of the old-fashioned, which happened to be my favorite drink. Miquel had made it perfectly with a burnt orange peel rubbed around the rim of the glass, just as I made them at home.

"It's very good. I think someone on this boat has done their homework on my drink of choice," I said with a chuckle.

He laughed and nodded, saying he was glad I liked it. Returning to the bar, he made another drink, set it on the edge of the bar, and disappeared back through the glass doors.

I was enjoying my old-fashioned when the glass doors opened once again. This time it was not the bartender. I stood as Jack Windham approached.

I don't think he was the kind of man who was easily caught off guard, but at that moment, he was. He stopped a few feet short of me and stared. In fact, we both just stood and stared. In most cases, that would have made for an awkward scene, but in this case, it did not.

I felt like I was looking into a mirror at my future self, and, by his expression, I knew he'd just been met by an image of the younger man he used to be.

He walked toward me with his hand extended, and I took his hand in mine.

CHAPTER TWENTY-TWO

Aubrey grabbed her bags from the Jeep, walked to the porch, and then had to wait in line to get any attention from her parents. The dogs squirmed and twisted, competing for head rubs, until one of them caught a whiff of something, and off to the woods they ran.

Aubrey's dad approached her with a big smile and a hug. "Hi, honey. Let me take those," he said, taking her bags and starting toward the house.

"Thanks, Dad. Have you put on some weight?"

Smirking, he stopped and looked at Aubrey and then at his wife with a shake of his head. He knew Aubrey's mother would jump in with a response, which she quickly did.

"See, John? Thank you, Aubrey! He comes out here so he can eat Beanee Weenees, pork rinds, and all kinds of junk food—like honey buns and candy bars—that I won't let him eat at home. I told him I'm going to trade him in if he doesn't start looking after himself," she said with a laugh. Aubrey laughed as well, knowing she'd had the same conversation over and over with Colby.

John and Mary Reese were in their early seventies and had been married for a long and happy forty-eight years. Much like

Aubrey and Colby, they met as teenagers and quickly fell in love. They grew up in a small community on the Savannah River, not far from the Georgia-South Carolina line. After high school, they both went to Atlanta for college.

Mary's heart's desire was to be a mother, and she had wanted a big family. She only attended college because it was more or less expected. Aubrey came along just as planned a couple of years after her parents graduated and got married, but then life got complicated. With John traveling a lot, time just seemed to fly, and along with it went Mary's dreams for a big family. But as it turned out, she and Aubrey were so close that Mary sometimes wondered if she would have had the same bond with any other children who might have come along.

The house in Jewell, which was always referred to as the river house, had belonged to John's parents. It was soon after returning from the South Pacific in World War Two that John's dad had bought the large antebellum home, which was wrapped with long, two-story porches and sat majestically high on a bluff over the Ogeechee River.

Then John took over the maintenance of the house after his parents became unable to take care of those chores. The house, the river, and the woods had been his playground as a kid and his refuge as an adult. He knew how much the home meant to his dad, and he took pride in keeping the property in perfect shape.

As an only child, he inherited the house when his parents passed. At the time, he and Mary were living in Augusta, but with the constant growth, traffic, and congestion, they decided it was time to move to Jewell.

They wanted Aubrey to experience growing up in a small community like they had. They wanted her to meet friends in school who would become friends for life. They wanted her to live in a place that was safe, where she could see the stars at night and have a big open space for all the pets she wanted.

Aubrey had been nine when they approached her with the idea of moving to the country. They won her approval quickly with the words "all the pets you want."

As for work, John was able to transfer to the department of transportation's regional office in Tennille, a town about forty-five minutes from Jewell. Mary took a job at the hospital in Thomson, which was only twenty minutes from the house. Aubrey started school at Briarwood, a private school in Warren County, and in no time, they had made a smooth transition to life in the country.

Aubrey entered the house with her parents and took her bags upstairs. Walking into her room was always like walking into a time capsule. Everything was exactly as it had been the day she left for college. She had tried to persuade her mom to put away all the bits and pieces of her youth and make the room into a guest room, but now she was glad she hadn't.

The room was a treasure trove of memories, and over the years, Aubrey had come to cherish the mementos of her past that now surrounded her. Her eyes moved from her cheerleading pictures to the trophies and ribbons she'd won running track. Those times had been some of the simplest and happiest of her life.

Then some pictures on her dresser quickly reminded Aubrey there were painful memories too. She gazed at a photo of her best friend—a moment frozen in time. They had been barely out of school the night it happened. Amy was riding on the back of a four-wheeler with her boyfriend after dark, and the vehicle flipped. No one knew how it happened. Both of them were killed. In Aubrey's mind, Amy would always be like she was in the photo— forever smiling and forever seventeen.

Her gaze moved to a picture of her and Colby at the home-coming dance her senior year. He was living in Athens by that time, attending the University of Georgia. He had earned enough credits to graduate from high school early at the end of fall quarter that year. And, against her wishes, he let his guidance counselor talk him into starting college early.

One tearful afternoon on the dock, she told him of her fears, that it would be too stressful for him—balancing college with a relationship while she was still in Jewell. Their two different worlds, she feared, would pull them apart. She asked him to wait so they could go to Athens at the same time and begin that new experience together.

He promised her that nothing would ever take priority over her or change their plans to build a future as a couple. Now, looking at the picture on her dresser, she could almost see the sadness in her smile. After a few weeks away, he had already started pulling away from her, and on the night of the dance, she sensed it would soon be over. It was the last picture made of the two of them together for almost thirty years.

Hearing a slight knock on her door, she turned to see her mother standing in the hallway.

"Can I come in for a minute?" Mary asked.

"Sure. I was just putting away my bags and about to come back down."

Her mom walked to the edge of the bed and sat, glancing around the room. "I like to come in here sometimes and just look at all the pictures of you—from when you were a little girl to the glamour shots we took at the Augusta mall back when you were sixteen. We thought we were hot stuff, and John said we looked like a pair of hookers!"

They both laughed at the memory.

Mary patted the edge of the bed next to her, inviting Aubrey to sit. "How are you feeling? Is the baby moving much?"

"She is. It's almost like she can read my moods. She's very perceptive about things and has some strong reactions." Aubrey paused. "If something is really wrong and her brain isn't developing,

I don't think she'd react the way she does. Mom, I think she's fine. It's like I can . . . almost feel it." Aubrey rubbed her hand protectively across her belly.

"When I was carrying you, I felt the same way, Aubrey. I knew what kind of foods you didn't like, and if I was upset, I could feel these jerky movements like you felt it too. If I was laughing and having fun, you seemed to move like you were dancing." She smiled and grabbed her daughter's hand. "I agree with you. Mothers are absolutely in tune with their babies, and a mother knows when something isn't right. Which makes me also feel that this little girl is going to be just fine." Mary leaned over and gave Aubrey a hug before standing up. "We'd better get downstairs before Mr. Needy starts hollering up for us. He is fixing lunch and wants to have it on the dock."

"Let's go smother him with attention, and I can tell you both why Colby has gone to the Bahamas."

CHAPTER TWENTY-THREE

Aubrey and Mary walked downstairs to find John with two red and black picnic baskets with pictures of his beloved University of Georgia bulldogs on the lids. Inside one, he had packed fried chicken, fried okra, buttermilk cornbread, and green beans. The other basket held a couple of bottles of wine, water bottles, plates, plasticware, napkins, and—most importantly—a chocolate cheesecake. He had been working tirelessly to prepare his feast.

Seeing the women enter the kitchen, he said, "All right, you two, Chef Reese has prepared a culinary delight for his two favorite customers. If you would please follow me to the dining room on the dock, lunch will now be served." Still wearing his white apron, he waved them toward the door.

"Mom, when did he become so corny?" Aubrey asked, laughing.

"Dear, you don't know the half of it. He's now telling me how to garden and cook, and he even bought lavender dryer sheets. I think he needs some of that hormone replacement they are advertising on TV," Mary reported with a laugh.

"You keep it up." John waved a spatula at Mary while shuffling them toward the door.

Down at the dock, John spread a red and black checkered tablecloth across the picnic table, unloaded the baskets, and opened a bottle of wine. While he was doing that, Aubrey filled up the dogs' bowls and called them to eat. They had been running the river since they got there, building up their appetites, and they dug right in.

With the water flowing lazily nearby and a blue sky watching over them, it was a beautiful day to be on the river. While Mary and John were setting up, Aubrey took a minute and walked over to the pavilion. No one knew exactly how long ago they were built, but both the dock and the pavilion had been there when John's parents bought the house. There were carvings on a cedar post at the pavilion dating back to the Civil War.

Knowing that Union soldiers passed through the area, according to local lore, one marking at the top of the post always caught her attention: "WTS 1864." William Tecumseh Sherman? It was possible. But more interesting to Aubrey was a carving on another post that read, "I love Aubrey forever" with "Colby" carved below it. She remembered him putting the marks there on their sixteenth birthday, which they shared. That was one of the best days of her life; she had been so sure then they would stay together—like his carving said—forever. She had no idea how much things would change only a year from then.

Pulling her away from the memory, John announced that lunch was ready. The three of them took their seats, and, after a short blessing, the chef served his ladies.

By the time they finished with dessert, Mary and John were a little tipsy from the wine. While Aubrey put away the food and cleaned up, Mary and John moved to the couch inside the pavilion. Aubrey watched as her dad put his arm around her mom, whispering something to her that earned him a kiss. Aubrey smiled, thinking how happy her parents were after so many years together.

It made her think about how much she missed Colby. She felt nervous for him, knowing that today was the day he would have his talk with the mysterious Jack Windham.

After cleaning up, she walked over and joined her parents.

Mary poured the rest of the bottle of wine into her glass and John's. "You said you had a story you wanted to tell us, Aubrey. Is now a good time?"

"Actually, it's a great time, and I'm glad you both have some wine; I think you may need it. And you might go ahead and pull the cork on the second one." She nodded to the bottle of wine on the table.

Then Aubrey told the story of the luxurious jet that brought a letter delivered by a stranger. She read them a copy from her phone and followed up with details of Colby's flight to the Bahamas. He could, she told her parents, be meeting with Jack Windham as they spoke.

When she was finished, a silence descended on the group. Mary was wiping tears, and John, a somber expression on his face, reached for the second bottle and filled their glasses once again.

Robert Cameron had been one of John's closest friends. The friendship dated back more than thirty years to the time they'd met through the hunting club. In addition to that, John had known Colby since Colby was a young teen, and the two of them were close. Aubrey could tell the revelation hit him hard.

Mary and Colby's mom had been friends almost as long as their husbands. Although they were not nearly as close as John and Robert, they had stayed in touch until it grew difficult for Colby's mom to communicate.

It was Mary who spoke first. "Is Colby okay, Aubrey? Do you think it was the right thing, for him to go to see that man?" Aubrey sensed her mom's reluctance to call Jack Windham by his name.

"Yes, I think it was. We had a long talk, and I encouraged him to go. Because, you see, the letter has brought up so many questions.

And, unfortunately, Colby can no longer ask his mom. The only way he could get any closure would be to talk to Jack Windham. And since this man apparently doesn't have much time— and we have the baby on the way—Colby didn't really have much time to think about it. No matter how it turns out, he had to go right now—or live the rest of his life wondering what the man might have told him."

Neither John nor Mary had a response to that.

After a minute or so, John stood and walked over to the picnic table. He picked up the baskets and, without any words, began walking toward the house. Mary motioned silently for them to follow.

As they left the dock, Aubrey thought about their reaction, which had come as a surprise. She had known they would be shocked, and she had expected a million questions. It was clear that the disloyalty of Colby's mom was heavy on John's mind. With the great love he had for Robert and Colby both, Aubrey knew it was hard for him to process the news she'd just delivered.

Men generally didn't handle things like that too well; women tended to be better at dealing with strong emotions. Aubrey knew her mom would want to talk about it. She loved Colby too, and Aubrey knew she would do whatever she could to help and comfort him.

CHAPTER TWENTY-FOUR

At the house, John and Mary went their separate ways, carrying with them the heaviness of the news. John got on his tractor and scraped the gravel up and down the driveway, even though the driveway was not in need of scraping. Mary busied herself pulling weeds and tending to the garden behind the house while Aubrey went upstairs for a nap.

Lying in bed, Aubrey wondered if it had been the right thing to tell the story to her parents. Maybe she should have waited and let Colby tell them. Maybe they should have done it together. She also wondered if Colby's family would have the same reaction. He had to eventually tell his sisters—but then again, maybe he didn't. Maybe after he got back, he'd decide to keep it all a secret, the way it had been his whole life.

Exhausted from it all, she dozed for a couple of hours and then was awakened by a tap on her door.

It was Mary. "Can I come in for a minute?"

Aubrey propped herself up and rubbed at her eyes, glancing at the clock on the bedside table. "Sure, come in. I didn't mean to sleep so long."

"Well, you're sleeping now for two, and it was quite an eventful day." Mary sat down on the bed next to her and took her daughter's hand. "Sweetheart, I want to apologize for the way John and I reacted to your story. It came as such a shock, and we were just at a loss as to what to say. But we never should have just walked away the way we did." She gave Aubrey's hand a squeeze. "But, Aubrey, we have talked, and we are so thankful that you told us without Colby being here. We wouldn't have wanted to be uncomfortable around him."

Aubrey took a breath, knowing she had made the right decision after all.

"The thought of him going through this is a bit overwhelming," Mary said. "It would be so easy to say that Robert was his father and all this other stuff that has surfaced shouldn't matter. But I realize there is more to it than just that." She paused and took a breath. "My concern is that this Jack-Windham person might latch on to Colby and want more of his time—you know, with him being close to death and all. That is the last thing either of you need with the baby on the way. I just wish none of this had happened."

Aubrey leaned over and hugged her mom. "I know. I've thought about the same things, but I think this is something that he had to do. Colby is not easily influenced, and I think he'll keep this in perspective. And who knows? It may go well and turn out to be something good. But whatever happens, we'll support him."

Aubrey was tired of the discussion and was ready to get up from her nap. She told her mom she would be downstairs in a bit and maybe they could take the dogs for a walk along the river.

But Mary didn't move and placed her hand on Aubrey's arm before she could get up. "Sit for a little longer. I have something I want to show you," Mary said as she took a small black Bible out of a cloth bag. "With the emotions of the day, this may be a bit too much, but it was the reason I wanted you to visit. I was going through some of your grandmother's things, and I found something tucked away in her Bible that was addressed to you. Judging by the date, it's a letter she wrote to you not long before she died. You were in college then, and I guess she never got the chance to get it to you. And I never knew she wrote it."

Mary removed some folded yellowed sheets of paper from the Bible along with a faded envelope. On it was Aubrey's name written in cursive. "I found it last week and wanted to get it to you as soon as I could. I'll leave it with you now." Mary put the letter back into the Bible and laid it on the bed. Then with a smile and a squeeze of Aubrey's hand, she left.

Aubrey stared at the Bible on the bed. With her being the only grandchild, she and her grandmother had a special bond, and Aubrey had been as close to her as she was to her mother. She thought back to the week her grandmother passed; Aubrey had always felt she'd let her grandmother down by not being there. She was at college in Milledgeville, taking her final exams. Now, she picked up the Bible and pulled out the letter.

My dear Aubrey, sitting in this old metal rocking chair overlooking the Savannah River, which has been my daily companion for at least fifty years, I can feel the end of my life approaching. This sickness has run its course, and I wanted to write to you while I still can.

I'll never forget that glorious day in May when you were brought into this world. It was one of the happiest days of my life. I was going to get to be your grandmother, and I only wish your grandfather had been alive to meet you. He would have been so proud of the person you have become. It's hard to believe he has been gone for thirty years. I will see him soon and give him a full update on you.

I think back to when you were a little girl and how grown-up you were. You did so many things that were well beyond your years, and you always took it upon yourself to look after others. When I reached the point that I needed extra

help, you selflessly drove from Madison to Augusta to be here
for me. Aubrey, you made that drive more times than I can
remember after you had worked all day. Your caring and
loving heart is such a blessing to me.

As I near the end, I have one more request of God before
I join Him and Mack. Aubrey, my final wish is for you to
one day become the person I know you are destined to be. I
have watched you from the days you took such tender care of
your dolls, and then I watched you give a loving home to all
the wonderful pets you rescued through the years. So, it is my
prayer, Aubrey, that you have the opportunity to become a
mother. You have so much love to give, and I also pray you
meet that special someone who can share that with you.

When you hold that precious baby in your arms, know
Mack and I are smiling down from heaven and that we are
so proud of you.

Aubrey, I love you, and my spirit will always be with
you. Until we meet again,
Grandmom

Tears streamed down Aubrey's cheeks as she finished the letter.
She knew God had a plan that she read the letter at this moment
in her life. And God's timing had been perfect. If the letter had
come to her thirty years before, it would have filled her with a huge
sense of loss. It would have hurt to read it knowing she had lost
the love of her life and the only person she could imagine having
a child with. Now, she was carrying Colby's baby, and she smiled,
thinking God and her grandmother must have conspired to make
that happen. If she had any doubts that her little girl would be
okay, those doubts were now gone. She placed her hand over her
baby, and, feeling calm and peaceful, she sent a silent thank you
to her grandmother.

CHAPTER TWENTY-FIVE

I looked into the eyes of the man I now knew was my biological father; there was no longer any doubt. I firmly shook his hand. After a few seconds of awkwardness, he let out a soft breath. His voice trembled as he spoke. "Colby, I have waited a lifetime for this moment, and words are not enough to tell you how I feel. I've played out this scene in my mind a thousand times, and I want to thank you so much for allowing me to see you. I know it wasn't an easy decision to come all this way after only receiving my letter last week."

I didn't know how to reply so I simply said, "Thank you for the invitation, Mr. Windham. I'm glad to be here." I knew he didn't want me calling him Mr. Windham, but I needed to let him be the one to establish which name I would use.

"*Jack*, Colby. Please call me Jack." He picked up the drink the bartender had left for him. Then he moved toward the couch and took a seat. Following his lead, I sat down in the chair across from him. When he raised his drink in my direction, I picked up mine and returned the gesture. I guess there should have been a formal toast, but we each took a sip and sat quietly, lost in thought. Here we were: A father who had with great sorrow given up his son, wanting that son to have the best future he could give him. And a son who was just now beginning to understand the complexities of that decision, which had dramatically changed the course of his life.

Love and compassion are powerful emotions, and in the way Jack looked at me, I could see how much he wished he could have been a part of my life. But this man's integrity had not allowed him to take that privilege from my father. I could not imagine the pain he must have felt watching me play ball and walk across the stage to graduate. How must it have felt to see the child he'd loved and held as a baby and to keep that love bottled up while he watched me from afar? I suddenly had a respect for him that went well beyond anything I had expected. I was wondering how to start a conversation more than forty-five years in the making when Jack spoke up first.

"I am sure you have a lot of questions, and I want to answer every one of them, but if you don't mind, I would like to start at the beginning and tell you who I am and where I'm from. A little background before we dive into what you came here to talk about. Is that okay with you?"

Still at a loss for words, I gave him a nod.

He took a long sip from his drink, crossed his legs, and stared into the sky, contemplating, I imagined, where to start. And then he began.

"I was born Jackson Samuel Windham in Stafford, Texas, in 1933. My father was James Jackson Windham, and he was born in 1902, and my mother was Emily Milhorne Morehouse. She was born the same year as my father. They were both from the outskirts of Stafford, which is a small oil town about twenty miles southwest of Houston.

They married in 1920, when they turned eighteen and moved from their families' farms to the city of Stafford. Dad got a job with an oil company and started as a tender for the inland oil rigs.

The oil business was booming with all the veterans returning from the war and needing oil for cars and heating.

My mom was a seamstress and made all our clothes, and she also took in sewing work for the community. She was happy being at home and taking care of her children. I am one of three. The first was my brother, Henry." Jack paused to sip his drink. I could tell by his expression that the ending to his brother's story wasn't good.

"Henry was born in 1920," he continued, "and he had my father's stocky frame as well as his work ethic. He wanted to create his own path, so instead of going into the oil business like my father, Henry saved his money and bought cattle throughout his teenage years. Dad owned a couple hundred acres in the country and let Henry use the pastures for his cows. Henry was successful with his herd, but he had to leave the cows behind in 1944. That's when he was drafted into the army to fight in World War Two." Jack shifted in his seat. "After basic training at Fort Sill in Oklahoma, he shipped off to England and was part of the Allied invasion of Normandy Beach—Operation Overlord.

"On June 9th, 1944, three days after the D-Day invasion, Henry was one of the many men who would lose their lives fighting for our freedom and our way of life. We never knew what happened to him, just that he was killed on the battlefield." Jack closed his eyes at a memory. "I will never forget the day an officer and a chaplain pulled up to our house with the news. That day took something from my parents' spirits that was never to return." He took his handkerchief out of his pocket and wiped at his eyes.

Thinking Jack needed a few minutes, I asked where the bathroom was to give him time to recover. He pointed to a door that was a few feet away. I knew very well how events from years before could hit hard at one's emotions. Whenever I thought about the night I found my dad in the deer stand—and about that final talk—I would tear up right away.

I returned from the bathroom to find Jack standing at the stern, looking out over the bay. He turned when he heard me enter. He was smiling now and seemed to have regained his composure. He moved back to his seat on the couch, and I found my chair. Then he continued with his story.

"My sister, Camille, was born a year after Henry and was always the glue of our family. She was a ball of energy and had the most loving spirit of anyone I've ever known. Had it not been for her, I think my parents would have mourned themselves to either death or divorce over the loss of Henry. She was always gentle and so compassionate." A smile spread across his face. "My sister was a nurse at a hospital in Houston when she met her husband, William. He was a returning wounded veteran and under her care. They fell in love and married soon after he recovered. But as much as they wanted to have children, that never happened for them. My sister had so much love to give, and she and William began to foster kids whose soldier fathers had shipped out, never to return to see their children born.

"Camille appealed to the state legislature about funding for a program for these kids and, with overwhelming support from them, she was able to establish the first organized department of family and children's services in Texas. It was so successful it became the model for the rest of the country." He paused. "Camille and William are no longer with us, but the legacy they left will be in place forever."

Just as he finished with his story about his sister, Miquel appeared with fresh drinks and placed them in front of us. When he left, Jack continued.

"As for me, I was the baby of the family. Henry passed when I was ten, and Camille was married and settled by the time I was barely in my teens. My father had done well with his company and built the engineering department mostly on his own—although without a title.

Without any formal education, he was never able to go any further. There was no doubt he had earned the right to be a VP or the director of engineering. He would have done well at those jobs, but he always said they wanted college-educated people at the top. For 'window dressing,' he told us." That's why he was determined that one of his kids would earn a college degree, and I was the only one left."

My own dad had used that same term, "window dressing," to describe the way the railroad favored college-educated people, often to the detriment of hardworking and more knowledgeable employees. He also was determined one of his kids would go to college. And with me being the last of the three, I was going whether I wanted to or not. It was ironic, really, how our stories paralleled.

"After a mediocre high school performance, I somehow got accepted to the University of Houston," Jack continued. "I was there for just two months when I was invited by my roommate to attend a rally for the ROTC. I had never considered the military or had any thoughts about joining until then. But it only took a few demonstrations on a large screen of an F-86 doing aerial maneuvers, and by the end of the night, I was so swept up in the hype that I found myself wanting to join the air force.

"Although I was eighteen and didn't need my parents' permission to join up, I went back to Stafford to let them know in person. When I told them I wanted to fly for the air force, my mother cried, and my dad got all quiet." His look turned serious. "This was in 1951 when we were in the middle of the Korean Conflict. Our military had already lost about twenty-five thousand men, and at least triple that amount had been wounded. I knew what they were thinking—that they couldn't bear to lose another child to war. They did their best to discourage me, but after completing my first quarter of college, I went anyway."

It was fascinating to see even more parallels between his life and mine. I had always wanted to fly jets, and only a few people knew that in my first year of college, I attempted to sign up for the air force. I didn't even tell my parents. And then in Atlanta at my all-day physical, the last test was for colorblindness—and I failed. That test abruptly ended my dreams of flying for the military.

Jack took a sip of his drink and continued. "I was sent to basic training and did well. Being in ROTC, even though it was only for one quarter, made me technically eligible for flight school. Normally, I would have had to have waited at least three years, but at that time they needed pilots. Many of them were leaving the military for civilian airline jobs, so the timing was right for me, and I got accepted." He leaned back in his seat. "Flight school was a year-long program with twelve-hour days. If we weren't flying, we were in class learning about flight systems, combat strategies, and even a bit of minor maintenance.

"After that year, I was assigned to a squadron that flew the F-86 Sabre. It was the first swept-wing jet and was being hailed as the greatest fighter aircraft of its time. Supposedly, it could stand up against the Russian MiG-15. And I was lucky enough to get to fly it!" Jack said with a big smile. I imagined he was waiting for the question he knew I was about to ask.

"Did you ever get into a fight with any of the MiGs?"

His face lit up with a bigger smile, and I knew the answer.

"I did. It was in May of 1953, right before I was to ship back home. We were on a mission up North, in the Changjin province, when we were intercepted by a skyful of MiGs. Our mission was to take out one of the hydroelectric dams. The B-29s had moved to night-only operations after they'd taken heavy losses during the day, and the F-86s were tasked with the daytime bombing runs. We were loaded with two bombs, a thousand pounds each, that severely cut down on our performance. The last thing we wanted was to get intercepted by the MiGs, but that is exactly what happened."

I leaned forward, fascinated.

"We were about thirty miles from our target," Jack continued, "which on that day was the Sui-ho Dam. And they showed up on our radar. They were about the same distance as we were to the dam, coming from the opposite direction. We were about three to four minutes away and had to make a decision. We could stay on the mission and drop the bombs over the target, or we could jettison them and either make a run back south or engage the MiGs."

With my heart racing. I knew there was no way he would stop the story now, but I couldn't help but ask, "What did you do?"

"We stayed on the mission, and with no time to spare, we dropped our bombs on the dam. It was not ten seconds later that we started taking on fire from the MiGs. They came in from a higher altitude and bore down on us," Jack said as his eyes met mine. "Two of our Sabres got hit immediately, and we were in a bad position. We couldn't lose airspeed and climb, and we couldn't outrun them with their altitude advantage, so we hit the deck and made them come after us.

"We knew we could out-maneuver them, so we kept the flight low and took it to a chain of mountains near the dam. Fortunately, we had just been outfitted with the new 20 mm M39 cannons, which had replaced the 50-caliber machine guns. Also, luckily, most of the squadron were experienced combat pilots. As for me, I was the least experienced of the group and had never engaged in a dogfight. We had trained to fly in pairs when engaged, but down in the canyons, that wasn't possible."

"I'll never forget, Colby, seeing the MiG coming up behind me on the radar screen. I didn't have a feeling of 'This is it; I'm about to die.' I knew my Sabre was superior to the MiG, and we had trained in the mountains of the desert for this scenario." He leaned closer to me. "Before he could get off a shot, I banked the Sabre around a sharp bend just feet over the surface of a mountain lake. I had the advantage of seeing the turns of the mountains up ahead, and he could only follow. I needed to get rid of him quickly and saw an artery of the mountains ahead that led to a canyon. I waited until the extreme last second and apexed the entrance to the canyon perfectly. I probably came within feet of hitting the outside wall of the cliff. He didn't react fast enough and missed the turn, and that was all I needed.

"I kept the jet in a hard-right bank and came in behind him as we both reentered the main channel of the mountains. He never saw me until I appeared on his radar, and then it was too late. I locked the M39 cannons on him and watched as the tracer rounds hit him at a quartering angle. He lost control of the MiG, and the thing exploded into the mountain.

"It was an adrenaline-filled minute, and nothing in my life has compared to it since." He let out a sigh. "I rejoined my squadron, and all but three of us made it back. I would leave for home the next month, and I have never forgotten the seriousness of that event. I lost three of my friends that day—someone's son, someone's husband, someone's father."

Jack stopped and took a long sip of his drink. I was still sitting on the edge of my seat, having just listened to one of the most amazing stories I had ever heard from a man I didn't know existed until the week before. In addition to being fascinated by the story, I found it surreal to watch this almost stranger and see myself in him, recognizing mannerisms and ways of saying things that had seemed unique to me.

I thought back to when I was a kid and had a desk in my room specifically set up for me to use when building models. Having a fascination for military airplanes, I only built airplanes and could clearly remember building the F-86 Sabre with the swept-back wings. It had been my favorite, and I think I built at least three of them. I had dreamed of flying one, and now sitting in front of me was a man who had—and on top of that, he'd shot down a MiG.

I knew Jack Windham's story was part of my own. It was from him I'd gotten my innate desire to fly airplanes and my love of flight.

I felt a sense of pride—but also of betrayal. I owed Robert Cameron the respect of not getting all worked up about this other man and the things we had in common. But that was hard to do. I took a long sip of my drink.

Then Jack changed the subject. "But in all my years of flying, I was never shot by ground troops while taking off from a narrow road—at night, in the middle of the jungle, with passengers on board. When I found out about all of that last year, I was seized with the thought that I had almost lost you—and almost lost the chance for us to have this talk. Although I had thought about it for years, it was mostly that event that prompted me to take a chance and write the letter. That and knowing that my time is near."

We took a needed pause when Miquel came in and whispered something to Jack, who answered with a nod.

"Miquel says they are ready for us in the dining room if you will follow me."

I nodded that I would.

CHAPTER TWENTY-SIX

We walked through the tinted black glass doors into a room that seemed a lot larger than it had from outside. The first thing I noticed was the floor, which was mahogany with fleur-de-lis marble inlays. The room was very masculine with wainscoted walls featuring a kind of wood I could not identify. Displayed under a flood of focused lights were statues and taxidermy of Southern woodland birds. As we moved through the foyer toward the dining room, the floors turned from mahogany to maroon-tinted marble.

We ended up at a large dining table that appeared to seat at least fourteen. Staff members, some of whom were present, had blocked most of the table with a row of fresh flowers, creating a more intimate space for two.

We took our seats, and the staff departed after some instructions from Jack. On the table were selections of red and white wine, decanted, and a row of wine glasses appropriate to the wine that was being served.

Jack picked up one of the decanters of red wine and poured us each a glass. "I know from my investigating—and no, I did not have someone go through your trash—that your favorite wine is from the Flanagan winery in Sonoma. One can find out just about anything these days on social media." He paused with what I would describe as a snicker; he even laughed the way that I did. "So, I ordered a few cases, and after some extensive sampling, I can see why you enjoy Mr. Flanagan's wine so much. I poured us a 2014 Serenity Way red from the Bennett Valley. And for a white, we will have one of my favorites, a 2012 Marcassin Vineyards Chardonnay. I think they will both pair well with the meal our chef has prepared." Jack raised his glass toward mine, and we both took a sip of the wine.

Right on cue, the chef entered the room and approached the table. He greeted us both and began his presentation of our meal.

As he spoke, I leaned back in my chair and studied him. He looked familiar, but a lot of people do, and I didn't know anyone from the Bahamas. So I just listened to his enticing descriptions of what we were about to eat.

In an English accent, he began telling us about the strawberry grouper that had been caught that afternoon by a Bahamian fisherman. It was against the law, he said, for anyone but a local to harvest that species of fish. He then described the Wagyu beef that he had cured and seasoned for a week with flavorings he had harvested from the Chub Cay gardens. He next presented the risotto with fresh peaches he had brought from home. Surprisingly, he mentioned a peach that comes almost exclusively from Georgia. And that is when I realized that I *did* know him—and wondered what he was doing on Jack's yacht.

It took me a second, but I recalled his name, and when he finished his presentation, I posed a question to him. "Andrew, that all sounds wonderful. You said you brought the peaches from 'home.' Where, may I ask, is home?" I put on my trademark crooked smile.

Since we had not yet been introduced, I could make out a bit of confusion on his face as he studied me. Just as he was beginning to answer my question, his sous chef walked into the room. Nick and I recognized each other right away, and I gave him a discreet nod along with a wink. He got the message and stayed behind Andrew, giving me a big grin.

"As I'm sure you know, peaches grow abundantly in Georgia, and we purchase them from a family farm in Perry, located in the appropriately named Peach County, Georgia," replied Andrew.

It was time for me to have a little fun. I knew Andrew and Nick from quail-hunting trips and attending several functions at an exclusive hunting preserve called The Burge Club in Mansfield, Georgia.

"Well, the best peach dish I've ever been served was a lot like what you've described at a place called The Burge Club. Have you ever heard of that place?" I asked with a wide grin.

Andrew stared at me blankly before he recognized me and broke out into a smile. "Colby Cameron, what in the world are you doing here? I thought you looked familiar, but my mind just couldn't make the connection." He approached, sticking out his hand. Nick also came over with a smile and handshake.

Before I could answer Andrew's question, he rushed to explain. "I want you to know this is all on the up and up. I have full permission from Burge to be down here. We have a few weeks a year when we are slow, and Mr. Windham grabs us and brings the whole staff to Chub Cay to cook for him and his guests." Andrew knew that Mr. Morehouse was strict about his quail club, and Andrew was not the type to take advantage.

"Andrew, I wouldn't say a word, if it was not on the up and up. I always look forward to your creations, whether they are contraband or not. My lips are sealed," I told him, laughing.

"What a small world," said Jack. "I met Andrew while shooting quail at the club about five years ago. After experiencing his amazing dishes, I worked out a deal with Mr. Morehouse to have them come to the boat between hunting seasons. But it wasn't cheap! He is a good negotiator, and I had to give up two weeks on the yacht and some good fishing for him and his family."

Andrew and Nick left the room, and Jack watched me from across the table. There was a lot of meaning in that stare. It was the first time he had seen me interact with anyone, and by his look, I sensed he was beginning to warm even more to the son he had known his whole life—but also never knew.

I looked down to give him a moment. Then we both reached for the decanter of red at the same time. We laughed, and I served us each another glass of the Serenity Way. We swirled the wine around the glasses a few times and before we drank, he spoke. "Maybe while we wait for dinner, if you want, I can start the conversation about what happened between your mother and me."

He sounded a little hesitant, and I wasn't quite ready either to go down that rabbit hole. "Maybe tell me first what happened after you and she made the decision to go your separate ways. Tell me about your life after that, and then we can circle back around. Is that okay?"

"Certainly. I think that's a good idea. Let's have dinner and then we can go back to the lounge and continue our discussion."

CHAPTER TWENTY-SEVEN

After a wonderful dinner, topped off with crème brûlée and small snifters of Cognac, we grabbed a bottle of wine and headed outside to the lounge. It was dark by then, and I could easily see all the stars and constellations of the southern sky. It reminded me of sitting on my dock in Warthen with Aubrey, looking at the same view of the heavens. Jack took a seat on the couch, and I sat in the same chair as earlier, facing him. We were silent for a moment, both collecting our thoughts on how to proceed with the discussion.

Jack picked up the bottle and was about to pour us each a glass of wine before he stopped. With a slight grin and a considerable sigh, he said, "I'm thinking that, considering where this conversation is headed, I might need a much stronger libation than wine. How about you?"

I laughed and, with no idea what I was getting myself into, I told him that sounded good to me.

Jack then motioned to Miquel to come and fix the drinks. I made the first request, sticking with an old-fashioned, and Jack asked for a bottle of Patron with a bowl full of limes. I was thinking he would probably regret that in the morning. But he was facing an emotional conversation with a son he had waited years to reconnect with. And only having less than a year to live, I imagined he thought, "What the hell?" This was shaping up to be an epic evening.

While waiting for Miquel to prepare my old-fashioned, Jack poured each of us a shot of the tequila, and we raised our glasses in a cheer before we drank. I had not done a shot of anything since my wedding, and I quickly threw it back and made a face while rushing to cover the taste with a big slice of lime. Jack calmly drank his in one slow swallow, paying no attention to the bowl of limes. It was interesting to see an eighty-one-year-old man do a shot of tequila.

"How about we start where we left off," he said. "You want to hear what happened after you were born?"

I replied with a nod.

Before he spoke, he lifted the bottle, poured another shot, this time just for himself, and slammed it like a college student.

"After we realized you were on the way—and after many tearful, heartfelt conversations about what to do—we decided it was best the two of us part ways, as painful as that was. Your dad was back in town after being in Greensboro, North Carolina, for a few months, and things with your family began to get back to normal. Your dad was excited that another child was on the way. I talked with him one weekend when we were both out doing yard work. He told me then about the pregnancy and how overjoyed he was and how he was hoping they would have a boy.

"Colby, I can't explain how hard it was to have that conversation. I longed with my whole being to be a father to you, to feel the thrill that he did, the anticipation. The emotions overwhelmed me—guilt and jealousy, both at the same time. I had to redirect the conversation before I blurted something that could have changed everything."

"What happened after that? Did you find someone else? I knew that, in fact, he had, and I wanted to steer the talk in that direction. It was too much too soon to hear about the interaction between him and my dad.

"I did. I knew I couldn't continue living next door to your parents, especially after you arrived. I sold my house and moved about five miles closer to Houston. As a distraction, I began throwing myself into my work in oil distribution. And one evening at a seminar, I met someone who reminded me so much of your mother. She had the same dark hair and blue eyes and was smart and interesting. We had a lot in common, and she was just the kind of person I needed in my life," he said as he poured himself a glass of wine.

"What did she think about you having a child on the way?" I asked.

"I didn't tell her right away. That was very private information for only your mom and me to know. But after about six months of dating, we began to get serious, and your due date was fast approaching. I knew at that point I wanted to marry her, and I knew we had to have the conversation.

"A lot was on the line. She and I ran in the same circles socially and had a lot of the same business contacts. If she had reacted in a bad way, I would have lost her, and everyone in Houston could have found out about your mom and me—and that meant your father too. I didn't think that was going to happen; we had built a trust between us, and we loved each other. But this was uncharted territory, so I had no idea what to expect. Aside from worrying about this conversation here with you, it was probably the most nervous and anxious I had ever been." He paused for a sip of wine.

"I had just bought my first boat, a new thirty-seven-foot Chris-Craft Constellation, and I kept it on Lake Houston. I decided to take Julia out on the boat for dinner and on the same evening, tell her about you and ask her to marry me. It was a lot at once, and I'm not sure what I would have done if she'd said no."

"You really didn't give her much of an option but to accept the story and say yes to your proposal. You had her out on the lake at night, and you were her only way back to shore."

Jack shook his head and laughed. "You make a good point. But even back at shore, she stuck with the yes and promised to support whatever I decided about you in the future." He paused. "But as much as I loved my new wife, I was not able to get you or your mother off my mind. From time to time, I would drive by your house, hoping for a glimpse of your mother out in the yard with you or loading you into the car. It was not fair to my wife, and she was smart enough to realize she deserved more from me.

"Almost a year into our marriage, she got pregnant, and we were blessed with our son Hunter. With my oil distribution business expanding all over Texas and the Midwest, I was busy traveling and signing up dozens of new dealers. And at the same time, I was buying land and drilling oil wells. The frantic pace of all of that allowed me to gradually let go of my thoughts about your mom, but it never stopped me from thinking about you." Jack wiped at his eyes. The poignant memories, combined with the alcohol, were hitting hard at his emotions. He quickly got a grip on them and continued.

"Growing up with wealth, Hunter was given anything a boy could ever want. Not that I didn't *try* to limit what we gave him in the way of material possessions, but it was impossible. His peers, who were the kids of our friends, were denied very little, and it was the same with Hunter. But even so, I taught and expected him to be respectful and courteous and to have good manners. And he was all of those things.

"In college at the University of Texas, he excelled in his finance studies and was primed to work for me and eventually take over the businesses. It was always my goal to have him run things and improve on my successes. Unfortunately, though, that's not how things panned out. About the time Hunter was graduating, I had a heart attack on the golf course. I was fifty-five.

"While recovering, I reexamined where I was in life and decided to change my priorities. For years, I had been working very stressful ten-hour days— sometimes even longer. If I wanted to live to see old age, I knew I needed to make a change. It was a knee-jerk decision predicated by the heart attack, but with their values at a high, I sold most of my companies. The few I kept pretty much ran themselves and didn't need attention from me on a daily basis." Jack let out a sigh. "If I could have a retake on that, I would have kept a couple for Hunter to run. Instead, I gave him a considerable amount of money from the sale of the businesses.

"I should have let him find a job and work awhile before I gave him anything. As far as I know, Hunter has never worked a day in his life. But he has used his finance and investing acumen to expand his wealth and maintain a kind of lifestyle the money I gave him would have never funded. I don't know exactly how much he has now, but he's never asked me for anything. I guess by some measure, he's been a success," said Jack as Miquel entered the lounge with a tray of much-needed bottles of water.

It all seemed surreal, hearing a story about a brother from a father I'd just met. If the twists of fate had turned a little differently, if the discussion with my mom or the encounter with my dad out in the yard had gone another way, my whole life might be different. Things for me could have taken on a whole new direction—and what a direction it would have been. Maybe good or maybe not. Having so much privilege and most anything I wanted could have turned me into a trust-fund kid with no accomplishments in my life.

Jack continued for the next half hour, telling me more stories about Hunter. And then after a while, I could tell he was starting to get tired. It was ten thirty by that point, and with the health challenges he faced, I thought it was about time we called it a night. I was about to suggest it when he brought up the subject of my mom. Although it was late, I think he wanted to get to the conversation that had brought me there. As he said in his letter, he had been waiting a long time to have this talk.

For this part of the story, he skipped the wine and poured us each a tall glass of water. He took a long drink then a deep breath, then he started on the story I had come to hear.

CHAPTER TWENTY-EIGHT

"**I** know I will probably repeat things I wrote in my letter, but please allow me that privilege," he said. "It was a special time in my life, and there aren't many people I've told this story to."

I told him to tell it any way he wanted, and he began.

"I had been renting a house downtown, but with my new business doing well, I was able to purchase my first house. It was on Sycamore Street, a few miles outside Stafford and next door to your mom and dad. It was the second day of moving in, and being the middle of July, it was at least a hundred degrees. I needed a break from the heat, so I got a glass of water from the faucet; we didn't have bottled water then. I took the drink and sat on the only chair I had moved into the den. That's when the doorbell rang, and when I opened the door, there stood your mother, holding a pitcher of iced tea and a plate of cookies.

"I didn't know who she was or where she came from, but I was immediately taken with her. She had the bluest eyes, and they warmed her whole face when she smiled. You have her eyes and her smile, by the way," he said. He looked at me as if at a memory, then he nodded and continued.

"She introduced herself, and I told her to come in. I pulled a couple of glasses from a box and asked her to join me for a glass of the tea, and she did. Thankfully, I had already moved in the kitchen table and chairs, so we sat and started talking. It was like I was talking to someone I had known my entire life. I could not take my eyes off her, and my heart was beating hard.

"But when she told me she was originally from Georgia—and that her husband had been transferred to Houston—my heart dropped to my stomach. I had been so captivated by her I hadn't even thought to look at her hand. And then I saw the wedding ring.

"I thought to myself of course it was too good to be true, that a beautiful, amazing woman would show up at my door, stop my world, and not be married. We talked for another half hour before she had to get back home to relieve her housekeeper from watching your sisters.

"After she left, Colby, I sat back in my chair and wondered what had just happened to me. I've never had anyone have an immediate effect on me like your mother did. And from that point on, I could think of nothing else but her."

He paused for a sip of water. "It was about a week after that when I met your dad. I wanted so much for him to be a jerk—a womanizer, maybe, who bragged about the women he had on the side when he traveled. I wanted to find that he was flawed in some important way, but he was the opposite. He was kind and funny, someone anybody would want as a friend." He looked down at the floor. "It was, ironically, my own flaws that could have torn apart a marriage.

"It all started slowly," he continued. "We'd throw our hands up to each other as we pulled out of our driveways. Then we'd talk out in the yard at night when she was outside watching your sisters play. She didn't talk about your dad much, but I sensed she was lonely. Your father was working hard at that point and was gone a lot.

"As the months went on, our talks out in the yard moved to my kitchen table. We would have tea or coffee and talk about anything and everything. She would often tell me how alone she felt and how she had been against the move to Texas away from all her family and friends. Robert had promised her the new job would mean less travel for him, but as things turned out, that was not the case. Within a few months of the move, he had more territory and was traveling even more than he had before. She felt like the family was no longer his top priority."

That made me think of conversations I'd had with my mother in my teenage years. She'd wanted so much for her and Dad to spend time with my aunts and uncles and socialize with other couples. She longed for us as a family to do things with other families. But the stresses and responsibilities of my father's job kept him tied to the railroad when she wanted him to be available for family time and time with her.

Maybe my mom and I had, in fact, been closer than I thought. At that time, my mind had been more on Aubrey than whatever concerns my mother might have been trying to share with me. But now I believed she was reaching out to me, hoping I could somehow appeal to my dad to spend more time with us. I probably spent more time with him than anyone except for his co-workers. I wished I had been mature enough to have picked up on her cues.

Jack continued. "One weekend, she and your dad were planning to attend a charity event. They were going to a ball, hosted by the railroad." He smiled slightly at a memory. "Your mother made me practice dancing with her in my kitchen. She was so afraid she might embarrass herself around the other wives. But then she came to me and told me the event got canceled."

He took a sip of water. "The truth of the matter was your dad had to stay late in St. Louis and could not get back in time. And your mom was devastated. With her days mostly spent caring for young children, she was so looking forward to adult time with her husband." He paused for a few seconds and looked at the floor. He and I both knew the direction this was about to take.

"That evening, she was already dressed up for the ball when she got the news. Weighed down with disappointment, she came to my house in her gorgeous gown. Then, after a couple of glasses of wine, she asked me to take her dancing. She had taken your sisters earlier to a friend's house for the night. And it just so happened that I had joined the River Oaks Country Club the month before, and as fate would have it, there was a dance that evening. I pulled out my tux, and in less than twenty minutes, we were headed to the club.

"We had dinner and then danced to the sounds of big band music until we could not dance anymore. I had never felt so alive, Colby, in my life." He paused for a moment, lost in the memory. "Natalie was breathtaking in her gown, and I was so proud to be with her. That night was like a fantasy, and when we got back to my house . . . well, let's just say it was the start of something from which there was no return.

"It didn't take long for me to fall even more in love. It was mutual, and we began to see more of each other. We dangerously dreamed about what it would be like to spend our lives together. We talked about traveling to see the world, relaxing at the lake, and even going grocery shopping as a couple.

Over the next few months, we'd meet when we could—when your sisters were at school or on the weekends when your father was out of town. Other than the night at the country club, we didn't take the risk of going out in public. We didn't really need to; all we really wanted was to be together. Mostly, when we could get away, we would spend time at my cabin on Lake Houston."

Jack paused, understanding the emotions he had just expressed were centered on my mom. With kindness in his voice, he asked me, "Are you okay with everything so far? I know this is a lot to process, and if you want to stop for a while, we can. Or if you have any questions, please just ask."

I told him I was fine and thanked him for his consideration.

He smiled and continued. "Sometime during those few months we were together, your mother became pregnant. The day I received that news was one of the most confusing and emotional days of my whole life. I was going to have a baby with the woman I so deeply loved and with whom I longed to spend the rest of my life. The situation just consumed me, and I wondered constantly how we could make it work.

"We talked about her telling Robert that we were in love and she was carrying our child. The hope was that he might get angry and demand she give him a divorce, but that was all just talk. Neither of us, Colby, could have done that to your dad. As the days and weeks went by, we were growing weary of debating what to do, and time wasn't on our side. We needed to make a decision and one day, it was made for us."

Jack stopped and rubbed his face. He looked tired and emotionally drained. I thought again about suggesting we call it a night and continue in the morning. But before I could, he poured himself a half shot of the tequila, downed it, and continued.

"Your dad had been in Atlanta for a week, and when he returned, he had a big announcement. He was being transferred back to Atlanta, and it was going to be an operations job that required no travel. This was to be a job that should keep him in Atlanta for possibly the rest of his career. He was so excited, and so was your mom. She could go back to her family and friends and get back to her old life.

"At that point, Natalie was about four months pregnant, and the transfer would not happen until the beginning of the next year. Meaning she was going to have the baby there in Texas.

"The next five months were torturous. We agreed to stop seeing each other, and it was killing me. Seeing her in the yard or in the car, when I could only wave or say a short few brief words, was tough." A soft look crossed his face as a memory came to him. "Sometimes when I was on my porch, I could hear her singing softly to herself as she worked in her garden. She loved plants more than anyone I've ever known." He paused and looked at me. "I couldn't take it, Colby, and in a few short weeks, I sold my house and moved across town."

That memory of my mother made me smile—and also made me sad. Mom did love her plants, and they seemed to love her back. I remembered how when I was around ten years old, she'd pulled the car to the side of the road so she could grab some half-dead plants from the top of someone's garbage. Then she took them home and nursed them back to life. Gardening was a passion she involved me in as well. I loved the time we spent in the vegetable garden she and I had together. There among the plants was where I bonded with my mother. Now, she only had a few plants and often forgot to water or take care of them. I wanted to tell Jack about her condition, but for some reason, I felt he already knew and had decided not to bring it up.

"When you were born," Jack continued, "I did get to see you, as I mentioned in the letter. Knowing it would probably be the only time I would ever hold my son, I rocked you in my arms and wept. In the hospital that day, I never wanted to put you down. I couldn't imagine having to let go of something that was so precious to me. I remember my mind racing as I tried to come up with some way to fix it so you could still be part of my life. I couldn't bear the thought that I might never see or hold my boy again."

We sat in silence for a while, the emotion of the memory heavy in the air. Then Jack continued softly. "As I told you in my letter, I followed your life, Colby, as much as I could. When you were about four years old, I reached out to your mom and asked her if she would tell me about your life and maybe give me updates every now and then. She never forgot how special our time together was, and she granted my request. I have in my safe in Houston every picture and article your mom ever sent me. I attended a few of your high school baseball games and was at your graduation at the University of Georgia. Always in the background but, Colby, I was there."

I was fighting back the tears by then; it was all too much.

With sadness and regret heavy in his eyes, he looked at me intently. "Colby, I want you to know how sorry I am for laying all of this on you, but while you never knew about me, I have thought about you every day. And I just couldn't leave this life without one more chance to see you." His voice was now the weak voice of an old man, and tears streamed down his cheeks. The strong man I had seen earlier on the yacht now seemed so frail and vulnerable. He had laid bare his emotions and put it all out on the table, the tenderest moments of his life.

He had one last request, he said, to ask of me that evening.

"Anything, Jack," I whispered, overcome.

No longer needing words, he stood and moved toward me, wrapping his arms around me. He placed his head on my shoulder, and the sobs came from a place deep within his chest. He sobbed for all the years he'd missed, and he sobbed in appreciation of this moment, when a dying man got to hold his son again.

I leaned my head against his, and I wept as well. I wept for the fierce love of a man who never once lost sight of the boy he cherished. And I wept in gratitude for the love and sacrifices of another man who had loved and cherished me as well.

CHAPTER TWENTY-NINE

After an emotional night, I left Jack and headed back to my cabana. When I reached the end of the pier, I was glad to see T. C. and his friends were not still hanging out on the dock. I had a lot on my mind and was not up to an interrogation.

Stepping onto the boardwalk, I realized I was unsure of how to get back to the cabana. As caught up as I had been with my anticipation of the meeting, I hadn't paid attention to how I had arrived. Oscar had told me he would pick me up, but I guessed at that late hour, he probably assumed I would just stay on the yacht. After all the alcohol and intense conversation, both Jack and I had forgotten to give him a call, and so there I was. I knew I needed to go left, but that was it.

Under the veil of night, all the trees, bushes, and vegetation looked the same, as did the maze of intersecting paths. It would be a total guess on where to go, so I decided to walk back through the hotel and ask the front desk clerk.

After making my way there, I walked up a long, wide set of steps and entered the back of the hotel through tall and heavy glass doors. It was late, and when I walked past the bar, it was crowded, mostly with men wearing fishing shirts and shorts. A weary-looking group was segregated in the corner, probably the captains and crew. The bar was exclusive and generally not open to the public. All of the people there were guests or people working for them. They all seemed to pause and take notice as I moved toward the reception desk. I didn't know if it was because I was dressed up like a yachtsman from a boating magazine or if it was something else. Did they somehow know I had been on Jack Windham's yacht, and were they wondering who I was?

At the front desk, I recognized the lady who had checked me in and explained my problem. She offered to call someone to drive me to the cabana, but I told her I would rather walk. She gave me directions, and I thanked her and stepped out the front door. Along the path were low-voltage landscape lights to lead the way. After making only one wrong turn that led to the wrong rental, I found my cabana. The first thing I did was strip down and take a long, hot shower. I was sticky from the walk home and being a bundle of nerves all evening. The hot water cascading over me helped to loosen me up.

Feeling refreshed after the shower, I pulled on a pair of shorts and a T-shirt, made myself a Scotch, and grabbed a cigar. Then I took a chair and walked the hundred or so feet to an open area on the beach where I had a full view of the sky. And what a view it was. Saturn and Jupiter were prominently visible, and just over the horizon, I could faintly recognize the red hue of Mars. Orion, the great hunter, was overhead as well, and to my right was Scorpius, the giant scorpion who defeated and killed Orion.

When I was a young man, one of my dad's contemporaries taught me to identify the seven most well-known constellations. He said it was something every man should know. He didn't tell me why, but I later found it very useful in the late-night company of females, who tended to be impressed with my knowledge of the night sky.

I had just set my drink carefully in the sand and was lighting my cigar when my phone rang. I didn't have to look to see who it was. I knew she wouldn't be able to wait until I called her in the morning.

"Hello, my dear," I answered.

"Hey," she said in a whispery voice. "Can you talk? Are you still with Jack?"

"Yes, I can talk, and no, I am not with Jack. I just got back to my cabana about half an hour ago, and I'm now sitting on the beach, trying to process everything he said. Aubrey, it was so surreal. I can't even begin to describe or explain the emotions I went through, and it was the same for him."

"Wow. I can only imagine. I've been nervous all day, wondering what was going to happen. I'm ready for the story, and don't leave out any details."

I paused, not knowing where to start or how to describe the waves of feelings that had hit me. But I had to try.

"I was escorted onto the yacht, which is a really big yacht, by Charles, the same guy who brought me the letter," I began. "He took me to a lounge on the rear of the boat and tried to reassure me things would be okay. Then a bartender came out, fixed a drink for me, and said that Mr. Windham would be out to join me shortly."

I paused for effect. "And then the glass doors opened, and walking out onto the deck, I swear, was an older version of myself. When he smiled, Aubrey, it was *my* smile. And when I shook his hand, it was like something biological took over, creating a connection just like that. I felt like I was shaking hands with someone I'd known my whole life." I stopped to give Aubrey time to respond, and I took a puff of my cigar.

"Colby, I have chill bumps hearing you describe that. Okay, what happened next?"

"We sat and had our drinks while we waited for our dinner. He told me about his family, which I guess is now my family. He had a brother, Henry, who was killed in World War Two, and a sister, Camille, who sounds like she was pretty much an angel. I'll tell you all about them and the family history when I get back home. Oh, and you will never believe who Jack's chef is."

"Let me guess. Some celebrity chef, like Emeril maybe?"

"Nope, although he might be a celebrity chef in his own mind," I replied, laughing. "It was Andrew from the Burge Club in Mansfield. He was the chef at Eric's wine event that we went to last year. I think he was just as shocked to see me as I was to see him."

"That is so cool! What a small world! So far it sounds amazing." Then her tone grew serious. "Now, tell me about the conversation about him and your mom."

I took a long sip of my drink and began. "It was a love story, Aubrey. One with all the twists and turns of a great book or play. It all started with a pitcher of tea and a plate of cookies for the new guy next door. And then it became a story about loneliness and the need to feel desired and loved. That's what my mom needed, and Jack was there for her."

I paused. "You know, what's interesting is that before I met him, I had Jack pegged as some kind of playboy who took advantage of a lonely housewife. But that's not the way it was. I think Jack was more hurt than anyone by everything that happened. Not to say she didn't love him, but she had a family, a husband who she also loved, and now a new baby on the way. And after getting the news that Dad was transferring back to Atlanta, she was excited about being back with her family and friends. She had a lot to keep her distracted; Jack had nothing.

"He said he couldn't eat or sleep; the guy was heartbroken, Aubrey. To know the woman he loved—who was carrying his child—was less than a hundred feet away and he had to keep his distance. It was all too much. He found a house on the other side of Houston and sold the one next to my parents."

"I can't imagine," Aubrey said, "knowing I may never see my child or get to be a part of his life."

"He said moving didn't help much, but at least he didn't have to see her every day. As you know, I was born in Houston, before the move back to Atlanta, and Jack did get to see me in the hospital once. My mother called and told him the day I was born, and he came to see me a few days later when Dad was at work. He got to hold me a few minutes and, as you can imagine, it was bittersweet—getting to hold your son and then knowing you might never see that son again." I paused, and Aubrey didn't say anything. I could hear her sniffling.

"It was overwhelming for him," I continued. "All of those memories and telling the story to the son he held forty-seven years ago and then had to hand back to his mother. It was overwhelming for us both. He was crying, Aubrey, when he embraced me at the end. And it was one of the most powerful and purest moments of my life. I cannot even come close to describing what I felt."

Aubrey was now sobbing and gasping. It took her a few seconds to respond. "I just don't know what to say," she began. "That is a beautiful story and not what I was expecting. I'm not sure what I was expecting, but not that. He sounds like a wonderful person, and I'm so glad you made the decision to go there and meet him."

She took a second and then said, "I think each person in that story was a victim: Your dad, whether he knew it or not, because of the betrayal. Jack, who lost his son and the woman he loved; and your mom for all those years of loneliness and having to make the hard decision to give Jack up and move on with her life and family.

"And also, Colby, you," she added in a shaky, tearful voice. "Now you will have to live with the consequences of knowing this new truth. A truth that changes everything you thought you knew about your life. I hope that after you have time to process everything, you can come home and find some peace." I could feel her warm heart spilling out into her voice, and that made me love her even more—if that was even possible.

"Thank you, my love. That was beautifully said, and I will try my hardest not to overanalyze all of this and take it for the story that it is. Oh, and as a little footnote, Jack told me I have a brother, Hunter, and if he makes it in tomorrow, I could meet him if I want to. He just found out about me as well, so it should be interesting."

I was tired of talking about me, so before Aubrey could respond, I asked, "How was your day? I've monopolized this conversation and haven't even asked about you and the baby. How are you feeling?"

"The baby and I feel great, and we both miss you. By the way, I told my parents why you're in the Bahamas . . . and it didn't go so well."

"What happened with your parents?"

"Well, they're from the old school where things like that were not supposed to happen. Neither of them really said very much, but I could tell they were both unsettled by it. They are worried about you. And they were concerned about what would happen when you met Jack—and about the repercussions for you if it didn't go well. You know how much they love you, and they just want the best for you. But I'm sure they'll feel better when you come home and tell them the story."

"Well, I hope so. I'm sure it was a shock for them, as it probably will be for anyone who knows us. Other than getting caught up in my drama, what have you been up to today? I'm sure the dogs are loving the river."

"They are, and we haven't seen much of them. Oh! I did have an interesting thing happen to me today. You're not the only one to get a letter from someone in your past," she said teasingly. Aubrey then went on to describe a letter her grandmother had written to her not long before she died. "I so wish you could have met her," she told me. "I regret I never took you to Augusta and that she never came to the river house when you were there.

"What was interesting, Colby, was that she—almost as if she was certain it would happen—talked about me being a great mother. Almost like it was a forgone conclusion. If I had read that letter at any other time in my life, I would have had different feelings about what she had to say. I think I was meant to read it now; with this challenge we are facing with our little girl. Colby, I felt such a sense of peace and comfort when I read her letter, and I'm sure it was a sign that everything is going to be okay."

With a smile and a full heart, I told her I felt the same.

CHAPTER THIRTY

I t was early morning, and I was startled awake by the crazy calls of some tropical bird. It took me several seconds to realize where I was.

I pulled the drapes, and the sun was higher in the sky than it usually was when I woke up. I had a slight headache from all the alcohol, and the aftertaste from the cigar was also a reminder of the night before. I squinted at the clock across the room and saw it was ten-thirty. I had never slept that late in my life. Aubrey had kept me in bed several times until late in the morning, but those extra hours had nothing to do with sleep. That made this a first.

I pulled the curtains shut to hopefully ease the headache and made my way to the kitchen for some coffee. I looked for a coffee maker but could only find a K-Cup dispenser and a Keurig. No one made normal coffee anymore. What happened to the good old days when we brewed coffee and drank half the pot before we were ready for the day? Nonetheless, I was glad to have it. I popped in a cup of something I had never heard of and pushed the button.

While I was waiting for it to brew, I noticed an envelope on the counter next to the door. I didn't remember it being there the night before, but being highly inebriated then, I couldn't say with any certainty it wasn't. I picked it up and saw it had a logo with Jack's boat in the upper left corner and handwritten in the center was my name. I looked around the room to see if there were any other signs of anybody having been there. It bothered me that someone had entered my cabana without me knowing.

I opened the envelope, and it was a note from Jack. He expressed how much he had enjoyed our evening and invited me for lunch at the hotel. It was my guess that Charles had been in to leave the note. I glanced at the clock, and it was already ten-forty-five. I had an hour to get a shower and get myself together.

At eleven-forty-five, I was dressed in my island garb and was heading out the door to walk to the hotel when the limo golf cart pulled up. It was the same driver, Oscar, who had picked me up the day before and delivered me to the marina.

He stepped out with a big smile, revealing a perfect gold tooth. "Good morning, Mr. Cameron. How are you?"

I replied that I was a little shaky from the night before but otherwise doing fine.

"Yes, I came by earlier to deliver the invitation from Mr. Windham, but I couldn't get you to come to the door. I hope you don't mind that I came in and placed it on your counter."

"Not at all. I'm just glad I found it." Mystery solved, and although I didn't think there was much crime on the island, I would remember from then on to always lock my door.

I got in the golf cart, and as we were leaving, Oscar handed me a fresh cup of coffee. "Black and brewed just the way you like it."

I was wondering if there was anything Jack didn't know about me.

After a five-minute drive, we pulled up to the front of the hotel. The first thing I noticed was the sweet, soft fragrance of the tropical flowers. The scent of the wet, fresh blooms reminded me of my favorite aunt's flower shop in Decatur, Georgia, a small city on the outskirts of Atlanta. While in high school, I delivered flowers for her in the afternoons, and on Fridays before I headed to Jewell, she would make up special floral arrangements for me to take to Aubrey. It was a good time in my life.

With the cool temperatures and the robin's-egg-colored sky, it looked to be the start of a great day. Oscar dropped me off with a smile and a wave. I waved back and walked up the stairs to the hotel.

I entered, and while I scanned the room for Jack, the lady behind the concierge desk approached and asked me to follow her. I nodded, and she led me across the lobby to the back of the restaurant to a private room. She parted long floor-to-ceiling curtains and motioned for me to enter. I did, to find Jack and another man sitting at a table.

Jack stood with a big smile and approached me for a handshake and a hug. I glanced at the other man, who neither smiled nor stood.

Jack then turned toward the gruff man and introduced him.

"Colby, I want you to meet Captain Alex Reyes. He has been my captain, fishing partner, and friend for almost thirty years."

I walked over to the captain, and he begrudgingly stood. When I moved toward him for a handshake, his big coarse and calloused hand engulfed mine. He looked directly into my eyes and seemed to squeeze my hand as hard as he could.

I clamped down with equal force and tried to read his stare. It was either distrusting toward me and protective of his longtime boss . . . or it was something else. Whichever the case might be, I had a bad feeling about the guy.

Jack interrupted the standoff and asked us both to sit.

"I was just telling Alex the story about us, and he was quite surprised, weren't you, Alex?"

Still pointing his stare at me, the man replied, "Yes, I was. It must have been quite a shock to suddenly find out you have a father—and one who happens to be very wealthy with his time running out. What do you think about that?" His tone was accusatory.

I looked at Jack before I answered; I could tell he wasn't happy with the question or the attitude. I also did not appreciate it, and I was not about to let this man, in his not-so-subtle way, accuse me of showing up for the money.

"Well, Alex, it is interesting that you don't seem to care that Jack has finally met the son he never had a chance to know. And that you just see this in terms of me coming to the island with bad motives. Jack's wealth, I will have you know, is none of my concern, and it should not be *your* concern. I'm here to spend time with the man who brought me into this world and who loved my mom during a very meaningful period in his life." I never took my cold stare off of him.

In his eyes I saw pure hatred, and if looks could kill, I would have just taken my last breath. I could tell he wanted to come across the table at me, but he knew he had to maintain control around Jack. I kept a half smile-half sneer on my face that said, "Give it your best shot if you dare."

It was crystal clear that he saw me as a threat and wanted to prove his dominance. I was not sure what, but I was betting there was a lot more to the story of Captain Alex Reyes.

Jack intervened, trying to smooth things out. "Alex, that was uncalled for, and do not ever speak another word to Colby in that tone," he said. "You know nothing about him or what his motives are. And I don't need you to protect me if that is what you think you're doing. This is a good thing, and I want everyone to get to know each other. And I certainly don't want to hear any further talk about my money or me being sick." He looked at us both for confirmation. I nodded, and so did Alex.

"Good. Hunter is flying in this afternoon, and I'm excited about the two of you meeting, Colby. And now I'm thinking these last-minute, surprise introductions aren't the best idea."

Alex shot a glance at me that seemed to say, "This is going to be interesting." I was thinking that if the captain was this blunt with his opinions, Hunter, with his closer ties to Jack, might be ten times worse. I knew Jack wanted me to meet everyone, but with the way things were turning out, it probably would have been better if just the two of us had met. I looked at Jack, and he seemed a little stressed—probably thinking the same thing.

"Alex," he decided, "why don't you go to the airport and wait on Hunter and then take him to the boat? He should arrive in the next hour or so. And later we can start this whole thing over. It was my fault for telling you about Colby just as you walked in the room. I should have told you earlier and given you time to express your concerns to me instead of him. I think you were being a little too overprotective, and Colby, you had every right to be defensive. You two got off on the wrong foot, but I think once you get to know each other, things will be just fine. Alex," he continued, "maybe tomorrow you can take Colby and Hunter fishing. It will give the three of you time to spend together." It was more of a directive than a question.

Alex just nodded, and without saying anything, he got up and left.

"I'm sorry you had to go through that, Colby. Alex is a little rough around the edges and is very protective of me. It's not just you; he doesn't trust anyone and thinks everyone is out to get my money. But enough of that. Let's have some lunch. I need something in my stomach after you got me drunk last night," he said with a laugh.

We ordered cheeseburgers and paired them with a couple of Bloody Marys to take the edge off our hangovers. When the food arrived, we dug in.

While we were eating, I asked Jack, "How do you think it will go when Alex tells Hunter that I'm here? I'm not sure it would be good for Hunter's first impression of his new brother to come from him."

Jack put his cheeseburger down and picked up his phone. He called Oscar and told him to go to the airport and wait on Hunter. He then called Alex and told him to go prep the fishing boat for the next day, that he had made other arrangements for Hunter to be picked up.

"I'm glad you thought of that," he said. "I'm not sure if he would have said anything, but it's not worth taking a chance. As for meeting Hunter, let's have dinner tonight, and this afternoon I'll tell him about you. I'll make sure he understands that I reached out to you and that you are here at my request. I promise there won't be a repeat of what you had to go through with Alex."

We continued our meal without talking much. It was not that there was any tension; it was quite the opposite. Jack finished with his meal, ordered us coffee, and then picked up the newspaper and started reading.

I sipped my coffee and turned my chair slightly toward the window. I pulled out my phone and checked for messages. Then I watched as guests outside the window put up their umbrellas and prepared for a day on the beach.

Every now and then, Jack would look up and smile. It was comfortable and pleasant, and I was hoping things would remain that way after I met Hunter.

Just as I finished my coffee, a large jet flew over the resort, so low that the cups and glasses on the table shook.

Jack lowered his paper, and shaking his head with an exasperated smile, he said, "Your brother has arrived."

My stomach tightened.

CHAPTER THIRTY-ONE

As we left the restaurant, Jack firmed up a time for me to join him and Hunter on the boat for dinner. Just like with the captain, it was more of a directive than it was a request.

I said I would be there, but, walking away, I was concerned. I had been prepared to meet a father who, until recently, I had no idea existed. But I never figured that a brother would be thrown into the mix so soon. What if he reacted the way that Alex had?

But, considering Jack's prognosis, I understood why he wanted to bring us all together now. I was sure one of his final wishes was that Hunter and I would come to terms and form a relationship. If I were in his shoes, I would wish for nothing more than to have my sons become true brothers.

I decided to walk back to the cabana, wanting to enjoy the sights and smells along the path and think some more about the upcoming dinner meeting. Hunter and I had lived totally different lives. He had been given part of his inheritance as soon as he graduated from college while my dad had given me a job with the railroad.

I wondered how I might have turned out if the roles had been reversed. Would I still have been the down-to-earth, simple man I thought myself to be, or would I be living a life of luxury with no ambition to ever get off the couch on my hundred-and-fifty-foot yacht? Hunter seemed to have made it work by investing his money well, never asking anything of Jack. I considered that success—and I might have been just a little envious, mostly that he had his own jet, which he flew himself. I found it interesting that all three of us were pilots.

If the two of us did bond enough to spend time together, I might pose the role-reversal question to my brother over drinks one day and get his take. Although I doubted he had ever wondered what it would be like to spend his weekends as I did, mowing the lawn and fixing leaky toilets. He probably never pondered what it would be like to swap fancy restaurants and premieres of Broadway plays for nights out at Ruby Tuesday followed by long strolls through the Home Depot aisles.

Back at the cabana, I decided on a nap. I had not slept much the night before, and this evening, I assumed, would be no different with a lot of alcohol and food—emphasis on alcohol.

I woke from my nap around four o'clock and threw on my swimsuit. I put a few beers in a cooler, grabbed a couple of towels, and headed for the beach. Thirty seconds later, I was looking over the most beautiful azure-colored water.

I walked to the surf, waded out about twenty feet, and dove in. The water felt so warm, and my first thought was to wish Aubrey was there with me. She was the beach person. A private cabana on a beach would have been just her thing. Under other circumstances, she would have come with me. So much of who I am and what's important in my life is centered around her.

Meeting Aubrey would have given Jack more insight into the person that I am. I could see the two of them staying up until all hours with Aubrey telling him every embarrassing and stupid thing I had ever done. I smiled at the thought of those two laughing at my expense. How I would have loved that, but with the issues with the baby, it was best she had stayed home. Maybe one day they would get the chance to meet.

I spent the next hour letting the warm sun soak into my skin. I freed my mind of everything except the sounds of the ocean and the wind and the squawking of the seagulls. After the upheavals of the past two weeks, my overthinking mind needed a rest, and it was a pleasant break. After a while, the cooler had been emptied, and the heat on my back and shoulders reminded me I'd forgotten to use sunscreen. It was time to head back.

I showered and put on a pair of khaki linen pants and a blue linen shirt. I had never owned anything made of linen until Aubrey decided that my wardrobe, consisting mostly of cargo pants and shorts, was seriously outdated. Both of us had laughed when she'd gone through my closet. "Why do all your pants and shorts have those hook things on the side to hold a hammer?" she asked me. "You don't build anything; why would you buy these?"

She decreed I could wear those pants to work, but she was not going to let me wear them when the two of us went out. She took me to a men's shop in Athens, and we spent half the day putting together my new look. It was one of the worst days of my life.

I had finished dressing and was in the kitchen reaching for a beer when I heard the golf cart pull up. I quickly poured the beer into a Solo cup and headed out, but not before I locked the door.

Oscar, with his big gold-toothed smile, was behind the wheel, and after the five-minute drive to the marina, he dropped me off at the same spot he'd left me the night before. He wished me a great evening before he pulled away.

Walking down the pier, I saw T. C. was set up in his portable rocking chair, smoking a big cigar. The same oversized Yeti container was in his other hand, containing, I was sure, an oversized cocktail.

He recognized me right away. "Colby Cameron! How are you today, my friend?" he asked, rocking in the chair as fast as it would go.

"I'm fine, T. C. How are you? Catch any fish today?" The flags on his boat didn't indicate a successful fishing trip. Looking up, I could see a few, but not nearly as many as were flying on the rest of the boats.

Following my eyes, he answered, "Yeah, we got a few sailfish in the cut and then we went deep lining for strawberry grouper. Overall, it was a great day. How was *your* day? Did you go fishing or have any great adventures?" He leaned forward in his chair, sounding genuinely interested. I knew better, though. He wanted to solve the mystery of why I had been on Jack Windham's yacht.

I was not about to give him the pleasure, but I had the itch to tease the guy a bit. "It was a really good day," I responded. "I spent it on the beach enjoying this weather. It's great to get away from the hot, humid climate I'm used to dealing with. It was nice of Mr. Windham to extend an invitation for a visit. Have a good evening, T. C." I began moving toward Jack's yacht before he could ask any other questions.

"Same to you, Colby. Stop by later for a nightcap if you want."

"Thanks. I might do that."

I got to the boat, and no one was in sight. I didn't know if I needed permission to go on board or if I could just walk onto the boat and announce that I was there. It felt like walking into someone's house without knocking.

Before I had to make the decision, Miquel walked out and threw up a hand. "Hi, Mr. Cameron. Please come aboard. Mr. Windham and Hunter are in the den waiting for you. Can I get you an old-fashioned?"

"Hi, Miquel. Yes, I think I'll definitely be needing an old-fashioned."

Noting my nervousness, he said, "I'll take care of that, and you don't have to worry about this evening. I have an idea what's on your mind, and Hunter's a great guy. You two will get along just fine."

I nodded my appreciation and boarded the yacht. As I approached the glass doors, they opened, and I walked in.

Jack and Hunter stopped their conversation and stood up. We all took a second to take in the moment. I didn't know if I was supposed to walk to them or if they would come to me. Should we meet in the middle? Finally, Jack said, "Colby, please come join us."

As I walked toward them, I decided I would take the lead since I was the older brother. I approached Hunter first and stuck out my hand. "Hi, Hunter. Colby Cameron." Which was kind of dumb, since, obviously, Hunter would know who I was.

He stepped forward with a big smile, and he shook my hand. "Hi, Colby. It's so nice to meet you."

I felt a bit awkward, but there are no books to tell you how to meet a brand-new brother not long after you have learned about your biological father. Jack told us to have a seat and he would arrange for our drinks.

But before we sat, I noticed the shared resemblance among the three of us. We all had the same small, squinty blue eyes, the same nose and mouth, and were exactly the same height. I wondered if either of them had noticed too.

Jack had taken a nap after Hunter arrived and had not had the chance to give him the story about me. He began telling Hunter about the letter he'd had Charles deliver to me at the Sandersville airport. He then gave Hunter a synopsis of what we'd discussed the night before. I was mostly silent, watching Hunter's reaction to Jack's story. From time to time, Hunter would glance at me, and I imagined he was trying to gauge my feelings too. He seemed to genuinely accept what he heard, and I saw no signs he had me labeled as someone who had shown up for an inheritance. I sensed he could see—and was thankful for—his father's newfound joy over our new connection.

About the time Jack finished the story, Andrew appeared to tell us that dinner was served. As he had the night before, he eloquently described the courses he'd prepared and then invited us to the table. We had a conch salad followed by grilled mahi-mahi that had been caught that day, sautéed asparagus topped with blue cheese, and lemon pasta paired with a Viognier from the Flanagan winery.

After dinner, we moved back to the lounge on the stern of the yacht. Jack had Miquel bring us a tray with three large cognac glasses, each one filled with about an ounce of golden-brown liquid. He handed us each a glass and stood. Then, after a few seconds of reflection, he made the most amazing toast I had ever heard.

"To my two sons. In different ways, I've watched as you each became men and developed integrity and strength of character, which I can take little credit for.

Hunter, I have failed you in so many ways, and despite that, you have become a remarkable person who has never allowed the things you have been given to change who you are. I have seen you volunteer and give to those less fortunate to help change their lives. I want you to know that I wish I had been around more to support you instead of working as much as I did. But you overcame that, and I am so proud of you."

Then he turned to me. "Colby, I cannot express how much I have loved you from afar and longed to be a part of your life. I watched you from the time you were a child and through your teenage years, and I was there when you graduated from college. But I never got the chance to tell you how proud I was of you.

"I wish the two of you could have known each other and had the chance to be brothers, but that was not to be—until now. Being here with both of you is a dream come true and has made my life complete. Now, it is my desire that you love each other and have the relationship I've always wanted for you."

Hunter and I stood and looked at each other. We both had tears in our eyes, and at that moment, a connection was born between us words cannot describe. Jack noticed what was happening, and

I think if his life had ended there, he would have died in peace, knowing his sons would from that point on be there for each other.

We raised our glasses then, basking in the warmth of the toast of a lifetime.

CHAPTER THIRTY-TWO

I t was getting close to eleven o'clock, and Jack was ready to call it a night. The previous night's excessive drinking had done him in, and he was tired. At least that is what he told us. He didn't *seem* to be tired and was probably making an early exit to give Hunter and me some time alone. He also said he had to make a run to Staniel Cay the next day for a little business but would see us in the evening. He gave us each a hug and said good night.

Hunter and I left the boat and decided to go to the bar at the resort to talk some more over drinks. As we got to the end of the pier, we saw that T. C.'s evening ritual was in full swing. People had set their chairs in a circle, and, as you would guess, he was the center of attention. He gestured and said something that brought on gales of laughter, and his rap music was way louder than I would have thought might be tolerated there. I was sure the fishermen and the people on the yachts would at some point tell him to keep the volume down or when to shut it off.

When T. C. saw us, he jumped up and grinned. "Hunter Windham, I figured you were here when we were about knocked off our boat by that low pass over the harbor. You know you piss off the old blue-haired ladies when you do that. If it were anyone else, they would be banned from the island."

"Hi, T. C. I know I should stop doing it, but I like to give you a break and give them someone else to talk about. I'm surprised they still let you have your little parties on the dock after the mishap with the topless girls. You're lucky *you're* still allowed here on the island."

With a laugh, T. C. agreed.

Hunter then turned and gestured toward me. "T. C., I want to introduce you to my brother, Colby Cameron."

T. C. slapped his leg and shook his head. "Colby and I have met, and now it all makes sense. You know I don't like anything going on around here that I don't know about, and when Colby headed to Jack's boat dressed like Judge Smails from *Caddyshack*, I wondered who he was. And now I know. Colby, how are you?"

"I did not look like Judge Smails," I said, laughing along with everyone else.

"I know. I'm just kidding. We are just about to shut this party down, being that the blue-hairs have given me a curfew of eleven. We are planning to head down to the Nauti Rooster. Why don't you two join us?"

The Nauti Rooster, as I'd found out earlier from Oscar, was the local bar where the fishermen and crews hung out. He said it could get quite rowdy.

"Hunter, what do you think?" I asked.

"I'm up for it if you are."

I looked at T. C. and told him we would meet him there.

"Great. We'll see you there in about an hour, and I will buy you both a drink. Brothers. I should have already figured that out. You two look a lot alike, and you both look like Jack."

We walked to the hotel and sat down for a quick drink before heading to the bar. Knowing it would probably be a long night, we skipped the hard stuff and ordered beers. When they arrived, we lifted them in a silent toast then we took our first sips.

"Did your dad really build all this?" I asked.

"You mean *our* dad, and, yes, he did—with a few of his oil friends from Texas. There used to be a small single-level hotel near the bar we'll be at tonight. Back then, it wasn't an exclusive island, more of a hidden secret that only the locals and seasoned fishermen knew about.

"The secret, you see, is a long, deep-sea gully that runs up the length of Andros Island. They call it 'The Pocket,' and it's just west of here. If the winds are right, it has some of the best billfish, blue and white marlin, tuna, and wahoo fishing in the Bahamas. The marina was about a quarter of its current size, and the harbor wasn't dredged to handle the big yachts. It wasn't until the late sixties that people started finding out how good the fishing was, and that's when this place got popular and when it started growing." He took a sip of his drink. "It did well for about ten years. They expanded and upgraded the hotel to cater to a higher-level clientele, and they even built a pool and lounge for the fishermen's families.

"But when Nassau became a main stop for the cruise ships and began to build resorts, it pulled the fishermen from Chub. Charter fishing companies were popping up everywhere, and it was only a short hop to fish in The Pocket. And, of course, the resorts in Nassau had all the shopping, waterslides, golf courses, and other amenities that kept the families busy while the fishermen did their thing.

"At some point, the hotel here closed and the marina all but shut down," he continued. "It looked like the end of an era for the island, and it upset Dad that everything was closing. For the people of the island, that would mean their main source of revenue would be lost. Dad had made some good friends here, and he was not about to let that happen. When he gets something on his mind, our father is committed.

"So, with a few of his contemporaries from Texas, he built this resort, expanded the marina, and dredged the harbor. He also persuaded a few of the fishing charter companies to come to the island and compete with Nassau. It took a few years, but as Nassau became more crowded and touristy, the wealthy fishermen began coming back to Chub in search of a more personal experience away from the crowds.

"Dad and his group bought most of the island and put it in a trust that prohibits the construction of any more resorts. Now, it's private and, for the most part, exclusive. There are only 860 acres and forty-six full-time residents. It's mostly booked for the entire fishing season but is available during the off-season, which is mostly in the winter months. And even then, it's difficult to get a reservation."

It was a great story, but what got my attention most was when he corrected me and called Jack "our" dad. I didn't think of Jack that way, but I was touched that Hunter had accepted me so quickly as his brother.

"What a story," I said. "And what an amazing man. I wish I'd had more time to get to know him."

"Oh, I do as well. I don't think I've ever seen our dad as happy as he was tonight. We can all be thankful for that." Hunter took a long sip of his beer and said, "I think we might need to wind things up here and head over to The Rooster. You ready?"

I told him I was, and he waved to the bartender and, without making a move to pay, he got up and left. I guessed since Jack owned part of the resort and island, he and Hunter didn't have to pay for anything, at least not by the item.

Hunter sent a text to Oscar to pick us up, and he was waiting out front when we got outside. It was about a five-minute ride to the bar, which was loud and crowded. A thatch-covered pavilion resembling a tiki bar was jammed with people dancing. As we got closer, I could see a band was playing. Judging by the steel drums, colorful clothing, and dreadlocks, I figured they must be from Jamaica or one of the islands.

As we made our way into the bar, I saw that it too was packed. I didn't know there were this many people on the boats or the island. I guessed since it was probably the only bar, it was the only place to go. We saw T. C. about the same time he saw us, and with a big wave, he motioned us over. He had two tables near the bar with two empty chairs waiting for us. We made our way over and sat, and a waitress immediately showed up and asked us what we would like to drink. I wasn't sure if she had hurried over because of who Hunter was, or if the bar was just that efficient.

We got our drinks and tried to talk, but it was too loud. T. C. motioned to the door and did a little pantomime of playing the drums and singing. I assumed that meant he wanted us to go outside and listen to the band. His group, about ten in number, filed out after him, and Hunter and I fell into step behind them.

T. C. and his boys went straight to the dance floor, found a group of girls, and started dancing. Hunter was approached by a couple who knew him, and they walked a few feet away so they could talk. He looked at me, and I motioned that I was going back into the bar where it was not so loud. He gave me a thumbs-up, and I walked back inside.

After all the years of flying, racing, and shooting guns without ear protection, my hearing was beginning to fail me, and I didn't want to speed up the process. Aubrey was getting tired of me always asking, "What?" after everything she said, and she was threatening to make me get hearing aids.

I found a semi-quiet spot at the end of the bar, pulled up a stool, ordered a beer, and began to people watch. Most of the patrons were under thirty, had dark tans, and were dressed in fishing clothes or beachwear. They appeared to be crews from the yachts or guests from the resort. Other than the bar staff, there did not appear to be a single islander, and I wondered where they might hang out on a weekend night. I imagined that on the other side of the island, there was a place similar to this, and it was probably packed as well.

I had been inside for about ten minutes when T. C. and his group, along with Hunter and a few of his friends, came back in, laughing hysterically about something. One of the guys gave T. C. a high five and then doubled over with laughter. It didn't take long for me to get a hint about what might have happened. Just as the guys got to their table, a knot of girls stormed in and made a beeline to the group. I was pretty sure they were the girls the guys had been dancing with, and I could tell by their expressions they were mad as hell. This was confirmed when one of them threw a drink in T. C.'s face and started yelling at him. He said something back that made his friends roar with laughter. She shot him a bird and headed toward a table near the front door.

Sitting at that table were a group of guys who didn't quite fit in with the Nauti Rooster crowd. They looked to be Italian or maybe South American. They had on nice shirts and slacks and were wearing big gold chains and had gold bracelets on their arms. The girls were American and a lot younger than the guys. I had a suspicion that the guys and girls hadn't known each other long.

The girl who'd shot T. C. the bird whispered something to one of the guys and pointed to T. C.'s group. Then all but one of the guys got up and walked over to the table.

Things escalated quickly after that. One of the guys started yelling with his finger jammed in Hunter's face. I suspected the girl had, in fact, complained about T. C. and the guy had gotten it all wrong. He shoved Hunter against a table, and Hunter shoved him back. The guy then took a wild swing, but he didn't have the reach to connect. Hunter shoved him a little harder, and he hit the floor. Then a melee broke out as everyone began shoving at each other.

For some reason, I took my eyes off the commotion and looked over at the table where the girls had been sitting. The one guy who had stayed back was now on his feet and moving toward the group. To borrow a line from the band Men at Work, "He was six foot four and full of muscle." He was zeroed in on Hunter and halfway across the floor when I jumped off my stool and went into big-brother mode.

I met the guy before he got to the group, and I put my hand on his arm to stop him. He gave me an incredulous look, seemingly in disbelief that I had the nerve to put my hand on him. When he raised his fist toward me, I already had my knife pulled and stuck it in his side with the tip barely piercing him. That got his attention, and he immediately put his hand back down.

With my knife still firmly in his side, I leaned toward him and whispered that he and his boys were about to make a big mistake. I told him if they harmed one hair on the head of the guy his friend was fighting, there was a good chance they would never make it off the island. I asked him if he understood, and he nodded that he did.

Everyone from his group had their eyes on him, obviously wondering why he'd stopped going after me. There was no doubt they were planning on him finishing what they'd started. He motioned for them to stop, and they did. He was apparently the leader, and I was impressed with the way he'd stopped the fighting by just holding up his hand.

I pulled back my knife and motioned for him to follow me to the bar. I apologized for sticking the knife in him and asked him if I could buy him a beer as a peace offering. He smiled and told me that would be nice.

We both glanced back at the table, where everyone was staring at us, shocked at the surprise ending of the fight. It had been a potentially tragic situation that had turned into a comedy. We both laughed and turned back toward the bar. About the time our beers arrived, I looked back at the table. The two groups were now laughing together as T. C. waved his arms in the air, in full storytelling mode.

"I assume that you're here fishing. Where are you from?" I asked my new friend.

"We are, and we are from Miami. I'm here with my cousins. And, as you've just seen, my job is more to look after them than it is to fish." He shook his head in frustration.

"What do you do in Miami?" I asked. Then I immediately regretted asking that. With the way the guys were dressed, where they were from, and how they acted, there was a fair chance of them being in the business of illegal drugs. In which case, the question would have put my new friend in an uncomfortable position.

"I'm a pilot," he replied.

I thought maybe I hadn't asked an unfortunate question after all. "Well, we have more in common than coming to the rescue of our families," I told him. "I am a pilot too. What do you fly and who do you fly for?"

Dodging my question, he asked me, "How about you tell me a bit about you first? Where are you from, and are you here fishing?"

I decided to be as transparent as possible. I had yet to tell anyone my story except for Aubrey, and I thought a total stranger might be a great start. "Are you ready for a story?" I asked him.

He motioned to the bartender, asking him to bring us two glasses and a bottle of bourbon. Then he poured us about two fingers and asked me to begin.

I told him where I was from, that I was married to the most beautiful girl in the world, and that we had a child on the way. I told him about the letter and why I was there, and then I pointed to Hunter. I explained he was a brother I hadn't known about until the night before. I explained about Jack's influence on the island and that if anyone had hurt Hunter, it would have caused real problems. I then said that Hunter was a great guy and that he was, in fact, not the one who had caused the problem with the girl. It was the bigger guy, I said. But I added quickly that T. C. was harmless and just loved to be the center of attention. I finished up by telling him I was a retired transportation guy and now a flight instructor.

"That's quite a story," he replied. "I can't imagine getting a letter like that with such life-changing news. I've heard about your dad, and even though I have a small hole in my side, I'm glad you stopped me from making a big mistake. We're docked across from your dad's yacht, and I think I saw you boarding it yesterday afternoon. How did it go meeting him? And how are things going with your brother? This must be big news to him as well."

"First, let me apologize again for the knife. I knew there was no way I could take you if you became aggressive, and all I wanted to do was protect my new brother. Also allow me to introduce myself. I'm Colby Cameron, and although we met under challenging circumstances, it's a pleasure to know you. As for meeting my father, it went well, and the same with my brother," I said, sticking my hand out for a formal introduction.

"Mark Azar, and it is a pleasure to meet you, Colby. Now that I know a little about you, I will tell you more about me. I clearly understand the position you were in tonight. Had that happened in Miami, I would have reacted the same way and given the same kind of warning that you did. My cousins' past behavior is the reason I knew to stand down and tell them to stop. They're a bunch of hotheads who get themselves in trouble that they can't get out of without me or someone from the family coming to their rescue.

"As for what I do, I am the pilot for the family, and in the old days, I flew a Cessna Caravan or a gutted-out King Air on some interesting trips from Central America to South Florida. Now I fly the family and their business partners in a Bombardier Global Express, which is less exciting but not quite as dangerous. And, like you, I am married—to the second most beautiful girl in the world, and I have three daughters who range in age from six to ten."

I had to laugh. How clever—and humble—of him to play off my remark about Aubrey and her beauty. I was beginning to really like this guy.

He then asked, "What do you fly, and where do you teach?"

I told him about my Cessna 182 and the 310, and I said my airplanes were nothing like the ones that he flew. I then told him I lived in a small town in Georgia and never had more than a couple of students at a time. Nodding toward Hunter, I told Mark that he and our father were also pilots, and that Hunter had a Gulfstream G550 and Jack had a G650.

Impressed, Mark let out a low whistle.

We talked about our upbringing and our families and what we both wanted out of life. I told him that despite the way we'd met, I hoped we could be friends. He said he hoped so too, and we exchanged contact information. He then invited me and Aubrey to visit him and his family at their vacation house in the Keys, and I extended the same invitation for Warthen. I thought that Aubrey and I would get the better end of that deal.

Before we left, we joined the group at the table for a little fun. I introduced Mark to Hunter and then we listened to T. C. and one of Mark's cousins compete to see who could tell the best story.

After a few minutes, I asked Hunter if he was ready to leave. He was, and I told Mark we would be heading out. He grabbed my hand and shook it and gave me a bear hug. Then with a sincere look in his eyes, he gave me some parting words. "Colby let's stay in touch, and if I can ever help you out in any way, you let me know. You understand?"

I told him I did and that it was the same deal with me.

Hunter called Oscar, who took us back to my cabana. Not ready for the night to end, I suggested we take a couple of chairs to the beach for a cigar and final nightcap. He agreed, and the conversation on the beach soon turned to our childhoods and the sports we'd played in high school. Then I told him about Aubrey, about breaking up with her when I went to college, and how it took twenty-five years to get her back. We talked a bit more, and then he got quiet. I asked him what he was thinking, and he hit me with a bombshell.

He said that right after college, his mom gave him a call when she was sick and nearing the end of her life. She told him what basically amounted to the story Jack had told me but without the details. She said she thought he should know he had a brother. She did not tell him my name but said that maybe one day it would work out for us to meet. She also cautioned him about bringing up the subject with his father. She said it was too painful for him and that lives could be ruined if the information were to get out.

Hunter said he had wondered all those years who I was, what I was like, and if he would ever get a chance to meet me. He also wondered if I knew. He'd regretted over the years not asking his mom what my name was, but she became too sick too fast, and he never got the chance. He said he felt like he would have tried to find me if he'd had that information. He also said he wished at some point he would have just asked Jack and tried to make a meeting happen.

We sat for a moment, both of us staring at the stars.

I then told him that I pretty much had done the same thing with Aubrey, let a lot of time go by without pursuing a connection I knew was important. I hadn't had the courage to do anything about it. I let almost thirty years slip by without trying to contact her, and it was my biggest regret.

I told him that maybe this was our time, and this was the way it was supposed to be. The past didn't matter; now that we had found each other, we could share the future and make the most of it. A few seconds passed, and then at the same time, we stood up and reached for each other; it was an embrace that closed the gap of all the years gone by. We were brothers now, and nothing would come between us.

CHAPTER THIRTY-THREE

C aptain Alex Reyes was sitting alone in the dimly lit corner in the back bar of the Chub Cay resort, and he was seething. It had been three long years since he'd had a drink, and sitting on the bar in front of him was a shot of bourbon. He stared at it and twisted the small glass around.

After almost getting fired years ago by Jack for inappropriate behavior with the wife of a guest—even though she had been the one to come on to him—Alex had been forced to give up the one thing he looked forward to after a long day on the water. Jack would certainly have fired him had Alex not blamed the incident on alcohol and promised Jack he'd quit. He always knew one day he would be at the crossroads where he now found himself; he just had not been sure what would get him to that point. He found out today.

He picked up the glass, holding it to the light and examining the brown liquid that had been his form of escape for so many years. He knew if he drank it, there would be no going back. And then, without hesitation, he slammed the warm alcohol down his throat. He closed his eyes, savoring the sting of the bourbon, and signaled the bartender for another.

He knew there was a good chance Jack would find out. He should have bought a bottle and drunk it in his cabin on the yacht, but a part of him really didn't care if he was caught. Because of how sick Jack was, Alex only had about six months of employment left, so what did it really matter?

Alex had been working for Jack Windham for the last thirty years. After a conviction by a military court martial and receiving a dishonorable discharge from the army, he spent two years in Leavenworth for crimes committed in Vietnam. He was imprisoned for taking part in an incident that was part of the My Lai massacre. During the event at which Alex had been present, a group of rogue American soldiers brutally killed twenty-two unarmed Vietnamese civilians and participated in other unspeakable crimes. He swore that he was not involved—and they couldn't prove he was—but being with the group and doing nothing to stop them got him two years in prison.

When he was released, he was broke, bitter, and unemployed. Being a felon, he found no opportunities for employment other than menial minimum-wage jobs, and he was not going to flip hamburgers. He contacted a few friends from South Florida he'd met in Vietnam, and they offered him employment. He took them up on the offer and got back into the shady business of distributing illegal drugs.

His job was running a drug boat, smuggling cocaine and heroin from Central America and the Caribbean to the States. He learned to navigate the waters, including dangerous sections of reefs, mostly traveling at night. He became very accomplished at the work and was always able to stay one step ahead of law enforcement. It was very lucrative for a while. What ended his career wasn't getting caught by the authorities but getting shot multiple times in a deal gone bad.

Fortunately for him, the incident did not take place out on the ocean, but in the backroom of a bar in downtown Miami. He spent a month in the hospital, and after his recovery, he decided to clean himself up and use his skills running a boat in a way that didn't put his life at risk.

He caught a break and was hired by a commercial passenger service running from Fort Lauderdale to Nassau. He did that for a year or two and then was hired by a private yacht owner. Alex ran the man's boat for a couple of years until the owner sold it. The yacht owner was a friend of Jack's and knew he was looking for a captain, so he recommended Alex. And thirty years later, here Alex was with nothing to show for that time.

He threw down the second shot of bourbon and thought about all the years of being at the beck and call of the Windham family. The first few years were the worst. He was more of a servant and babysitter than a captain. He spent more time running to the liquor store or picking up groceries than running the boat. Jack would play host to couples who couldn't care less about boating or fishing; they just wanted to get drunk and never leave the harbor. Or Jack's wife would bring down her friends and their spoiled-brat kids. More than once, Alex had to save one of the little cretins from falling overboard. The only benefit was that every now and then one of the women would get drunk and make advances toward him. He obliged them all.

What made him stay was Jack. When there were no guests, they would take out the fifty-five-foot Hatteras and fish from the time the sun came up, sometimes into the night. Jack always pulled his weight on the boat and did not accept laziness. Alex had to fire more than one mate for spending too much time on their phones instead of watching and tending to the lines. But mostly what made him stay was that Jack understood him. He knew Jack didn't know the whole story about Alex's past life, but he knew enough—and still gave him a chance. Jack respected Alex as a captain and never looked down on him.

With Jack only having a short time to live, Alex knew he would soon be without a job. His health wasn't the greatest, and he was ready to retire. He knew there was no way he could take on a new owner on a new yacht. After working for Jack, he wouldn't have the patience to deal with some rich wannabe fisherman who just wanted to reel in the fish and knew nothing about fishing or the sea.

But until now, Alex had never felt he had to worry about that. Jack had always taken care of him, and on several occasions, he had assured him he didn't need to be concerned about his retirement, that he would reward him for all his years of service. Alex had never been bold enough to ask him exactly what he meant by "reward" or to ask for something formal to be put in writing. He had no assurance that Jack had, in fact, taken any steps to provide for his retirement, either in a retirement account or in his will.

If he *wasn't* in the will, he wondered if Hunter would voluntarily follow through with his dad's wishes or if he would need a bit of "persuading." Alex kept in touch with acquaintances in South Florida who routinely worked outside the law, and they could make things happen. With a few well-placed threats, Alex knew that Hunter would cave to whatever Alex wanted. Hunter was soft and not the type to stand up to confrontation. Hunter wouldn't risk his safety to hold on to a few million dollars.

But Colby Cameron was the reason Alex was at the bar, having the drink he knew would throw him over the edge and possibly get him fired. When he met Colby at breakfast, he knew he would be a problem. He was not like Hunter. Colby had stood up to him and even challenged him. It was possible there was a new threat to his financial future, and now more than ever, he needed to have that talk with Jack about his retirement.

CHAPTER THIRTY-FOUR

After all the drinking and almost stabbing Mark Azar in the ribs with a knife, I woke up the next morning tired and with a serious hangover. It was the second morning I had slept past nine. If Aubrey ever found out, I wouldn't hear the end of it.

I coaxed myself out of bed at nine-thirty, stumbled into the kitchen, and plopped one of the plastic containers of coffee into the machine. I was sleepily taking my first sip when I heard a horn outside, not like a car horn, but more like a motorcycle.

I walked to the door and looked out. It was Hunter in Oscar's golf cart, and he was all smiles. He gave me a wave, and I waved back and motioned for him to come inside. He bounded up the walkway like he had not had the same experience that I had the night before. As he walked through the door, even though it hurt my head, I just had to laugh. He was dressed in a safari hunting outfit.

"Why are you dressed like that? Are we going big-game hunting?"

"No, smart-ass. I'm going to show you around the island, and we may go on a hike."

"Hunter, the island is only eight hundred acres, and most of that is the resort, airport, and marina. Where are we going to hike?"

I asked, laughing. Then I studied him and asked, "You don't hike much, do you?"

"No, I don't, but there are trails around the beaches, and don't act like you're Paul Bunyan," he said defensively.

I had to laugh again. "Hunter, Paul Bunyan was a *lumberjack*. He was not a hiker, and I'm guessing you haven't hiked much farther than the buffet line at the country club."

"Okay, so maybe I'm not a hiker, but I sure look good in hiking clothes," he told me proudly, waving an arm to indicate his crazy outfit.

I just rolled my eyes and took a sip of coffee. "You want a cup?"

"Sure, the caffeine will give me more energy to hike."

We both laughed, and I put another plastic cup in the machine. "So, seriously, what do you want to do today? Is there really anything to see on the island?"

"Not much, but I can take you on some cart paths that go all through the island, and some of the views are honestly pretty incredible to see. And also remote beaches only the locals know about. I can show you where they are, and maybe you can come back and bring Aubrey. They are great places to get lucky, and I'll even throw in a few lessons on how to make it a successful outing if you know what I mean."

As was becoming a habit after Hunter spoke, I shook my head. The last thing I could imagine was Hunter teaching me anything about romance.

"Have a seat and enjoy your coffee, Don Juan," I told him. "I'm going to get dressed. Unfortunately, I didn't pack my safari outfit. I let Biff at the club borrow it, along with my pith helmet."

Hunter replied with instructions on what I could do with the pith helmet. A few minutes later I emerged wearing a pair of khaki shorts and a fishing shirt. I immediately felt his critical eye on me.

"Dude, those cargo shorts went out in the nineties. And why are you wearing socks with loafers? Doesn't your wife teach you how to dress?" Although he looked like Ernest Hemingway on a safari hunt, he was probably right. I had heard it all before from Aubrey, and I was not going to give him the satisfaction of knowing she was on his side. When she bought my new clothes a few months ago, she gave away all my cargo shorts—except for my favorite pair, which I managed to hide.

After commenting on my clothes, he pulled a bottle of rum from the cabinet and poured a generous amount into his coffee. Before I could stop him, he poured a few fingers into my mug and then jokingly asked me if I wanted some.

"Why not? I've had alcohol streaming through my blood since I got here, so why should I stop now?"

"I knew you were my brother."

We left the cabana in Oscar's limo golf cart and headed to the other side of the island. It took every bit of five minutes, and if I'd stood on top of the golf cart, I could have almost looked down at the whole island all at once.

Hunter stopped the cart at a clump of palm trees and studied them a minute. He then walked to the shore and carefully splashed his shirt and face with water before walking back. "This should be good," he said. "Take a picture of me in front of these trees and try to get them all in the picture." He took off his helmet and put it over his chest, making a horrible, strained face.

I took several pictures and asked him what he was doing.

"I told a special lady friend from New Zealand I was going on a backwoods trek on my dad's island, and she sent me these clothes. Colby, she is hot, and I don't want to disappoint her." He again posed like he was exhausted, this time with his hand on his knee. "Take a few more," he said.

"I assume she doesn't know the island is the size of a Walmart parking lot? And how is it that you have a girlfriend in New Zealand? That is an extreme long-distance relationship."

"I didn't say she lived in New Zealand; I said she was from there. She actually lives in Brussels. She's the sister of a girl I used to date in Paris," he said as if all of that was as normal as could be. I wanted to call him an international playboy, but I knew he would take it as a compliment.

"Life is an illusion," he continued. "She has no idea that we didn't hike twenty miles through an alligator-infested swamp. As a matter of fact, that is probably what she wants to believe, and she'd probably never research what the island's really like. It's all about the fantasy of believing what one wants to believe. I can clearly see that you don't know women. You've spent too much time behind a computer or driving trucks or whatever you did in Canada to know about such things. Stick with your worldly brother, and I'll teach you a few tricks."

Jack had obviously not filled him in about the more extreme chapters of my life, and I decided to let him have his fun. One day I would share with him some true-life worldly tales.

We left the dangerous alligator-infested swamp and drove to the most beautiful private beach I had ever seen. It was even prettier than the pink-sand beach on Grand Cayman where Aubrey and I had spent our honeymoon. Set back in a little cove with bleached white sand leading to cobalt-blue water, it was beautifully protected by a semicircular stand of palm trees.

Hunter parked the limo and pulled a cooler and a couple of chairs from the back of the cart. He set the chairs up under the palm trees so that they faced the beach. He then grabbed us each a beer from the cooler and cut the ends of two cigars and handed one to me.

"I call this Hunter's Hideaway. It's the place where many young maids lost their baubles to my trade," he said, a look of mock smugness on his face. He took a sip from his beer and puffed on his cigar. I think he liked setting himself up for me to make fun of him. He had a self-effacing way of not taking himself too seriously.

"So, you are also a highwayman?" I asked, acknowledging his reference to the song.

We spent the next couple of hours drinking beer and talking about our lives. He told me how he'd planned to learn the real world of business from Jack after college and hopefully take over for him one day, but that had not worked out. He said it was a disappointment—not just the loss of the business opportunity, but missing out on spending time with and getting to know his father.

I understood exactly what he meant. As kind as he had been, my own father had worked a lot and was not around that much when I was young. Our time to bond had come when I was out of college and he was retired. Railroad men were a different breed. They were generally married to their jobs and weren't home much with their families—which could lead to wives becoming lonely.

Hunter said he'd thought about starting his own company but hadn't had the nerve to risk the money Jack had given him after graduation. Instead, he invested the money with a friend's firm. He said he felt like a failure for never doing anything substantial with his life.

We sat quietly for a while. I wanted to tell him that I probably would have done the same thing.

He asked me about my life, and we picked up where we'd left off the previous evening on the beach. I told him more about moving to Canada and starting the logistics company. He said he couldn't imagine picking up and moving that far from home. I told him that had not been easy and that I had almost backed out more than once. In the end, it had been my dad who gave me the encouragement I needed to firm up my plans and go.

That should have been an omen, a sign for me to stay. By listening to my dad, I became like him: married to my job. With that decision, I gave up on what should have mattered most. I told Hunter I had always wondered what life would have been like if

I had not made the decisions that caused me to lose Aubrey for so long.

If I'd stayed, I might have reconnected with her after college, and maybe we would be getting ready now to send some kids to college. I'd always felt like a failure, I told Hunter, for not following my heart and giving up on me and Aubrey.

But we all make our paths in life, and they seldom lead us where we think they will. It was interesting that now my life and my brother's had led us to this place, a small island in the Bahamas, where our paths finally merged.

I asked him if there had ever been someone special in his life. And after a deep sigh, he told me about a girl from Mississippi he fell in love with not long after college. But, much like me, he'd allowed true love to slip away as his life moved from one stage to the next. Once Hunter's plans to work with Jack fell through, he bought a boat and a jet and took off to discover the world while she took a job in Atlanta. I asked him where she was now, and a shadow moved across his face when he said he didn't know. I didn't go so far as to tell him to look her up, but I did tell him that life seemed to offer second chances.

What started as a fun-in-the-sun, lighthearted day had turned into a time for introspection. We delved into parts of our lives we didn't share a lot with others. Hunter stared out into the sea, and after a minute or two of silence, I learned what was on his mind. With his eyes still pointed at the view, he asked me softly, "Do you think he knew?"

"I've asked myself that question at least a thousand times. It was unmistakable that, physically, I did not fit in. I was taller than anyone on either side of the family. But there was always talk of an uncle or great-uncle on someone's side who had reached six feet. No one knew who he was, but they were sure of it." I paused. "Whether he knew or not, he loved me and cared for me, and he was a great father. I was with him when he died, and in our last conversation, he said everything a son could want to hear. He smiled at me, Hunter, as he took his final breaths, and it was my honor that I got to be with him in that moment to wipe away his tears." Now it was my turn to stare out at the sea as the memories engulfed me. "I got to tell him then how he had shaped me to become the man I am. I got to tell my dad how much I'd always wanted to be just like him. I told him that no son could love his father more than I loved him—and that I would be forever proud that he was my dad."

I looked over at Hunter, and, like me, he had tears running down his cheeks. He stood and embraced me in a way that said more than words.

We talked a little more on the subject and then, having reached our emotional threshold for the day, we just enjoyed the beach as we drank our beers and puffed on the cigars. There was nothing better than sitting quietly by the surf next to my brother.

After achieving a nice beer buzz and an adequate sunburn, we loaded up the limo cart with the chairs and empty cooler. Hunter drove me on what I called his ride of shame, telling me the name of every girl he had romanced in each cove we passed. I told him he should have been a fiction writer. After circling the island, we arrived at the resort.

Oscar was standing out front with his arms folded across his chest. He did not look happy, and I could only think of one reason why.

"You didn't ask him first about borrowing his cart?"

"Well, technically it's our cart, and, hey, it was right out front with the keys in the ignition. And he was mostly just using it to take you around. I didn't think he'd mind."

"That was what I said—some of it almost verbatim—when I got caught stealing my mother's car when I was fifteen. It didn't work then, and it's not going to work now. You'd better come up with something else."

Oscar walked to the cart with his arms still folded and said to Hunter, "You took my cart without asking. I had deliveries to make today."

I am ashamed to say that Hunter took my advice.

"Oscar, I am so sorry, but it was an emergency. Colby had way too much to drink last night, and when he didn't answer his phone, I got really worried. I needed to check on him, and when I ran out of the hotel, there was your cart. I knew you wouldn't mind under the circumstances, and I rushed over to his cabana. I blew the horn several times to try and wake him. Then, when he didn't come out, I rushed in and found him sleeping on his back—and he was turning blue. I think he must have thrown up and almost suffocated. I got there just in time. Thank you so much for helping by offering your cart. Both of us saved him, Oscar. Jack will be so proud." That last dramatic flourish could have fit right into an Academy-Award-winning scene.

Oscar stood there for a minute, looked at Hunter, and then turned to me. I thought he was about to tell us to get our narrow asses out of his limo before he called Jack. But instead he wiped his eyes, made the sign of the cross over his chest, and said, "Oh, thank God that Mr. Colby is all right. With all that drinking at that bar, I always worry that something like that could happen. Mr. Jack would have died if something had happened to Mr. Colby. Thank you, Mr. Hunter, for acting so fast to save Mr. Colby."

"Anything for my new brother. He hasn't been many places other than a cornfield in Georgia, and he isn't used to life outside the farm. Oscar, I'll keep an eye on him and make sure nothing happens."

"Oh, thank you, Mr. Hunter. Why don't you keep the limo, and I'll use the smaller cart."

"You're welcome, Oscar."

After Oscar left, Hunter turned to me with a big grin, holding his arms out in an expansive gesture. "Any questions for the master?"

"You are quite a piece of work. Of course, back in the cornfield, dressed in our overalls, we would have another way to say that. We would say you are a lying piece of something that comes out of the south end of a cow," I said with a laugh.

As we were walking up the steps to the hotel, he put his arm around me and peered down at me over his sunglasses. "Hate the game, but don't hate the player."

I shook my head and laughed. "That worn-out cliché, which was overused by thirteen-year-old boys back in the eighties, still sounds just as stupid. And it also sounds like something T. C. might spout off."

"I can take your jealous criticism, but that really hurts, comparing me to T. C. To repair that, you will need to buy me lunch and two margaritas."

We were instantly greeted by several of the staff in the lobby, and they were beaming. We said we would like to have lunch, and three of them escorted us to the same table in the back room where Jack and I had eaten breakfast the previous morning. It was obvious the word was out about us being brothers. Our waitress arrived, smiling, and could not stop staring as she took our order and left.

"You know what they are thinking," I said.

Hunter looked up from his phone, genuinely curious, and asked, "What?"

"That it's intriguing how one of Jack Windham's sons could turn out to be so tall and handsome while the other turned out . . . well, you know what I mean. But I'm sure they think you are very nice, so at least you have that." I said it with a straight face, turning my attention to my phone. I could feel him staring at me, trying to come up with a clever comeback, but I knew I had him. A smile formed slowly on my face, and when I looked up, he mouthed, "F-Y" and shot me a bird, concealing it behind his phone from any passersby.

"Classy."

While waiting on our lunch, I noticed Captain Alex enter the restaurant through the back door. He looked around the room and when he saw us, he walked over to our table. Surprisingly, the captain was all smiles and seemed glad to see us. Hunter got up, and they hugged each other. Hunter then turned to me and said,

"Colby, this is Dad's captain, Alex Reyes. Alex, I'm sure you've heard the news from Dad that I have a new brother." It was apparent Jack had not told Hunter about my contentious introduction to the captain.

"I had the pleasure of meeting Alex yesterday at breakfast," I said with a little edge on the word *pleasure*.

"The pleasure, Colby, was all mine. I know we got off to a rough start, and I want to apologize for my behavior. I had no right to act the way I did and say the things I said. You are a blessing to Jack and Hunter, and I'm glad the three of you found each other," he said with a warm smile.

I smiled back and nodded. I was still not sure about this captain, but I appreciated the apology, and I was willing to give him another chance.

Hunter looked confused but went along with it. "Well, I'm glad that's all straightened out. Alex, how's the fishing?"

"Not so good. The winds for the last few weeks have been out of the northwest. Everyone is having to go miles offshore to catch anything, and then not many billfish. The Tongue and The Pocket have produced almost nothing," he reported. But then with a big smile, he pointed out the window. "Look outside," he told us, "and tell me what you see."

Normally, not being a fisherman, I would not have any idea what he meant. But both aviators and mariners are obsessed with

the wind, and from the movement of the flags outside, I could see
the winds were coming in from the southeast. If northwest winds
were bad, this could only be a good thing.

"Southeast winds, and with the low tide coming in, the baitfish are going to be pushed up The Tongue and into The Pocket,"
Hunter said with the excitement of a kid. "We need to be out there
first thing in the morning."

"No, we need to be out there as soon as possible and fish until
sundown with the first low tide," replied the captain. "Every fisherman in the entire region has been waiting for the wind to shift.
It will be like a boat show out there tomorrow, so we need to get a
head start. Jets are already flying into Nassau, and all the captains
are preparing their boats."

No sooner did he get those words out of his mouth than we
heard a jet landing at Chub.

Alex pointed up. "See there. They're coming. I already have
the bait ready, and I say we go slay them for a few hours and then
come back to the dock later this evening. What do you think?"

Hunter hesitated with his response. "Well, I don't like the idea
of coming back at night, but it should be fine. I'll ask Jack and
see what he says. He may have plans for me and Colby tonight."

"Jack is who suggested I take you and Colby fishing. If we hit it
right, Colby can catch a blue and a white on his first trip out. This
may be a once-in-a-lifetime opportunity." Alex *was* convincing. "And,
besides," he added, "Jack is sleeping, so we may not want to disturb
him. He had a long morning at Staniel Cay and probably won't be up
before we'd need to leave. It's your call, though. Let me know what you
decide. I'm going to the boat to check on some last-minute things."

Alex left and our lunch arrived. I noticed that Hunter had
gone quiet, which was odd.

"Are you thinking it might not be a good idea to go fishing?"
I asked him.

"I think it would be great, but I hate to go without talking to Dad. If this really is an epic, don't-miss kind of setup with the winds and tide, I think he should be there with us. I know he would love to watch you catch your first marlin. But if he's been out all morning, it may be too much for him. I'm trying to decide if I should wake him up and ask him."

"It's still only noon. Why don't we wait an hour or so and see if he wakes up and ask him? He may want us to wait until tomorrow so he can go with us."

"Yeah, that's a good idea. I'll go down to the boat and let Alex know, and I'll call you when we have a plan. It will take us about an hour to get to the fishing area and then about twenty minutes to get the rigs in place, so we would need to leave no later than three."

"Okay, that sounds good. I'm going back to my cabana for a little siesta. I need at least a couple of hours on this trip where I'm not drinking."

CHAPTER THIRTY-FIVE

We finished lunch, and Hunter walked down to the marina while I headed back to the cabana. On my way, I couldn't help but think about the seemingly sudden change of heart in Alex. The evil and hatred I'd seen earlier in his eyes had either genuinely disappeared or he was doing a good job of disguising how he felt. Either Jack had convinced him that I was not a threat and had no ill intentions, or Alex had decided it would be a shame to get fired with a few months to go in a thirty-year career. Or maybe it was all an act.

I arrived at my little paradise in the cove and decided I was not yet ready for a nap. I grabbed a couple of beach towels, a book from the bookcase, and a chair and took them to the beach. I figured I would get some sun and return home so bronzed and tanned that it might lead to a little more activity around the Cameron compound.

With the beach to myself, I sprayed the body parts I could with the SPF 15 sunscreen—including, unfortunately, my eyes. Then I plopped down in the chair to enjoy the sounds and smells of the ocean and beach. The southeast winds were in my face and made me think again about the fishing trip. I was hoping it would get worked out. This was my third day on Chub, and my plan was to fly back the next afternoon. Hunter was only in for a day or two, and if we got to fish that afternoon, it would give him more time to spend with Jack.

The thought of flying home the next day made me think of the ultrasound that was coming up. I was sure Aubrey was anxious about that as well, and I wanted to get back so we could worry about it together. With her on my mind, I decided to give her a call. She was probably at the shop putting the finishing touches on the Downs project.

She answered on the first ring. "Well, well, look who finally decided to call. The last I heard from you was Sunday night. I've been wondering for two days if you got to meet your brother and how things were going with Jack. Did you forget you had a wife at home who can't stand to be ignored?" she asked playfully.

"Hi, honey. I miss you too, and it is always *such* a pleasure to hear your voice."

"Oh, shut up! You know you should have called me. I think you do these things on purpose. Now, fill me in or you will be coming back home to the newly created Cameron Convent."

So much for the suntan.

"I did meet my brother, Hunter, and what a great guy, Aubrey. He was so accepting with never a suspicion that I was here for the wrong reasons, like to grab the family fortune. We've had a great time hanging out, and we're a lot alike. It's fun to banter back and forth with him, and we've even started to finish each other's sentences."

"So, he is basically like you, a smart-ass who thinks too much of himself."

"Yep, I would say that about sums it up," I replied, laughing.

"What else? And you know I want details."

I told her about the great dinner with Jack and how we almost got in trouble at the Nauti Rooster. She gasped when I told her about sticking the knife in Mark's side. I told her I'd had long talks with Hunter, catching him up on my life and hearing about his. And then I moved on to Hunter's revelation that he had known about me since he was twenty.

"You know, it's strange. I've known him for less than a day, and already I feel so connected to him—like we've always known each other." It was the same way I felt with Jack. The pull, maybe, of genetics? I really didn't know, but it had changed my life; it had changed *me*.

My only regret, I told Aubrey, was that she wasn't there.

"I'm getting teary listening to you tell the story, and I wish I *could* be there. If everything goes well in the next couple of weeks, maybe we can fly out together. Do you think Hunter would have the opportunity to fly back to Chub?"

"I think that would be great, and Hunter is a self-proclaimed playboy without a job, so I'm sure he would be able to make it back to meet you. On another note, Hunter and I are planning a fishing trip this afternoon. Jack's captain, Alex, is going to take us to a spot nearby that's supposed to have some of the best marlin fishing in the Bahamas. From what he said, the fishing's been pretty bad this summer until now. The plan is to fish this afternoon until sundown, before all the fishermen show up tomorrow and fill up the place."

"That sounds fun. Be sure to take a lot of pictures if you catch anything, and I want pictures of you and Jack and Hunter. I want to see the resemblance. And I will be the judge on whether you are the better-looking brother."

"I will, but it will be no contest with Hunter, bless his heart." I could almost feel the eye roll over the phone. "What have you been doing since dropping the bomb on your parents about me? I know it was an emotional and exhausting weekend for you."

"It was. I'm glad to be back in my shop, and I finished Scott Downs's project this morning. The baby and I feel great, and we're

looking forward to you coming home. Are you still planning on
flying back tomorrow?"

"Definitely. I miss you both, and my plan is to get out of
here in the morning and get back to Florida before the afternoon
thunderstorms pop up over the Atlantic. I'll call or text you before
I leave and then when I land in Fort Pierce. I should be home by
midafternoon."

"Great! Have fun fishing, and I can't wait to see you tomorrow.
Be careful out there and be sure to wear your life vest. Call or text
me when you get back. I love you!"

"I sure will, and I love you, too."

I ended the call and thought what a lucky man I was. Everything
was going so right in my life, and the only thing that could make
it perfect was for our little baby to be healthy. Just like Aubrey, I
felt sure she would.

I spent another hour soaking up the sun. Then it was nearly
three o'clock, and I had not heard back from Hunter. It was time
to get back to the cabana, take a shower, and find out if we were
going fishing.

After a shower that alerted me the SPF 15 hadn't done its job, I
checked my phone to find a text from Hunter. He said the fishing
trip was on and to meet him at Jack's boat at three. He also said
to wear shorts, deck shoes, and a long-sleeved fishing shirt and to
leave my Thurston Howell III yachting outfit in the closet. I had
to laugh because that was just like something I would say to him.
I texted back that he could kiss my ass and that I would be there
at three.

I got dressed and made the short walk to the marina. I met
Hunter at Jack's boat and found that Jack had woken from his
nap. He said he would take a pass on the trip but was glad we were
getting to go. Like Aubrey, he said he wanted pictures. We told him
we would take some and planned to see him for breakfast at nine.

Hunter and I left Jack and walked back up the pier to the fishing boat. It, according to Hunter, was a fifty-five-foot Hatteras and was mostly used for longer, overnight excursions. But the forty-two-foot Boston Whaler they used to fish locally was down for maintenance. The largest boat I had ever ridden on was my Uncle Pete's twenty-two-foot Bowrider on Lake Lanier back home in Georgia. It held eight people in a pinch. As Hunter gave more specifics about the boat, I had no idea what he was going on about. So I simply nodded like I understood.

When we got to the boat, Alex walked out of the cabin and met us on the pier. He was wiping his hands, which looked to be covered with grease and oil. "Hey guys, how's it going?"

We both replied that things were fine and returned the question.

"I've been working on the fuel lines. We haven't taken the Hatteras out for a while, and the fuel lines to the auxiliary tanks were leaking, but I think I've got them fixed," he said, continuing to wipe the grease and gas off his hands onto a dirty rag.

I looked at Hunter, not liking the idea of going out on a boat with leaking fuel lines the captain *thought* were fixed. Hunter didn't seem to be concerned.

"Also, we have a change of plans," said Alex. "I've been talking to the fishermen who were out earlier, and The Tongue and The Pocket haven't hit yet. Hunter, as you know, it takes a day or two for the winds to push the baitfish off the banks and into The Pocket, and then another day for the marlin to show up. The winds have only been coming from the southeast for a day or two, and, unfortunately, the marlin haven't reached The Pocket. But I did get a report that they are active in the Gulf Stream, north of Walker's Cay.

"I'm thinking if we leave now, we can get through during high tide and have enough daylight to get us into the harbor. I thought about anchoring around Triangle Rocks and getting a head start in the morning, but I don't know those waters and tide levels well enough, and I don't want to risk getting into the rocks. But from what I've heard, they've fixed the entrance into the harbor and made it much easier to navigate.

"If we don't leave today," he continued, "we'll have to wait until late morning for the next high tide. I've got everything we need on board. What do you think? You want to head out now, stay on the boat at Walker's, and be ready to hit it first thing in the morning?"

Hunter asked me what I wanted to do, and I wasn't sure. I'd told Aubrey I'd be home the next afternoon. But I thought about it for a second and knew she would understand. Another day would not be a big deal. I would text her about the change of plans and told Hunter the plan was good with me.

We grabbed our gear and boarded the Hatteras, which was named "Crude," referring, I assumed, to Jack's business. Alex fired up the diesel engines, and we began easing out of the harbor. I saw Hunter look toward the bow of the boat, and he had a puzzled look. I asked him if anything was wrong.

"Nothing is wrong. I'm just wondering why the Zodiac is here. It's our little center-console launch vessel we use on longer trips when we need to take it to an island or a sandbar. But we won't need it on this trip, and it just seems odd that Alex thought to bring it."

I didn't have an answer.

Leaving Chub, we took a right and headed north past Mama Rhoda Rock, which Hunter said was a favorite spot for snorkeling and diving. Reaching the foot of Great Abaco Island, we turned east through the Berry Islands channel with Bimini to our south. We then ran the strait between Florida and Grand Bahamas, and three hours later, we made the turn at Little Bahama Bay and headed for Walker's Cay.

Walker's Cay is a small island of only a hundred acres and is the northernmost island in the Bahamas. Walker's, like Chub, had fallen on hard times. It was demolished in 2004 by hurricanes Frances and Jeanne and was abandoned for fourteen years. Coincidentally, a Texas businessman bought the island and rebuilt the resort, airstrip, harbor, and marina. It can now hold up to six one-hundred-and-eighty-foot yachts and has seventy slips for fishing boats. Also like Chub, Walker's is famous for its billfish and marlin fishing. It's just up from Little Bahama Bank, a large area of shallow water with vast expanses of coral heads that is about forty miles long and full of small aquatic nutrients that hold baitfish. When southern winds are prevailing, the baitfish are pushed off the banks into deeper water, attracting the marlin.

When we reached the harbor, Hunter and I guided Alex past the rocks and sandbars. As tricky as that was, I couldn't imagine trying to bring a big boat there in the old days before they fixed the entrance, as Alex had explained they'd done. After careful navigation, we got the boat safely into a slip and tied it down. Of the seventy slips, about half were taken, and the closest boat was about six or eight slips away.

Once we were settled, Alex brought up a spread of cold-cut sandwiches and chips. While we were eating, we discussed the plan for fishing the next day. Alex sat with us a few minutes and then said he needed to finish getting everything prepared for the next day. After that, he planned to call it a night.

Once we were alone, I fixed a Scotch, and Hunter poured Tito's into a tall glass along with a pink sugar-free fake lemonade mixture from a packet. We then grabbed a couple of cigars and headed to the stern to watch the night sky and wind down the day.

We talked about my time in Canada and his life traveling. As we told the stories of our lives, we both wondered what it would have been like to be in each other's shoes. He had never known what it was like to live in one place with the responsibilities of a job, going through the same routine one day after the next. He knew nothing of what I thought of as a normal life: meeting up with friends to golf at a public course amid talk of raising kids, where to spend the only two weeks of vacation most families got a year, and which riding lawn mowers were the most affordable.

And I had no idea about the jet-set life of traveling from house to boat to exotic island, hanging out with movie stars and models. I told him that, with the exception of me being with Aubrey, I thought he had ended up in the better pair of shoes. And he didn't argue.

We talked a little longer and finished our drinks, then Hunter headed off to bed. I stayed back and sent Aubrey a text explaining what had happened and where we were. I told her the weather looked good over the next few days and to expect me home in two days. I waited a few minutes to see if she would return my text, but she didn't and had probably gone to bed.

I looked at the stars a final time and eased down into the bedroom. Alex and Hunter seemed to be competing to see who could snore the loudest. Thankfully, I had remembered to bring a pair of earplugs. I got into my bunk, and as the boat swayed gently, I closed my eyes on another wonderful day that just the week before, I would not have thought was possible.

CHAPTER THIRTY-SIX

After a good night's sleep thanks to the earplugs, I was awakened by Hunter brushing by me to go to the bathroom. I looked at my watch to see it was a little before seven. I pulled out my earplugs just in time to hear noises coming from the bathroom that I would rather not have heard. In those tight quarters, I knew what was coming next, so I quickly jumped out of my bunk and went up top. Alex was setting up the rods and placing them in the rod holders on the sides of the boat. I asked him how it all worked.

"We will be using what is called the bait-and-switch method," he explained. "We start with four teasers, two on the outriggers up top on the tower controlled by electric reels, and two flat lines down here, controlled by you and Hunter. Teasers don't have hooks and are only used to attract the marlin. We will run two Black Barts up top." He held two teasers that were about a foot long and were red and purple.

"Down here, we will run two Hatteras Eye Catchers. Those are my good luck charms. I hardly ever miss with them." As he held them up, I could see they were the same size as the others, but they were blue and white.

"We will run the lines at different intervals, starting at forty feet to sixty feet, behind the boat at around ten knots. A marlin will come to the surface and whack the teaser with its bill, trying to kill it. When we see the marlin chasing the teaser, we'll start reeling in the teaser fast enough to keep it ahead of the fish. When he gets about fifteen or twenty feet from the boat, we snatch in the teaser and replace it with a mackerel on a circle hook. The marlin takes the bait and gets hooked. That is why we call it the bait and switch."

After hearing his explanation, I was not impressed. "Marlin must not be very smart," I said.

I could tell he took offense, and he asked me why I thought that.

Not trying to be a smart-ass (just stating the obvious), I explained. "Well, I have never fished in the ocean, but I have fished a lot for freshwater fish; I've fished for bass and trout. And all of those fish spook really easy if there's any noise or if something seems unnatural in the way the bait's presented. So let me get this straight. First, we have a marlin swimming behind a big noisy boat, chasing something that is getting progressively *closer* to the big noisy boat—filled with excited fishermen. Then this thing the fish is chasing disappears, only to be replaced with something else—and this fish still bites the hook?"

The captain looked at me with disgust, like I was an idiot, but before he could reply, Hunter opened the hatch and climbed the stairs to the stern. "I'm done down there," he said, "if anyone needs to use the head."

"I would like to have some coffee, but I don't think that place will be inhabitable for the next hour or so," I said, motioning to the cabin.

"Life on board a boat, son. You'd better get used to it," said Hunter, then he turned to Alex. "Are we ready to go? What can I do?"

"We're ready, and everything is in order. You and Colby remove the lines, and I'll start us up."

We removed the lines and fenders, and Alex slowly pulled us from the slip. We motored out of the harbor carefully at a few knots, navigating much more easily than we had at night. Once we cleared the marina and got into the channel, Alex poured the fuel to the twin diesel engines, and we quickly sped up to thirty knots. We then settled in for the forty-minute ride out to the banks.

After a pleasant trip, we arrived to find no other boats around. Apparently, we were the early birds. Alex positioned the boat just over the banks, which dropped from six hundred to twelve hundred feet. The banks were a long ledge that ran for miles, and baitfish were known to hang out there.

Ready to fish, Alex climbed the tower and let out the short riggers, and Hunter did the same with the flat lines on the sides of the stern.

All the teasers were dancing across the top of the water at different intervals as Alex steered the boat from the tower. That gave him a great perch to spot any marlin. Hunter, though, said it could be a while before we had any action. So, hoping the air had cleared in the skunk hole, I went down and made a large cup of coffee. Then I came back up with it to watch the teasers.

It took about thirty minutes, but Alex finally yelled that we had a marlin following a teaser. He pointed to the port-side outrigger, and I followed the line to the water. Sure enough, a marlin was pounding the teaser with its bill. Hunter quickly began to reel in the teaser and told me to start dropping the mackerel for the bait and switch. Just as the teaser got about twenty feet from the boat, Hunter pulled it out. I handed him the loaded rod, and he put it right in front of the marlin. The marlin smashed the mackerel. Fish on!

The marlin dove straight down, and the line was zinging as it was pulled from the reel. When the marlin began moving away from the boat, Alex reversed the engines to keep up with it. When it would turn, I would reel in as much line as I could, and then the fish would run again and take away my gains. It got within fifty yards of the boat once, and we could see it was a blue marlin. Everyone was excited.

We played tug-of-war for about two hours, and just when I thought my arms were about to fall off, the marlin gave up. I reeled him to the boat, and Hunter said he was about three hundred pounds. He reached down and tried to remove the circle hook from the marlin's mouth, but it was lodged in such a way he couldn't. He took a pair of pliers and cut the line as close as he could to the hook. I watched with concern, thinking it couldn't be good for the fish, being released with a big hook stuck in its mouth. Hunter laughed and told me not to worry; the saltwater would have the hook rusted out in a matter of days.

About twenty minutes later, Alex yelled again and pointed to the starboard-side outrigger. This time a white marlin was chasing the teaser. As we had done with the blue, Hunter pulled in the teaser, and when I presented the mackerel, the fish took it. This was a smaller marlin, and, thankfully, it stayed near the surface. I had him to the boat in about thirty minutes. I held the rod while Hunter prepared to remove the hook.

Alex told us to wait so he could come down and take pictures of us on our first fishing trip together. We smiled for the camera, and I could already see the picture framed and sitting on my desk in the hangar.

We took a break for sandwiches and beer, and Alex said he wanted to fish a little further out to see if we could catch something bigger. We were riding high on catching fish and said we were up for whatever he wanted to do. It took us only twenty minutes to get to the spot where Alex thought we might have the best luck. We had barely gotten the lines out when a big blue marlin started banging its bill on the teaser of the port-side flat line. Just as the other two had done, this one took the bait when it was presented. Hunter grabbed the rod and fought the fish for over two hours.

Then he handed the rod to me for a few minutes while he chugged down a bottle of water.

He took the rod back and, finally, after almost three hours, the fish wore out and Hunter brought it to the boat. It was the biggest catch of the day, weighing in at about four hundred and fifty pounds. Alex got a great picture of us in front of it. That would be another for the desk.

Alex went back up to the tower and yelled down that he had spotted seagulls over by a weed line north of our location. Seeing the birds meant that tuna had pushed sardines or baitfish to the surface. Alex told us to put the billfish rods up, that we were going tuna fishing. He grabbed the ones on the outriggers and brought them down. Hunter and I removed the rods from the slots on the sides of the boat and stowed them away. We then brought out the tuna rods and reels, which to me looked just like the ones we had put up. Maybe fishing rods were like the guns we used to hunt; they all looked about the same but had much different functions.

Hunter and Alex baited up the rods with blue runners and then tossed them over the side. The baitfish immediately dove down and swam toward the weed line. They had only been out of the boat for a few minutes before a tuna crashed the sardine. Hunter looked at me with a crooked smile and said that one was all mine.

It didn't take me long to figure out why. Pulling in tuna is like pulling up an anvil. They are heavy oval balls that dive straight for the bottom. While I was tugging that one up from the depths for almost an hour, I would have sworn it was three hundred pounds. As it turned out, it was maybe seventy-five.

Over the next hour or two, we caught three more, and after having to pull all of them in, I decided I wanted to be a marlin fisherman.

The sun was beginning to set by then, and Alex said it was time to call it a day and head back to Chub.

CHAPTER THIRTY-SEVEN

It had been the day of all days. I had never caught a marlin or tuna, and now I had caught a blue and a white and a handful of tuna. It had been amazing to watch the marlin chase the teaser, brutally go for the mackerel, and then jump and twist out of the water trying to dislodge the hook.

Alex had been a good captain, finding us the perfect spot for marlins and then spotting the shorebirds to alert us it was time to fish for tuna. He had cleaned one of them right after it was caught, and we'd had fresh tuna for a snack in the late afternoon. He had also kept us supplied with cold beer, and when I had caught the last tuna of the day, he poured tequila shots for me and Hunter to celebrate our successful day of fishing.

Alex had us pull in all the rods and stow them in the holders in place around the boat. Then he went down into the cabin while we cleaned up the stern.

Just as we were finishing spraying down the floor, I began feeling a little light-headed; it felt like I was drunk. I looked at Hunter and noticed he was a little shaky too. Maybe it was from being on a boat all day with the tossing and turning, but I could barely stand. Hunter staggered over to me, and he looked like he was about to get sick.

It was at that moment I began to feel uneasy. With the small amount we'd had to drink, we should not be feeling like we were. And that is when it happened.

Alex appeared from the cabin with that evil look of hatred I had seen at our first meeting. I saw a gun in his hand, and Hunter saw it too. Even in my sickened state, I understood what was going on. There had been more in that shot of tequila than tequila.

This had all been a clever setup. Alex had never planned for us to fish The Tongue or The Pocket; he had just dangled that idea to get us all excited about a "quick afternoon fishing trip." We would have been less likely to come all the way to Walker's and spend the night on the boat had he not first baited us with talk about changing winds and the prospects of an epic marlin catch.

I walked back to the stern and leaned up against the side of the boat, waiting to see what would happen. Hunter eased over to the other side of the stern and did the same.

Alex just stared at me for a few seconds. "You didn't think I was going to let you get away with it, did you? I've worked my ass off for Jack Windham for thirty years and put up with more shit than anyone would believe." Then he turned to point at Hunter. "I've had to take care of that snot-nose and all his spoiled rich friends, who treated me like I was nothing but their servant." He was yelling now.

"I've had to cater to a whole parade of rich whores and their kids. I've had to clean up vomit and shit, and I never got a thank you or even a 'Kiss my ass.' I was supposed to be invisible and do what I was told. I put up with all of that, knowing that Jack would take care of me when the time came. And if he didn't, I knew I could get what I wanted from this weak, miserable son of his." Alex waved the gun toward Hunter.

Hunter hung his head and would not make eye contact with his father's captain, now suddenly turned enemy.

"But that all changed when you showed up," continued Alex, directing his vitriol to me. "The golden bastard child appeared out of nowhere. Just because Jack stuck it to some lonely woman forty-five years ago does not give you the right to show up now and mess up everything. Jack thinks this is some sort of fate shit, but I know you're only here to play the long-lost son and steal his fortune. Hunter should have figured that one out, but the boy is always too drunk to see what should be plain as day—too drunk and too stupid. You have played it well to this point, but someone had to see this for what it is and take care of the problem." Alex raised the gun and pointed it at me.

I needed to say something. I could not see any way to change the mind of this maniac, but I had to try. "Alex," I began, "I can see how you could think that, but I can promise you that is not the case. I want nothing from Jack or Hunter. I have been successful, and I don't need Jack's money. You're about to make a big mistake, one you don't need to make. I am sure Jack has a plan to take care of you. Put the gun away, and let's just talk about this. Even if Jack did not include you in his arrangements, I'm sure Hunter would take care of your retirement. Isn't that right, Hunter?"

With his arms folded around him tightly, Hunter still had his head down, and I wasn't sure if he had heard much of what we were saying. Whatever Alex had put in our tequila shots was having a stronger effect on him, but I needed him to help.

"I told you he was a drunk, and you can forget him helping you get out of this. He will do exactly as I tell him." Alex walked over to Hunter and kicked him in his side.

My brother cried out in pain, and it seemed to bring him back. He stood up straight and stared at Alex. "As good as Dad has been to you over all these years, and you pull this shit? You think you are doing me and Dad a favor by killing his son and my brother? You are a worthless son of a bitch, and I told Dad he should have fired you years ago. All you do is complain about your job and how bad you have it, but where would you be if Dad hadn't hired you? Probably rotting in some prison or—even better—dead," Hunter said defiantly.

Alex's face went red, and a darkness glinted in his eyes. In a flash, he rushed toward Hunter and pounded the butt of the gun into my brother's head. Hunter fell to the floor, and I was moving toward him when Alex raised the gun to me. I stopped, and Alex turned and spoke to Hunter.

"The best thing you can do is go down to the cabin and let me finish what I came here to do. You can go along with what I tell you and carry on with your pitiful life—with more money than you deserve—or you can die like your brother here."

At that point I knew I had no chance of talking our way out of the situation. We were miles offshore and even if I did survive being shot, there would be no one to find me except the sharks. I thought of Aubrey raising our baby girl all on her own, having to explain what had happened to me when our daughter was old enough to ask. I thought about the pain Jack would feel, knowing I'd still be alive if he had not reached out. I wondered what story Alex and Hunter would tell him. *If* Hunter went along with this atrocious scheme Alex had dreamed up.

Instead of being scared, I was furious. This lowlife piece of shit was about to rob me of everything good that had finally lined up in my life. I looked out past the boat and saw the weed line, which was at least a hundred feet wide and seemed to go on for miles. There was more trash floating in the weed line than you'd find in a landfill. I saw a refrigerator, a few plastic coolers, and several large boxes that all looked like good cover. I decided right then I was not going to let this monster shoot me. I would take my chances in the ocean. I needed a distraction, and it had to be Hunter.

"Hunter, you know he won't let you live with this secret," I said to my brother. "He will wait long enough for Jack to buy the story, and then you will have an 'accident.' Stand up to him now. There is no way he can pull this off without your cooperation. Tell him he has to stop." I knew, of course, that Alex wasn't going to stop, but I had to get Hunter engaged so I could buy some time.

That's when Hunter stood up, covered in blood, and proved himself to be the man Alex said he wasn't.

"You're right, Colby. I will not stand for this. He will have to kill us both, and that will be hard to explain to Jack. Alex, put the gun down, and let's go back to Chub and let Jack handle this. He may be lenient with you, or maybe not, but that's what has to happen. Killing his two sons will not get you anything but the rest of your life in jail. Either that or death."

Alex shook his head and with an evil smile, he said, "Oh, that is where you're wrong. Remember that fuel leak? The one I was working on and talking to Jack about? There will be an explosion on this boat—in the middle of The Pocket for every fisherman and anyone outside on Chub to see. Hell, maybe Jack will see the explosion and fire that will kill his sons. You two will have been below, drinking too much and smoking your cigars, which will conveniently provide the catalyst for the explosion that will kill you.

"I will try my best to save you, even getting badly burned on my arms in the process. I will be so remorseful when I tell Jack, and being his good friend, I will help him through his loss. And I will have on my phone pictures of you and Colby catching fish and having the best day of your lives. Or should I say, 'the last day' of your lives?" He glared at Hunter. "I'm tired of listening to you both. It's time to wrap this up."

As Alex was raising his gun toward me, I scooted to the edge of the boat and knew I had only half a second to fall overboard before he pulled the trigger. But I had timed it too late. The gun went off just as I was rolling to my left toward the water. The last thing I saw was Hunter jumping in front of me, and I heard him yell.

I fell into the water and began diving down as quickly and deeply as I could. But Alex was at the edge of the boat, firing into the water. I could sense the bullets piercing the surface and moving past me in the water. He must have fired at least ten times, and then the bullets stopped. I was steadily swimming toward the dark, deep water that I knew was the bottom of the weed line. I was almost out of breath and had just begun to surface underneath a plastic box when I heard a loud splash at the edge of the weed line. It was Hunter with a pool of blood around him.

He was motionless and sinking. I took a quick breath and dove down to try to catch him before he slipped away into two thousand feet of water. Just as I reached him, I heard Alex crank the engines.

I put my arm around Hunter's neck and kicked frantically toward the surface. But with every kick, we seemed to be sinking more than rising. I knew if I could not kick harder, I would have a decision to make. I felt the same anxiety that had come over me while Aubrey and I were snorkeling at Cemetery Beach on our honeymoon in the Caymans. I remembered feeling mad at myself later that I had been willing to give up so easily.

Had it not been for Aubrey finding a perch of coral for me to swim to for safety, I would have died that day. I told myself if I ever got that close to death again, I would fight with every ounce of my being to survive. Well, now here I was, and I felt an adrenaline rush, the kind a mother feels when she finds the strength to overturn a car to save her child.

I kicked like hell with both legs and started moving upward. When we made it to the surface, I saw the old rusty refrigerator floating a few yards from us. I held on to Hunter and moved behind it, hoping it would hide us. I was treading water for us both and didn't know how much longer I would last.

Alex, in the meantime, was turning the boat around to make a run toward the place where I was hiding. He couldn't have seen us surface and probably thought we were dead and sinking to the depths, but I imagined he wanted to make sure.

I took a quick second to check on Hunter. He appeared to have a gunshot wound to the head—from the bullet I knew had been meant for me. Blood was everywhere. He was still unconscious, and all I could do was try to stay out of Alex's sight and hope Hunter would survive.

Driving crazily, Alex approached the weed line. He zigzagged the boat through the trash, trying to make sure that if we surfaced, he could finish the job he'd started. He crashed through empty propane tanks, wood pallets, boxes, and all the other trash, searching anywhere he thought we might be hiding. He just missed us on the first run, coming within a few feet of the refrigerator. Now, he was turning around for a second pass. If he hit the refrigerator, it would be the end.

During the commotion, Hunter had regained consciousness. Mindful of Alex being close, I spoke into Hunter's ear, telling him to take a deep breath. He heard me and took in some air before I pulled him under the water.

Alex soon came tearing back and ran directly over the refrigerator. A loud screech filled the air as the hull made contact with the refrigerator, which bobbed under the boat. It couldn't have missed our heads by more than two feet.

After that, he made at least five more runs as he moved his way up the weed line and on from there. He finally, I supposed, figured he had done enough and headed west toward Grand Bahama.

Suddenly it was silent except for Hunter's labored breathing, and I swam back with him to the refrigerator. As I opened the door, the hinges were so rusty the whole thing broke off. I eased it over onto its back and slid Hunter into it, facing up. It was a large refrigerator and made the perfect little boat to keep his bleeding body out of the water. I held on to the door, which, with its heavy insulation, acted as a raft.

It must have been around nine o'clock since it was getting dark, and I knew I had to locate the source of Hunter's wound and survey the damage. He had either fallen asleep by then or slipped back into unconsciousness. Needing something to wrap around his head, I pulled off my long-sleeved shirt and started looking for the wound. I wiped the clotted blood from his head to find a six-inch cigar-shaped gash just above his ear. It didn't appear to have penetrated his skull, but with all the blood and hair, I couldn't tell for sure.

I wrapped the shirt around his head. Using the sleeves to double back, I pulled them tightly to put pressure on the wound. Then I pressed down with my hand as well and waited. It took a few minutes, but the bleeding stopped. His breathing was getting a little better. His pulse was weak, but it was there. Hopefully, he was just in shock and would wake up soon.

With Hunter stabilized, I traded the refrigerator door for a large piece of Styrofoam that had probably been used to hold up a dock somewhere. I climbed up on it and looked for any lights from land or boats, but I saw only black. I could feel us being pulled along the weed line that was part of the Gulf Stream heading toward Africa. By morning, we could be miles from that point, and I wondered if Hunter would still be alive.

Exhausted, I lay across the hunk of Styrofoam and closed my eyes. I thought about Aubrey and what she might be doing now. She was probably still at her shop, maybe thinking about me coming home the next day. With my eyes still closed, I said a prayer that—maybe not the next day but one day soon—I would get back home.

Chapter Thirty-Eight

Alex left Grand Bahama feeling a freedom he had not felt in years. He was sure Colby and Hunter were dead and by now they had sunk to the bottom of the ocean. Hunter had taken a direct shot to the head, and if he had survived, the blood would surely have attracted sharks to finish the job. Even if he had gone along with Alex, Hunter's time would have been short. No way would he have ever let Hunter have a chance to rat him out to Jack. Somewhere between Walker's Cay and Grand Bahama, he would have shot and dumped him. The plan all along had been to return alone, with a sad tale of both brothers being killed in the explosion.

As for Colby, he had to have been hit in the hail of bullets Alex fired into the water. But if he had somehow missed him, there was no way Colby could have survived in that weed line. Alex had carved through every inch, and there had been nowhere to hide.

Satisfied that his problems were behind him, Alex idled down the boat and went to the galley to grab one of the bottles of bourbon he had brought on board for this special occasion. Back at the helm, he turned up the bottle, drinking the contents down to the top of the label. Just like at the bar, the burn felt good going down. No one would ever tell him again that he couldn't drink, and he would never again be anyone's servant. It was time he took control of his life and got what he deserved.

He thought about his time in Vietnam and the My Lai massacre that had gotten him locked up. They called it a massacre, but they got what they deserved. He had never regretted killing the women, children, and old men who had stood in the way of him escaping that hell hole. The government had placed him there to kill, and that is what he did. He hated that place and the people in it.

Around the turn at Grand Bahama, he made his way through the Straits of Florida. Then he turned east, moving past the Berry Islands toward The Pocket. It had been dark for a couple of hours, and he didn't see any other boats. When he got to The Pocket, it was empty as well. It was now time to execute his plan.

His depth radar indicated he had reached the deepest part of The Pocket. It was more than fifteen hundred feet to the bottom, and when he sunk the boat, there would be no practical way for anyone to retrieve it. He then began the process of creating the scenario of the explosion and the deaths of Hunter and Colby.

First, he unshackled the Zodiac from the cable that held it to the bow and slid it to the edge of the boat. He needed it to easily go overboard during the explosion. Then he went under and opened the hatch to the engines, loosening the fuel line to the gasoline tanks that provided fuel for the Zodiac and auxiliary generator. He had made it a point to tell Jack there were issues involving a fuel leak, which would validate his story.

Near the gas tanks were several propane tanks that were used for the grill and heat lamps during the winter months. It was not the best place to store them, but due to a lack of space, that is where they were. Their location would work well for his plan.

At the beginning of the trip, he had not worked out a way to explain the spontaneous combustion that would come with the ignition of the fuel vapors—until he saw Hunter and Colby smoking their cigars on the stern. Instantly, problem solved. It would be believable that the brothers had caused the explosion by lighting up to smoke their cigars in the closed cabin and galley area.

Alex knew he would have to convince Jack that he had tried hard to save the boys. And to help convince him, he had brought a portable propane tank to use to burn his arms.

He looked around the boat one final time before he took out his Zippo lighter from his days in Vietnam. He lit a twisted roll of paper, opened the door to the cabin, and threw the flaming paper in. Within seconds, it ignited the fuel vapors. With fresh oxygen coming off the ocean and the opened valves of the propane tanks, an inferno was unleashed.

Knowing he had a minute or so before the tanks exploded, he quickly downed half the remaining bourbon and ran the flaming torch of the portable propane tank up and down his arms. The pain was excruciating, and the smell of his burning flesh made the bourbon rise up in his stomach, and he threw it up. Only the urgency of the moment kept him from passing out. He knew if he didn't move, he would be caught up in his own trap and blown up.

He ran to the bow, and the tanks blew just as he rolled into the Zodiac, escaping into the water. It was much more of an explosion than he had expected, blasting the Zodiac into the air and throwing Alex out. Soon, with the seawater stinging his burned arms, he lost sight of the Zodiac. For a few seconds, he panicked, until he spotted it about twenty feet behind him. He swam toward the small boat, and with all the energy he had, pulled himself back in. In the darkness, he found the handle to the small engine and brought the Zodiac to life. By then, the Hatteras was fully engulfed, and he was sure anyone within ten miles could see the fire.

He knew his next actions would be pivotal to the outcome of his story. He pulled his phone out of his pocket. It was wet, but it still worked, and he dialed 919, which is the equivalent of 911 in the States. The operator answered right away.

"This is Captain Alex Reyes of the boat Crude, and we have an emergency," he yelled. "My location is north of Andros Island and west of Chub in the middle of The Pocket."

"What is your emergency?" the operator asked.

"We have had an explosion on the boat, and the boat is now on fire."

"How many souls on board?"

"There are two on board. I tried to save them, but I couldn't get to them. Please come now! They are going to die if someone doesn't get here quick!" Alex made sure to add a note of desperation to his voice.

"Sir, where are you? Are you on the boat?"

"No, I was thrown off by the explosion, and I am in the small tender. I am burned badly, but I'm going to try and get back on the boat to save them."

"Captain, stay where you are, and we will get the coast guard there immediately. Do you understand? Do not board the boat," the operator told him forcefully.

"But the boat is sinking, so they need to hurry! Please! Oh God, I cannot believe this is happening. These are my friends," Alex replied, weeping.

In a solemn voice, the operator said, "I'm sorry, Captain. We will be there as quickly as we can."

Alex disconnected the call, lay back in the boat, and watched the Crude burn. It was starting to list to the starboard side, and he hoped it would sink before the coast guard arrived. Knowing the efficiency of the coast guard, he had no doubt it would be at the bottom of the sea before they got there.

As he waited, he pulled the cap off the extra bottle of bourbon he had stowed in the console of the Zodiac. He took a sip and thought about his actions. He had just taken the lives of two people, one of whom he had known since he was a kid. He had even changed Hunter's diaper a couple of times and watched him when Jack and Julia had gone into town. They had trusted him to look after their son, and now he had just taken his life.

In a rare moment, Alex thought about the man he had turned out to be. His mind went to his childhood, much of it spent on the docks in Miami. His dad had been a longshoreman, and for a while they lived in a nice house in a nice neighborhood near the harbor. Alex didn't do badly in school and even lettered in wrestling his junior year. He assumed he would finish school and, like his dad, be a dock worker with the union.

That was the plan until his dad and mom started arguing a lot, which, for his dad, led to increased drinking, multiple DUIs, and getting kicked out of the union. The family lost their house and had to move to a row of government houses further from the city. Alex's dad got a job at the warehouses and worked twelve hours a day loading trucks for half the money he'd made at the docks.

His increasing bitterness took a toll, and the drinking became worse. Then the abuse began. He would come home drunk and take out his failures on his wife, and when that was not enough, he beat his son. Alex lay in bed at night trying to think of some way to get out. After a while, his father beat a man hard enough it landed him in prison, and Alex and his mother were left alone without any means of income.

Lying in the dinghy while the bourbon did its job, he thought about how he had become just like his father, bitter and causing harm to others. But then very quickly, he dismissed that idea, reminding himself that he spent had thirty years of his life serving Jack and his family, and now they had turned on him. They were getting what they deserved.

He then thought about his mother. After his dad went to jail, she fell apart mentally and emotionally, and that left her unable to hold down a job. At seventeen, Alex started dealing drugs to support himself and his mother. Her health got worse, and she died from pneumonia the winter he graduated from high school. He blamed the loss of his mother on the government for not providing enough heat in the shitty little house they lived in.

It was at that point his life changed. He no longer saw the future he had hoped for. It was now a matter of survival.

With his mom gone, he moved in with a group of drug dealers, and things immediately got worse. He had been there less than a week when the house was raided by the cops, and he was arrested for possession and dealing narcotics. He had a choice: spending ten years in prison or going to Vietnam to fight for his country. He could care less about his country, but a trip overseas with the military would beat doing time.

In Vietnam, he found a group of guys who were in the military for the same reason he was. He quickly resumed his life of crime, including dealing drugs, and that life came easy to him. The year he spent in Southeast Asia, he was mostly high on pot or heroin. He was given a dishonorable discharge for his criminal actions and sent home. After a brief time in a military prison, he tried to change his direction, but the old temptations were too strong, and the pull to the path of least resistance was even stronger.

While waiting for the coast guard, feeling the effects of the bourbon, Alex had a moment. He wiped at the tears streaming from his eyes. Gazing into the water, he allowed himself to wonder what life would have been like if he'd pushed himself to set higher goals. In some ways, he guessed he had. He had managed to work for the same man for almost thirty years and was a professional captain. He had mostly stayed out of trouble and performed his duties well. But bad decisions had always seemed to follow him, and today he had made the worst decision of them all. He had panicked, thinking he would be left with no provisions for the future, and he had killed the sons of his friend and employer. Jack could have had a generous retirement planned for Alex. Perhaps he was waiting until his final days to unveil the details to his longtime captain. But now it was too late. Alex had no choice but to follow through with his plan.

He took a deep breath and began to think about the story he'd tell Jack. Colby and Hunter, he would say, had, against his advice, gone down below for cocktails and cigars. He would weep as he told Jack how he'd tried desperately to save them, and the burns on his arms would be the proof.

It took them about an hour, but he could at last see the lights of boats coming toward him. The Crude had long disappeared into the depths, and Alex was thankful there would be no evidence to contradict his story. When the coast guard got closer, he lay back in the boat, pretending to be unconscious.

The rescue team kept yelling at him. "Captain, can you hear us?"

Alex barely raised his head and acted like he was trying to reach out to them but couldn't hold his arm up. Within seconds, the rescue squad descended on him and began first aid. As they lifted him out of the Zodiac and hoisted him onto the coast guard boat, he heard one of the men say, "With those burns on his arms, I think he's in shock. Wrap him in blankets and start an IV and oxygen. He may have internal injuries, and we need to get him to Nassau as quick as we can."

It was going just as he had planned.

At some point they put a painkiller in his IV, and he didn't remember anything after that until he woke up in the hospital. His arms were heavily bandaged, and a team of people were discussing his condition and why he was still not responsive. He kept his eyes closed and just listened. They concluded he was probably still in shock because of the severity of the burns. In addition to that, the pain medication was keeping him sedated.

In time, one staffer said, Alex would wake up and be able to tell his story to the authorities.

Alex opened one eye to see a police officer in the room. No doubt this case was high profile, and they wanted answers. He wondered if Jack knew what had happened yet.

—

The doctors and police officer finally left his room, and Alex looked to see if the door was closed. When he saw it was, he rolled out of the bed and found his clothes in a closet by the bathroom. He searched his pants for his cell phone. He reached to retrieve it but had second thoughts; he didn't want to be caught with his phone if someone came back in. He knew time was on his side, so he decided to lay back down and enjoy the high of the pain meds.

He woke a couple of hours later and was feeling no pain. He thought some more about how his plan would unfold. When a nurse or doctor came in, he would ask to speak to the police and Jack. He would shed a few tears and tell them how he had done everything he possibly could to save Colby and Hunter. He was sure the cops would have already listened to the recording from the 919 call, which would back up his story. Jack would see his bandaged arms and would thank him tearfully for his attempts to save his boys.

While he was polishing the details of his scheme, the door opened. He expected a nurse or doctor, but it was just some orderlies coming in to take the trash and replenish supplies. He kept his eyes shut and was paying little attention to them until something that they said made his heart almost stop. Two fishermen, they said, had been brought in a couple of hours earlier on a helicopter. One had been shot in the head and was in surgery, barely alive. The other was uninjured and had saved the life of his friend.

Alex froze. At that moment, his once-flawless plan imploded. Now, it would just be a matter of time before everybody knew the truth. He had to get out of there. He waited for the orderlies to leave, then he hurriedly grabbed his clothes and dressed. He pulled out his cell phone and called a friend who lived on the island. His friend answered on the third ring.

"Hermano, I need you to come immediately and pick me up at the hospital. I'm in trouble and have no time to explain. Pick me up in the back. Understand?"

"Si, amigo. I'm on my way."

Alex opened the door and peeked down the hallway. He saw the orderlies pushing the cart full of trash bags through a door across the hall. From the view out the windows, he knew he was on the first floor, so he assumed that door led outside to the back of the building. He waited a couple of minutes then slipped out of his room, and in three leaps he was across the hall and at the door. Throwing it open, he could see the red ends of two cigarettes about twenty feet away. The smokers were half hidden behind the dumpsters; Alex could hear them talking.

On the other side of the dumpsters was the parking lot—which was where he would text his friend to pick him up. The far corner of the lot was dark and secluded, the perfect place to wait and make his escape. Maybe if he could get to Jack before anyone else, his plan could still work. He would no longer get to be the hero, but he could still get what he wanted, and that was the money.

CHAPTER THIRTY-NINE

I wasn't sure how long I dozed, but I was suddenly awakened by a disturbance coming from the direction of the refrigerator. I had drifted a few feet and quickly paddled back to Hunter, who seemed to be having a seizure. I grabbed the side of the fridge and tried to keep it stable. I knew if he rolled out, he would sink a thousand feet to the bottom.

I couldn't hold it steady from my place on the Styrofoam float, so I slipped into the water and held on to him, feeling helpless. The seizure went on for about thirty seconds and then stopped. I put my hand over his chest and although his breaths were shallow, they were there. I felt his pulse, and it was weak. Maybe he had lost a lot of blood, or the wound had been deeper than I thought, but, for whatever reason, he was getting worse.

I was thinking we could probably find something to drink in the hundreds of water and soda bottles floating all around us. We could go days without food, and maybe in that time, a ship or a boat would find us. But I now had doubts that Hunter would make it through the night. I couldn't help but think how tragic it would be for us to perish in the ocean with Jack dying soon after that in a hospital bed. Maybe this had all been fate. A little pre-party meet and greet in the Bahamas followed by a big reunion up in Heaven.

But I drove those thoughts from my mind. I was not ready to go. I had Aubrey and a baby on the way, and I was not going to die.

I was so tired, and all I wanted to do was get back on top of that piece of Styrofoam and sleep. But I couldn't take a chance on Hunter having another seizure and falling out of the makeshift boat. So I wrapped my arm around his and laid my head on the edge of the refrigerator, and then I just waited.

It was maybe another hour or so when the fridge shook violently and jarred me awake. Hunter was jerking in five-second intervals and making a gurgling noise. I put my hand under his mouth and felt something wet. I couldn't tell if it was blood or if he was regurgitating water. In my gut, I felt his time was near. I ran my hands through his hair and told him how much I loved him and how immensely grateful I was we had gotten to spend time as brothers. I told him I would do the best I could to look after Jack. I think he might have heard me; he let out a moan. Then he calmed down for a while and we both drifted to sleep.

At some point, I was again startled awake, this time by something bumping against my leg. I jerked my leg away and waited to see what would happen next. If it was a shark, I would have to make an impossible decision to get back on my raft and let go of Hunter.

A second later, it happened again. This time it was more of a buzz than a bump. I couldn't figure out where it was coming from. But when it happened a third time, I realized it was coming from the side pocket of my cargo shorts. It hit me then—it was my cell. Before I left the dock, I had sealed it in a Ziploc bag and forgotten all about it. I had put the thing on vibrate, and now someone was calling.

I pulled it from my pocket and carefully removed it from the bag and held it over Hunter. That way if I dropped it, it would fall into the fridge and not the bottom of the Atlantic. I know this is crazy, but my first thought was that it was probably a telemarketer trying to sell me an extended warranty on my vehicle. Fortunately, it wasn't. It was Nathan. I dried my finger the best I could and slid the phone to life.

"Nathan!" I yelled into the phone.

"Hey, I know it's late, but I wanted to call and see how your trip is going. Did you get to meet your father?" His normal, calm voice sounded out of place in the middle of my nightmare.

"Whatever you do, do not hang up or take another call," I rushed to say. "If we get disconnected, Nathan, call me back. Do you understand?"

"I understand. What's wrong?"

"Hunter has been shot and isn't doing well. We are in the ocean and floating north of Walker's Cay, and we need help right away."

"What happened? Are you on a boat? I tried to find you on the location thing, but it's not connecting."

"No, we are in the water, drifting in the Gulf Stream. I'm going to try and drop a pin on our location. Do you think you can use your resources to send a rescue team? We can't wait on the coast guard or any kind of local help. Nathan, I don't think Hunter can hang on for that long." As a retired CIA agent, Nathan understood exactly what I meant by his resources.

"Colby, what is a pin?"

Any other time I would have shaken my head and laughed about his digital skill set being stuck somewhere in the eighties. Nathan was old-school and would never have traded his flip phone for a smart phone if I hadn't done it for him.

"I am going to mark my latitude and longitude on Google Maps and text you the location," I told him. "Open the text, and it will pull up Google Maps with a pin for our location." I pulled up the GPS and placed a pin on the spot where we were floating. In only a few seconds, it was off to Nathan.

"I got it. It looks like you are northwest of Grand Bahama and about thirty miles north of Walker's Cay. I will call the station chief in Nassau and have a rescue helicopter on the way. Or should I call the coast guard?"

"No, don't call the coast guard. Jack's captain was the one who shot Hunter and abandoned us, and I'm afraid he'll panic if he hears over the radio that we're being rescued. And then he might hurt Jack. We need to keep this quiet for now."

"Understood. Stand by, and I'll make the call. I will have someone there as quick as possible. You hang tough and take care of your friend, Hunter."

"Brother. Hunter is my brother," I said in a quiet voice. There was a moment of silence on the line.

"I'm making the call now and then catching a flight to Nassau. I'll send you a text when they are moving, and you reply back, okay?"

"Roger that and thank you. Oh, and Nathan, don't call Aubrey. I don't want her worrying. I'll call her when we're safe."

We floated in the dead calm of the sea for another ten minutes before I heard my phone buzz once again. Again, it was Nathan, and his text said help was on the way. For some silly reason, I replied with a smiley face.

As we waited, I thought about Alex and his scheme. I was sure he planned to play on Jack's emotions and "support" him as he mourned the loss of his sons. He was probably thinking Jack would lean on him until he passed and then leave him his fortune since there was no one else. Time seemed to move slowly as I anxiously awaited help. I tried to think positively about Hunter getting better and me getting home to Aubrey. Those thoughts filled my mind for a while. Then as I was making my own plan for how I was going to deal with Alex, I could hear in the distance the low thumping of a helicopter.

It arrived in total blackness, and it was not until they were directly over us that they turned on the lights. Suddenly, the whole ocean lit up. In a matter of seconds, two dark figures jumped into the sea. They were in full SCUBA gear and swam over to us. One pulled his regulator from his mouth and asked, "Mr. Cameron?"

I nodded, thinking, who else would I be? Any other time I would have made a joke, but this was not the time.

"Let's get you out of here." He looked over at Hunter and spoke into his handheld device, asking them to send down a stretcher. They lowered what looked like a long canvas hammock and then explained to me that they were going to roll Hunter into it. I asked if I could help, and they told me to steady the appliance on the other side to counterbalance it as they eased Hunter out. I complied, and it worked perfectly. They kept his head above water, secured him into the hammock, and then lifted him into the belly of the helicopter. They then sent down the harness for me. I was lifted, and then the medics were brought back up so we could quickly leave.

As we departed, the medics began working on Hunter. One took his blood pressure and pulse and listened to his chest with a stethoscope while the other started an IV and began unwinding the shirt I had tied around his head. When he removed it and cleaned his head, I could see Hunter was in worse shape than I'd thought. He had both an entrance and an exit wound. He was pale and unresponsive, and I thought it would be a miracle if he made it.

On the way to Nassau, one of the pilots gave me a comm set. I put it on and asked one of the medics, "How do you think he's doing?"

"He is critical. He's lost a lot of blood, and his blood pressure and pulse are low. I think there may be some internal bleeding and swelling on his brain that are causing his problems. We won't know until they do a scan at the hospital." He looked at his watch and said, "We are twenty minutes out. If he can hang on, we're flying in a neurosurgeon from Miami, and he should be there when we land. I called in the request when I saw Mr. Windham's condition while we were in the water."

I put a hand on his shoulder and told him thank you.

Chapter Forty

We arrived in Nassau, and the pilots set the helicopter down on a landing pad on the roof of the four-story hospital. I could see a team of medical personnel awaiting our arrival. As soon as we were shut down, they rushed over, loaded Hunter onto a stretcher, and steered him toward an open elevator. I jumped out just as the pilots were restarting the engines. Since they had on their headsets and wouldn't be able to hear me with the engine noise, I mouthed the words *thank you*, and they acknowledged me with salutes. I could not recall exactly who Nathan called for help or where they had come from, but because of them, Hunter had a chance.

I walked toward the elevator but was afraid to push the button. I didn't want to disrupt it while it took Hunter to wherever he needed to be. Instead, I took the stairs and walked down to the lobby. It was now close to midnight, and it was hard to believe that just a few hours before, we were finishing up a great day of fishing and having a cocktail while watching the sun set.

I located the nurses' desk to ask where I needed to wait to be updated as soon as possible about my brother. They pointed to a waiting room down the hall and said to check back in half an hour.

I thanked them and decided to find the cafeteria and see if I could get a cup of coffee. It would be a long night, and I needed the caffeine.

The cafeteria turned out to be closed, but the dining area was open with several coffee stations. I grabbed a large cup, filled it to the rim, and found a table. I drank about half of it, but it was not doing its job. My eyes felt heavy, and I decided to lay my head on the table for a few minutes.

I didn't think I had been asleep for long when I felt someone gently shake my shoulder. I quickly jerked awake, thinking it was a doctor or nurse with information about Hunter. I turned, and it was Nathan.

"Mind if I join you?"

"Hey! Yes. Please," I said, wiping sleep from my eyes and trying to wake up. "How in the world did you get here so fast?"

"I may be retired, but I still have a few special perks and privileges. I hopped on a King Air 300 in Athens, and they had me here in less than two hours. How is Hunter, and how are you holding up?"

"Hunter is in bad shape. He took a bullet to his head, and it went through the left side. I'm not sure where he is and what they are doing. The nurses said to check back with them in half an hour." I looked at my watch and was shocked to see it was almost five o'clock. I had slept for a little over three hours and was upset with myself. I needed to go check on Hunter, but first I needed to give Nathan a quick update. Alex was out there somewhere, and I was sure his plan was to find Jack. We needed to get to him before he found out we'd been rescued. I needed Nathan to start putting together a plan.

He must have read my mind.

"Do you mind filling me in briefly on what happened? You said your father's captain shot Hunter and dumped him overboard. Is that right?"

"Well, something like that. Let me start from the beginning." I told him about the first confrontation between me and Alex, when he accused me of being there to steal the family fortune. Then I moved on to his seeming change of heart and how he'd lured us out to sea with talk of tides and wind direction. And I briefly summarized the nightmare on the boat.

I told Nathan I should have known something was up when Alex was so persistent about the fishing trip. Why should he have cared if I caught a marlin? I told Nathan that I'd felt something wasn't right, but never did I think he was up to murdering us at sea and dumping our bodies in the Gulf Stream. Had we not been found, it would have been the perfect plan, I said.

"So many of the schemes I've seen these guys plot over the years are like that—*almost* perfect. There is usually one small detail that is overlooked, and that's what gets them locked up or maybe gets them killed. In his case, it was your cell phone. Plus, they could have found Hunter's body with a hole in his head, which would have been hard to explain.

"Speaking of the captain, where do you think he is? If you say his plan was to burn himself to look like he tried to save you and Hunter, he would have contacted the authorities or Jack by now. And if he was burned bad enough to be convincing, where do you think is the logical place for him to be?" Nathan folded his arms with a crooked little smile. "You go check on Hunter and meet me back here in ten or fifteen minutes. I'm going to make some inquiries." He stood and walked toward the elevator.

The staff had changed at the nurses' station, where I was greeted by a young nurse with a friendly smile. I asked her if she could check on Hunter, and she entered his name into the computer. I held my breath and waited. Then she looked up, and I tried to read her expression. Her smile had disappeared.

"Mr. Windham is still in surgery. It looks like he has been in there for four hours," she said, looking at her watch. It being a small hospital, and since it wasn't every day a patient with a bullet wound arrives by helicopter, she probably knew why he was in surgery, and four hours was a long time.

"I can call up there, but they usually won't give out any information till they're done. Check back with me in a little while, and I'll see what I can find out." She gave me another smile.

I thanked her and returned to my table. It was now five thirty, and I thought about calling Aubrey. I needed to let her know what was happening, but she would still be asleep. I decided to wait until later when she was up.

After about twenty minutes, Nathan returned and sat down. He had a Coke in his hand and was still wearing a crooked smile.

"Would you like to guess who is currently a patient in room 110?"

"I'm guessing it would be Captain Alex Reyes," I replied, not believing the luck. If everything fell into place, Alex could be arrested and Hunter out of surgery before Jack woke up and found out what had happened.

"I've alerted the police, and they are meeting us in the lobby. Then we are going to pay Mr. Reyes a little visit. I can't wait to see his face when you walk through the door. I also checked on Hunter, and he is still in surgery. I gave the staff the number for my cell, and I told them to call with any updates. Let's head to the lobby. The police should be here soon."

I thanked him for checking on Hunter and told him I had received the same news. I should have thought about giving my cell number to the nurse.

After meeting the police and the hospital security guard in the lobby, we received a report from a nurse on Alex's injuries and what to expect when we went into his room. She told us that he had been sluggish and not very responsive since he arrived. His blood-alcohol level could probably explain that, along with the morphine he'd been given. The burns were bad, she said, but not enough to keep him in a state of shock. They expected him to wake up soon and be coherent.

We proceeded down the hallway to room 110 without the police drawing their weapons; they did not seem to be concerned they would meet resistance. At the door, we decided Nathan and I would enter first.

But when we opened it, we were stunned. Alex was not there. We then noticed the door to the bathroom was closed, and the light and exhaust fan were on. I knocked and then tried to open it, but it was locked.

"Alex, this is Colby. You need to come out. The police are here, and it's over." I waited a few seconds and repeated my command. Still nothing.

Nathan noted that the bathroom was on an exterior wall and could possibly have a window to the outside. He went into the hallway and motioned for everyone to come inside. He then asked the nurse, "Does the bathroom have a window?"

"No, sir. The only window is in the room."

He then asked the police to force the door open. That was accomplished fairly easily with a shove from one of the larger policemen.

The bathroom was empty.

Nathan ran to the window next to the bed and found it to be locked shut. "Put a guard at every exit door, and I want a complete room-to-room search of the hospital," he said.

I assumed the police had been told who he was. They rushed out of the room to comply with his requests.

He then looked at me. "If his wounds are as bad as they said, and he was heavily medicated, where could he have gone? He must still be in the building. He could not have just walked out."

"Don't underestimate him, Nathan. We are talking about a ruthless man who is in survival mode and capable of anything.

He must have found out we're still alive. It's the only explanation why he would take off, and I don't think we will find him in the hospital."

Nathan looked over at the nurse, who was still in the room, and asked, "Where are his clothes?"

She pointed to a small door next to the bathroom, and I opened it. Just like the bathroom, it was empty—except for a hospital gown.

Nathan yelled over his radio, giving instructions that the outside of the building should be searched as well.

After being questioned, the nurse told us no one had been in his room for at least several hours. I could feel the panic rushing over me, and Nathan said the very thing that I was thinking.

"We need to call Jack."

I pulled out my phone and dialed his number. It was nearing six o'clock, and I wasn't sure if he slept late or got up early. I breathed a long sigh of relief when he answered on the second ring.

CHAPTER FORTY-ONE

Alex slipped past the orderlies, who were throwing bags of trash into the dumpster. He crouched down, taking cover behind a row of bushes as he watched for his friend. After a long five minutes, the orderlies finally went inside, and a few minutes later, Alex could see headlights at the entrance of the parking lot.

His friend Angel's truck was spitting and sputtering as he pulled into the parking lot, and then the damned thing shut off. Angel repeatedly tried to crank it, and each time, the headlights grew dimmer. Alex was thinking about what direction he would need to start walking in to get to the marina when the truck finally cranked. It was time to move.

With one quick glance back toward the hospital door, he made a dash to the truck. He opened the passenger door and jumped in, and Angel took off right away. He had been in enough situations himself to know there was no time to waste.

"Where to?" Angel asked.

"To the marina. And just drive normally; I don't want to attract attention."

No one spoke during the drive, which took less than five minutes. Alex needed Angel—and his boat— to get to Chub, and he was trying to figure out the best way to ask.

Just as they pulled into the parking lot, the engine stalled again. Angel pounded his fist on the dash and cussed the truck, which gave Alex an idea about how to entice his friend to go along with his plan.

He turned to him and said, "Angel, the two of us have worked our whole lives on boats for rich bosses, and where has it gotten us? We work day and night for what amounts to almost nothing. They use us for their fun and then leave us at the docks to clean their boats until late in the night. Then they expect us to be ready to do it all again the next morning. All while they are drinking and dining in their fancy restaurants and bragging about the fish they caught, never giving us any thanks or credit.

"I'm getting tired of it, and you should be too. Look at this truck you're driving. It's old and barely runs. You deserve better than that, Angel, and they could care less about you or me. It's time for us to get what we deserve, and I have a plan to shove it back at them. What do you think?"

"First, why don't you tell me why I picked you up at the hospital?" he asked, looking at Alex's bandaged arms.

Alex knew he couldn't tell him the real story, so he told him that Jack's sons had gotten drunk on the boat and that there had been a gas leak and explosion. He said he got burned trying to save them. And how had they thanked him? By insinuating it was all his fault for not keeping the boat safe. He knew if he stayed, he would end up taking the fall and probably get convicted of some made-up crime. He told Angel he was not going back to jail.

"Okay, so what's your plan?"

"My plan is to make us both rich, for us not to have to work for those rich bastards one more day, and for you not to have to drive a piece-of-crap truck that will maybe start and maybe not. And to never have to answer to anyone again."

"And how exactly would we do that?"

Alex noticed he said "we," and that was a good sign.

"First, what's the status of your boat?" he asked. "Is the owner here in town?"

"No, he's in Texas and won't be back until next week."

"Good. Where is the captain? "

"He's taken his family on vacation to Grand Bahama. I'm the only one on the boat."

"Well, then this is going to work out better than I thought. Here's what we're going to do." Alex laid out his plan to Angel and waited on his reply. Now that he knew the boat owner and captain were both out of town, one way or the other, he was taking that boat to Chub. He hoped Angel would make the right decision.

Angel didn't have to think for long before he turned to Alex. "I'm in debt over my head, and with what little I make, I can't see any way out of it. You probably don't know, but Maria left me last month and is talking about filing for divorce. She was tired of living in poverty and moved back to Miami. She asked me to go with her, but I can't with all the money that I owe. What you say is right. All my life I've worked hard, and what has it gotten me? Like you said, I am nothing more than just a slave for the rich."

He paused and then continued. "I'm about your age, and I don't think I can do this kind of work much longer. And what will they care? When I can't do it anymore, they'll just get rid of me and find someone else. If this is the way out, I'm in."

Alex was relieved. "Good. You won't regret it. You can leave this hellhole behind and make a life for you and Maria wherever you want to go. And, trust me, I do have a plan to get my hands on the money."

They left the truck hidden behind a row of abandoned boat parts and cautiously walked down to the boat that would carry them to Chub. It was just after five, and other than a few fishermen preparing for the day's fishing trips, there wasn't anyone around.

Without any trouble, they managed to board the boat, which was a Hatteras, similar to Jack's boat that was now resting in the depths of The Pocket. They eased it out of the harbor and set a course for Chub Cay.

Ironically, the boat belonged to one of Jack's friends from Texas, and Alex had been the one to recommend Angel when the captain was looking for a first mate. Now, Alex was thinking if he could get to Chub before anyone else had a chance to contact Jack, his plan would work out fine. He nervously watched the time of arrival tick down on the GPS.

They entered the harbor close to six a.m., and, to Alex's relief, there were no police or welcoming parties waiting on them. Most of the boats had already left for the day. Angel pulled into a slip located across and a few spaces down from Jack's yacht. Alex stayed hidden while Angel moored the boat. He then instructed him what to do.

Chapter Forty-Two

Jack had just woken up, and for a change, it was quiet on the boat. With the boys on an overnight fishing trip, he had given the crew a much-needed day off. He had even instructed Charles, who was there every morning, to sleep in and meet him around lunchtime. He fixed a cup of coffee and walked to the lounge on the stern with his phone; he would catch up on emails and read the *Houston Chronicle*.

Watching a fishing boat come into the harbor (odd at this time of day), he wondered how the fishing trip had gone. He hoped Colby had gotten a chance to catch his first marlin. He wished he could have made the trip with them, but he felt it was more important for the boys to spend time together. When he was gone, he hoped they would have a lifelong relationship.

He picked up his phone and was checking his emails when it started ringing. He looked at the caller ID to see it was Colby. He smiled as he answered. "Good morning. I was just having a cup of coffee and wondering if you caught a marlin."

Colby hesitated, not wanting to scare him. "Yeah, Jack, I did catch a marlin. I caught a blue and a white, but that's not why I'm calling. Look, there's been—"

Jack was so excited that he interrupted. "That is fantastic! It took me several years before I caught a white marlin. They don't fight as much as the blue, but what a beautiful fish. Did Hunter catch . . . Hey, hold on a second."

Shouts came from the dock.

"Colby, I've got to run. Something seems to be going on. Someone is yelling for me on the dock. I'll call you back in a minute."

Colby yelled into his cell for Jack to stay on the phone and not go anywhere, but he had already hung up.

Jack put down his coffee and stepped from the boat to the dock. A man he recognized was jogging toward him—his friend Paul Keen's first mate. He was out of breath and panicked.

"Mr. Jack, we need your help," said the man. "Mr. Paul has had an accident on the boat, and he's not moving. Come and help us, please."

Jack knew Paul had not been well, and he feared the worst. Probably a heart attack. It seemed he was hearing weekly about the passing of one of his peers. They were at that age, he thought. He followed the mate to the boat and stepped inside. And right away he understood something wasn't right.

There was no sign of Paul, but sitting in the captain's chair was Alex.

"What is going on?" asked Jack. "Where is Paul, and why are you on his boat?"

"From what I understand, Paul is in Texas," Alex said. "As for what is going on, have a seat, and I'll explain it as we leave."

"Leave? I'm not going anywhere. Alex, you'd better explain yourself right now." Jack moved back toward the exit, but the first mate stepped in front of him.

"Jack, you *are* going somewhere, and I told you to sit!" yelled Alex. "And I will explain when I am ready." There was a raw anger in his voice Jack had never heard in all the years Alex had worked for him.

Jack knew in his weakened state he couldn't challenge him and sat on the couch. As they left the harbor and reached open water, he glanced at the compass, and it was pointing northwest. They were headed straight for Miami. He wondered what Alex had planned and what his motive might be. He noticed his arms were wrapped heavily in bandages. He seemed to be in pain and was steadily pulling sips of bourbon. He knew how Alex got when he drank, and a drunk Alex was bad news.

After about an hour, Alex turned the helm over to Angel. He'd waited until he calmed down, not wanting to let his anger take over as he spoke to Jack. He was fortunate that no one had contacted his employer before Alex got to him. So instead of having to tell him what really happened, he could spin his own version of events. He took Jack to the back of the boat where Angel could not hear him. He didn't want Angel hearing the version of events he would describe to Jack. Although it really didn't matter; at this point, they were not turning back.

"Jack, I am so sorry it has come to this, but after what happened yesterday, I have to do what I have to do. My body is broken, and I can't take enough meds to stop the arthritic pain in my hands and joints. You have always said you would take care of me, but here we are at the end, and nothing has been done. Yesterday, I took your sons fishing, and I saw what the future looked like. I now agree with you that alcohol brings out the worst in people." Alex tried his best to sound sad and betrayed.

"Those two drank all day, and by the afternoon, they were drunk and acting recklessly on the boat. Hunter almost gaffed Colby when we were pulling in a tuna. As captain of the boat, I told them their behavior was unacceptable and to straighten up." Alex closed his eyes, pretending to be hurt. "Hunter told me then exactly how he felt about me, and it wasn't kind. He told me as soon as you are gone, he plans to fire me and make sure I never work again as a captain.

"And Colby, your little golden boy, just stood back and laughed like it was some joke. He said I had better learn to flip burgers because I was not about to get a dime from them." He leaned forward in his seat, his eyes intent on Jack. "Then they were smoking their cigars and set fire to the galley, and I had to put it out and got burned in the process. I left them on the boat this morning, and after all of that—plus this excruciating pain—I'd had enough. So, while this may be a bad decision, it's better than what I wanted to do to those sons of yours." Alex leaned back in the chair and waited for Jack to respond.

"So, what decision did you make?"

"We are going to Miami, and you are going to get ten million dollars from wherever you get that from. And after you do that and I receive it with no trouble, you will be free to leave. Jack, I don't want to hurt you. You've always treated me fairly, and I respect you for that. I really hate to do this, but as I said, I have no choice."

"Alex, you should have come and talked to me before doing this," said Jack. "Do you really believe I was not going to make provisions for your retirement? I've told you for years that I had something set aside for you. When have I ever not been a man of my word? You have an account in your name at Merrill Lynch that I have been putting funds into for the last ten years. The balance is somewhere around two million dollars. You need to turn this boat around and take us back to Chub. At this point, I'm not sure what will happen, but I do know this won't end well if you continue with your plan."

"It's too late for that." Taking a deep breath, Alex reflected on the fact that this decision was no different than all the other bad decisions in his life. He had jumped in too quickly, fueled by his anger. If he had only talked to Jack . . . But he hadn't done that, and, as he just said, it was now too late.

"We *will* go to Miami," he barked, "and you *will* get the ten million, which is just a blip on your radar, and then you can go back to Chub or Texas or wherever you want to go." He looked down at the floor. "You should be ashamed of how your sons acted and just go along with this."

"I'm not sure how one would go about getting ten million dollars in cash, but if I'm able, you can have it. I could not care less about the money. And I don't believe for a second my boys acted the way you said they did. But at this point, it doesn't matter. I will get you whatever I can, and then I hope you'll be true to your word and let me go. I only have a few more months before I get a lot worse, according to the doctors, and I want to spend that time with my sons—in peace."

"You get the money, and you can go home." Alex then took the helm from Angel. After about an hour, he could see Miami on the horizon and needed to figure out what they were going to do when they got to the dock. By now, he had to assume everyone knew what had really happened, but there was no way they could know he was in Miami. Time was on his side.

Chapter Forty-Three

I tried calling Jack back several times, but his phone went straight to voicemail.

Having heard my end of the conversation, Nathan asked me what was up.

"I have no idea. He seemed just fine at first. He was asking me about the fishing trip, and then he said someone was calling for him to come out on the dock. He said he'd call right back." I paused, a wave of dread filling up my chest. "There is no way that person being out there was a coincidence. I think Alex got to him." I called Charles, and he picked up on the first ring.

"Charles, where are you?"

"I'm in the restaurant having breakfast. Colby, what's the matter?" He could tell something had happened from the tone of my voice.

"Have you seen or talked to Jack today?"

"No, he gave the crew the day off and told me to meet him at the boat for lunch. Tell me what's happening," Charles said, concerned.

"Charles, go to the boat right now! Find Jack. I will update you when you get there, but you must get there now. Alex has done something that's horrific, and Jack is in real danger."

I knew what Charles would find—or not find—when he got there. The only way Alex could salvage his plan would be to kidnap Jack and extort money from him.

It only took Charles a few minutes to run from the restaurant to the marina and quickly call me back. "Colby, he's not here. What did Alex do?"

"I don't even know where to begin." I let out a sigh. "It started on the morning Jack and I had breakfast with him. That's when he accused me of being there to steal the family fortune, and I guess he somehow thought that would keep him from getting anything from Jack. Yesterday, on our fishing trip, he tried to take Hunter and me both out of the financial equation, so to speak. He shot Hunter in the head with a bullet that was meant for me. Hunter is in surgery, and, Charles, I'm not sure if he's going to make it." I then told him about Alex escaping from the hospital in Nassau. I told him about the phone call to Jack and the distraction on the dock.

"I think he has been taken," Charles said. "His coffee is here on the table with a newspaper and his cell phone. Nothing has been disturbed. It's like he just walked away—which fits in with what you said about him going out to talk to someone on the dock." There was an urgency in his voice. "I am going to make a sweep of the boats here and see if anyone saw or heard anything. Most of the fishermen have already gone out, but the sailors are usually up and around at this time of day.

"If Alex was here, he had to have come by boat," he continued thoughtfully, "but he could be headed in any direction, to any of the islands." He paused. "But we don't know what kind of boat, and it would be impossible to search them all. Why don't you go check the harbor there and see if any boats are missing? I'll call back when I know more, and you do the same," Charles said as he hung up.

Nathan and I caught a ride with the police and left the hospital for the marina. When we arrived, we split up, attempting to find anything that might be out of place—hopefully, a stolen or unaccounted-for boat. I found the harbormaster, who reported that nothing out of the ordinary had gone on that morning, just the usual fishing boats going out without a lot of transient traffic. I asked him about any other marinas that might be nearby. He said there were dozens of private docks and several small marinas further up the island.

When I met back up with the others, I looked at them, discouraged. The police had also come up with no information about suspicious goings-on. I was not sure of our next move and could only hope Charles had learned something.

CHAPTER FORTY-FOUR

C harles knew every boat owner who had a slip at the marina, even those who were there on a temporary basis. He made it his job to keep an eye on Jack's surroundings, including who was in the area and what activities might be going on. Everyone assumed he was just the assistant and took care of all Jack's personal and administrative needs, but he was much more than that.

He walked up and down the dock, looking to see if anything seemed out of place or if he could spot any unfamiliar boats. Everything seemed calm, and nothing appeared to be out of the ordinary. He asked around at a few of the boats that were near Jack's yacht. No one had seen anything suspicious, but one person had heard yelling and some kind of commotion near his yacht. When he came out to check, he'd seen no one on the dock, but he had seen a Hatteras leaving the harbor. Charles's worst fears now seemed likely to be true. Alex had taken Jack.

Back at the yacht, he was about to call Colby when he glanced down at the open newspaper on the table next to Jack's chair. Charles, too, always started his day with the *Houston Chronicle*. It reminded him of an article fifteen years earlier that had reconnected him with Jack.

Charles Westcott had been a Texas Ranger or, more correctly, was still a Texas Ranger. Retired or not, one always was a Ranger. His dad and grandfather had been Rangers, and he was the third generation to join the most respected and elite group of lawmen in Texas. The Rangers have jurisdiction over the entire state; they protect the governor and even function as a paramilitary force. Of the seventy-eight thousand lawmen in Texas, only 166 were active Rangers.

It was his tough-minded resourcefulness—essential for any Ranger—that first connected Charles with Jack Windham in 1996.

It was Friday, August 23, and Texas had been experiencing a drought for several months when Hurricane Dolly slammed into Tampico, Mexico, and began its way up the coastline. It made an early-morning landfall in Corpus Christi, and more than ten inches of rain poured down on Southern Texas in less than an hour. The hurricane, with gale-force winds, was headed north toward Austin.

As the hours turned to early evening, Julia Windham was hoping she would not be late for the first football game of Hunter's senior year. They were playing Westlake in Austin, which was North Houston's bitter rival. Hunter had traveled to Austin on the bus with the team, and Julia had waited on Jack so they could ride together. Jack, however, ended up with a last-minute meeting. He had called to tell Julia to go ahead without him, that he would meet her there, hopefully by the end of the first quarter.

Fortunately, the hurricane had turned east earlier in the day, leaving nothing but mild rain and floods. Julia heard on the radio a few roads were being closed, so she felt an urgency to get to Austin. Not much, including a hurricane elsewhere in the state, could stop Friday-night high school football in Texas. She was Hunter's biggest fan, and she did not want to miss one second of the game.

It was 6:35 p.m., and she had just taken the Highway 290 exit off Highway 35, meaning she was only about twenty minutes from Chaparral Stadium. The traffic wasn't bad for an early Friday night, and she breathed a little easier, knowing she would get there in time for the game at seven. And parking should be easy. She'd come up with a little trick, slipping her SUV inside the area marked off by cones so she could park next to the North Houston buses. They were always parked right next to the stadium, and she knew she would be long gone before they loaded to come home. She had been doing it for years, and it always saved her at least fifteen minutes of walking time. Jack told her it was cheating, but with the money they gave the school, they had probably *bought* the buses.

Now, she turned onto Highway 360 and could see flooding on both sides of the road. Barton Creek, which was more the size of a river, had overflowed its banks and was almost to the road. It was unnerving to see, and she gripped the steering wheel a little tighter.

Just as she began to cross the Barton Creek Bridge, she felt a rumble beneath her and immediately slammed on the brakes. But it was too late. The bridge suddenly buckled and twisted and was quickly swallowed into the turbulent water. Julia's Land Rover flipped, and everything went dark. The vehicle was swept away by the water and slammed into trees and rocks. Julia screamed, overcome with a claustrophobic panic. She didn't know if she was right side up or upside down and could not see anything, but she could feel the water coming in. Trapped by her seatbelt, she knew this was the end.

—

Charles in the meantime was on his way to the same game. His nephew would be playing the saxophone in the halftime show with the Westlake band. It had been years since he'd seen a high school football game, and he'd been looking forward to the game all week.

Charles had played football at Westlake and had been an all-state fullback. He had hoped one day he might watch his own son play, perhaps sitting in the stands and cheering with his wife and daughter. But he had chosen the life of a Texas Ranger, and with the dangers of the job, he worried he might leave a wife without a husband and children fatherless. Now, driving to the game, he wondered if he had made the right decision.

He had also taken the Highway 360 route to the game and was pulling up to a line of cars just before the highway got to Barton Creek. People were standing on the side of the road, pointing. Something had happened just ahead, and Charles knew he wouldn't make the game.

Being a Ranger, he was always on duty. It was more of a calling than a job.

He unbuckled his seat belt and got out of his truck, quickly jogging the twenty yards to the gathered crowd. Looking toward the creek, he saw a vehicle caught up in the current; it was upside down and wedged between two trees. Everyone was yelling, and Charles could feel the sense of panic spreading among the group. A couple of men had edged to the side of the road and were trying to figure out a way to get to the SUV. It was at least thirty yards off the road, and the water was moving rapidly.

Jumping immediately into action, Charles told the men to move away from the water and get back near their vehicles. He then ran back to jump into the bed of his truck and open the toolbox. In it was everything one might need in any emergency—except for this one. He knew he couldn't swim to the vehicle without wearing a life vest, and then he would need one more—or several more—for the people in the car.

Then he had a thought. It was Friday, and Lake Travis was only a few miles away. Charles stood on the roof of his truck and looked down the row of stalled cars and trucks until he spotted what he was looking for.

He took off at a run, and when he reached a truck pulling a boat, he told the driver what he needed. Eager to help, the driver helped him carry five life vests and a couple of long ski ropes back to the scene. By then he could hear emergency sirens in the distance, but there was no time to wait. He connected the ski ropes to make them long enough to reach the vehicle and then tied them around his waist, put on a life vest, and entered the water upstream from where the vehicle was still pinned between the trees. The water level was getting higher, and he hoped he was not too late. With a crowbar he had pulled from his toolbox, he signaled to the men holding the rope to play it out. His goal was to have enough rope to reach the cluster of trees where the vehicle was trapped. Then, hopefully, he could ease his way from tree to tree to reach it and not get swept away by the water.

Everything was going fine, and the angle of the drift would put him just above the vehicle he now could see was a Land Rover. He was almost to the tree line when something suddenly struck him from underneath the water. It wrapped around his legs, and he felt himself about to be pulled under.

He took in a mouthful of water and choked. If he didn't get it off of him before the drift took him past the trees, he'd never get to that Land Rover. In one hand he held the life vests that were keeping him from going under, and with the other, he reached into the water and took hold of a chain. It was connected to what felt like a child's swing and was whipping wildly around his legs. He took a deep breath, went under as far as the buoyant life vest would let him, and with one hand, untangled the chain, got himself free of it, and popped back up.

Thanks to the rope and the men controlling it, he was still in good shape. He reached the tree line and signaled for them to hold the rope. He would need it to get the Land Rover's occupants back to the road. He then began working his way to the vehicle.

When he got there, he tried to open the door, but the pressure was too much. Taking hold of the crowbar, he punched against the glass and knew he'd have to act quickly when it broke. He already had his waterproof flashlight turned on and knew he'd have very little time to get the people out. He prayed they were still alive and that he had enough life vests.

The water, in the meantime, had come up past Julia's head. She was still trapped in the seat belt and had to use her arms to grab what she thought was the gear-shift lever to pull herself up and keep her head above the water. The muscles in her upper body were now screaming. She would pull herself up for as long as she could and then, holding her breath, go back under the water to rest. She had been doing this for what seemed like forever and knew her strength was running out.

Then, as she came up for what she figured would be the last time, she heard something tapping against the SUV. She had been hearing things crash into the vehicle throughout her ordeal, but this was different, more rhythmic. She was trying to figure out where the noise was coming from when something crashed through the window.

Water rushed in, rapidly filling the last bit of precious space that still held air. There was also a bright light, but that did not make sense. In her confused, oxygen-depleted mind, she couldn't process what she was seeing. Maybe it was the light one sees just before the end as they move on to Heaven. She had always heard there was a light. And then she heard the voice of an angel.

Feeling determined as he broke the window open, Charles took a deep breath and stuck his head in. His light shone directly into the eyes of a woman. There was barely enough space for her to keep her chin above the water. He had to act fast.

"Ma'am, I'm going to get you out of here. Are you alone?"

Her voice was calm. He wasn't sure if it was relief he heard or whether she had given up on getting out on time and come to a kind of acceptance. "It's just me," she said.

The next few seconds were a blur. Charles took a last big breath then pushed his head through the window as the water rushed in to completely fill the space. He pulled his knife from the sheath on his belt and cut the woman's safety belt. He felt her break free from its hold, and he expected her to panic and fight him to get out. Instead, she just floated.

He pulled her out the window and brought her to the surface. She took a big gulp of air like she was being raised from the dead. Charles untied one of the life vests he had secured to the ski rope and put it on the woman. He was about to instruct her on how they would use the rope to be pulled to the road when more help arrived.

He turned to see two firemen paddling toward them in a yellow raft. They pulled Charles and Julia into the raft with them and navigated safely to the road.

Upon their arrival, Charles was met with a huge round of applause from the hundred or more people standing around the parked cars and along the edge of the road.

Charles Westcott was a hero that day, and Jack Windham would never forget that he had saved his wife.

It was seven years later when Charles would again come to the attention of the Windham family. Jack and Julia had kept in touch with Charles, but their contact had dwindled to quick notes on Christmas cards. On that day, it was a story on the front page of the *Houston Chronicle* that reminded Jack of the heroic Texas Ranger to whom Julia owed her life. The story was about the abduction of a fifteen-year-old girl taken by human traffickers from a relative's house near Brownsville. With interest, Jack read about the events that unfolded after that.

Frantic, the parents of the girl had alerted the police, who then contacted the Texas Rangers about the situation. If the abductors crossed the border, the distraught parents understood they would never again see their daughter, and her life from that point on would be hell on earth. The girl's phone indicated a location not far from the border, and, at least for the time being, the victim and her captors seemed to be staying put.

Charles had been in Brownsville to testify in court when he got the call. He rushed to the location and, easing up a narrow dirt drive, he came upon a shack next to the Rio Grande. Parked next to it were vehicles matching the descriptions of the ones the relatives had seen. Backup was on the way, but they were nowhere close, and the border with Mexico was just a hundred yards away. Charles felt he couldn't wait.

Parking his truck where it would be hidden, he put on his Kevlar vest and pulled his AR-15 from the cargo area, loading it with a fifteen-round magazine. Next, he loaded his .45 Colt 1911 and put four spare magazines in his vest. He knew he couldn't wait for the abductors to come out. With the number of cars they were traveling in, there was no way he could stop them by himself if they were to leave, and they could easily escape to the border with the girl. He had no idea how many people were inside, but at least could catch them by surprise.

But just as he was about to burst through the door, it opened. He was face to face with four of the gang members, and they got the draw on him. He took one round in his leg and another in his shoulder. Several bullets hit his chest, but the vest saved him.

He fell back behind one of the cars and could feel the blood running out of him. But he had to move! He had to get to the girl. He pulled himself up and stumbled around to the back door. He half-expected them to rush him, but they didn't; they had remained inside the shack, probably trying to figure out what their next move should be.

Charles slowly turned the knob and then kicked open the door. He had both weapons in his hands and began firing at anyone who didn't look like a girl.

He took down six of them, but the last one standing was holding the girl in front of him. She was sobbing as he tapped a pistol against her head, yelling at her to shut up. Charles waited for him to raise the barrel just a couple of inches away from her head; then he would take his shot. That needed to happen soon before he lost consciousness; he was light-headed now. The girl got more aggressive, struggling to get free, and the gang member slapped her with the same hand that held the gun.

Big mistake. A second later, a hole had formed in the middle of the guy's head. Charles ran to the girl as her captor collapsed onto the ground—and he remembered nothing after that.

He woke up in the hospital and was told a bullet had nicked his liver and his kidney, and he shouldn't be alive. Every law enforcement officer in the fifty-mile radius showed up to donate their blood.

Charles Westwood was once again a hero, but this episode would cost him. With the damage to his body, he would be unable to return to active duty. He had seen several of his friends go out like this, but he never thought it would happen to him.

After reading the article about Charles in the *Houston Chronicle*, Jack Windham paid him a visit in the hospital. When he found out Charles would not be returning to active duty, Jack offered him a position as his personal administrator at twice his Ranger salary. He felt he owed it to him for saving his wife, but Jack also needed Charles.

Charles was still on heavy pain medication, and his mind wasn't clear enough for him to make a decision. He was still in denial about the need to leave a profession that was part of his family legacy and that had come to define him.

As the weeks passed, he slowly began to build back his strength. The doctors finally felt he had improved enough to go home. But back at his ranch, he found it hard to do the chores that had always been just part of his life. He hung around the barn, and each day he would barely manage to get in his John Deere Gator and ride the fences. When he found a breach in a fence, he didn't have the energy to fix it and had to call for assistance.

After a few weeks, although he was slowly getting better, he finally accepted the hard truth; his days as an active Ranger had come to an end. The last thing he wanted was to be a liability by staying on the job when he could not protect those he had made an oath to serve.

With much sadness, he packed his uniform into a canvas bag along with the Cinco Peso badge that had been handed down to him by his father. He stowed the bag in the closest. Then he picked up his phone and told Jack he would take the job.

CHAPTER FORTY-FIVE

They arrived in Miami around noon and docked at the Fifth Street marina in Paul Keen's slip. Angel knew all the fuel workers and had the yacht refueled in case they needed to leave quickly.

Alex had already worked out where they were going to stay. Angel's cousin had an apartment above a warehouse for overnight guests, ones he didn't want his wife finding out about. The warehouse was right up from the marina, a short walk away. The question was whether Jack was going to cooperate or if they would have to take him there by force. Being that Jack was eighty-one years old, Alex didn't think there would be a problem, but he had also learned to never underestimate Jack Windham.

They made it from the marina to the warehouse, and everything went smoothly. Angel's cousin met them there, and they managed to hide the fact that Jack was being held against his will. Although Alex really doubted the cousin would have cared. He told them if they needed anything to call, and Alex felt it was a safe place. He was within a few blocks of where he grew up, and he knew the surrounding streets.

Being back in the area, he wondered what had happened to all the friends of his youth. Alex had lived there in the days before the move to government housing, before his dad became a drunk and beat up his mom and anyone else who got in his way. He was sure most of those friends had gone on to college, had good jobs, and were respected in the community. He should have been one of them.

It was now midafternoon, and they were getting hungry. Angel ordered a couple of pizzas from a restaurant on the docks and went to pick them up. Alex took the opportunity to talk with Jack in private. "So, how is this supposed to go? How do we get the money?"

"How should I know? I have never been kidnapped. You should have had all of this worked out. You should be telling *me* these things."

"Well, I have never kidnapped anyone before, so we will just have to figure this thing out together. Let's say you're buying something—like an island maybe—for ten million dollars, and the seller wants you to pay in cash. How would you handle that?" Alex poured himself a tall glass of bourbon from the apartment bar.

"First of all, that would never happen, unless maybe it's a foreign seller who didn't trust an American buyer. Take, for example, the Bahamians; they never trust Americans. I've had to do cash purchases with them before. But ten million, Alex, is a lot of money, and I have never seen that much in cash. You might be able to get a couple million without raising any red flags, but the rest would have to be wired to an account. I suggest, if you don't have one, setting one up in the Caymans. I can help you do that.

"As for the cash, my main bank is in New York, and I'm not sure if they have a branch here in Miami. If they do, we may be able to arrange it."

'Well, it's Monday afternoon," said Alex, "and the banks haven't closed, so why don't you call them and see what they say. Also, what will I need to set up an account in the Caymans? Will I need a computer?"

"Normally one has to go there in person, but I have a long-standing relationship with a banker in George Town, and all I need to do is call and tell them I'm setting up an account for a friend. It shouldn't be a problem."

Alex pulled out his cell phone and handed it to Jack. After looking up the numbers for the bank, Jack called the main office in New York and found out they did have a branch in Miami. He explained he wanted to complete a real estate deal and that the seller would only accept cash.

They confirmed they could handle his request, but they would need until noon the next day to raise that much cash. After telling them he was sick and too weak to come in person, he said he'd be sending his courier and would send the courier's credentials to the bank later in the afternoon. He then called the bank in the Caymans, and after he explained why he and Alex could not appear in person, they agreed to set up an account in the name of Alex Reyes. He told the banker to expect an eight-million-dollar wire transfer sometime in the next day or so. He then called the bank and arranged the wire transfer to Alex's new account.

Alex took a sip of bourbon as he studied Jack. He was a bit surprised at how accommodating Jack had been in making the arrangements. When Jack had finished with the call, Alex asked him why he was making it so easy.

"I don't care about the money," Jack replied. "If you had asked for twenty million, it would have been much harder to get, and a much longer process, but I would have done it. Money doesn't mean a thing to me right now. I don't have long to live, and I want to get back to my boys as quick as possible." Jack took a long sip of water from a bottle on the coffee table before he continued.

"Alex, I do want you to know how disappointed I am in you. I thought we had a better relationship than this. No matter how anyone else may have treated you, I always made it a point to show you respect and treat you as a friend, not just as an employee. But I guess I was wrong. When I hired you so many years ago and gave you a chance when nobody would, I should have listened to my friends. So many of them told me that people like you never change and that one day you would turn on me." He leaned back on the couch and closed his eyes.

Alex felt his anger welling up, but deep inside, he knew the things Jack said were true. At this point, though, it didn't matter what he thought. All he needed was to get his hands on that money without getting caught. That meant keeping Jack rested and relatively healthy, and at the moment, Jack wasn't looking good. Alex helped him off the couch and put him in a bedroom, where he went right to sleep.

Angel returned with the pizzas and asked where Jack was. Alex told him he had gone to bed and updated Angel on the plans to get the money.

"I was wondering how he was going to get that much cash without the feds and everyone else wanting to know why," said Angel. "At least he can get the two million. Split between us, it's more money than most guys like us could ever dream of having. How do you plan on picking up the money? I'm sure someone will be watching the bank now that they know Jack is missing and may have been kidnapped." Alex had decided to keep the eight-million wire transfer for himself. Like Angel said, a million dollars was more than Angel would have ever seen if not for Alex, and that should be enough for Angel.

"I've been thinking about that, and I'm not sure," said Alex. "It will need to be picked up by someone who's familiar with the area and who can elude the cops or anybody else who might try to follow him. Someone who has a network of contacts and doesn't mind getting involved in this kind of thing. It will obviously need to be someone who has no aversion to breaking a law or two, like a drug dealer maybe, but the problem is, you can't trust those kinds of people." Alex took a piece of pizza for himself and handed one to Angel.

"I think I do know someone who fits that description," Angel said. "We could ask Maria's cousin. His family has a warehouse and a boat storage place that's right around the corner. He's a little shady and will do anything for money. I'm not crazy about the guy, but he has the means to pull this off, and he probably would do it. For the right price, of course."

"Yeah, but can we trust him?"

"Absolutely not. I wouldn't trust this guy for anything, but I do trust his father, who owns the warehouse business. The father is a man of honor in the shady world they live in. Luis would never do anything to hurt his dad's reputation—at least not again. A few years ago, he did a little drug dealing on the side. And when he got busted, a lot of his dad's clients at the marina started to get nervous. Maria never told me exactly what the story was, but Luis disappeared for a while and came back with a few scars and a different point of view. All I have to do is ask how his father is— and tell him that I hope we don't have to talk with him during this deal—and the guy will get the message."

"How much do you think he would charge?"

"I don't think we need to tell him how much we are getting. Maybe we tell him he is picking up one million dollars, and we'll give him ten percent for a couple hours of work."

"That sounds about right. We can have the cash put into two bags at the bank, and then Luis can put it into a couple of suitcases. One for me and one for you. We can give him fifty K from each of our cuts. I think Jack can have it set up for them to give the money to a courier. Luis would need to get an ID and give us the info so Jack can call it in. And tell him not to wear any dog chains, oversized rings, or any kind of gangster bullshit—to try to look professional. And he should take some type of secure box to put his cash into.

"With Jack cooperating, this is not a heist; it's just a courier picking up a package for a client. I doubt anyone will get alerted that it might be something more. Tell him the pickup will be at noon, and we will let him know which bank in the morning."

Angel took his phone and went outside to call his cousin. Alex could hear a lot of laughing and yelling. He hoped that was a good sign. A few minutes later, Angel came back inside and told Alex that the cousin was on board and that he would do it for the hundred K. He was texting a picture of an ID he'd be using. "We can write down the info for Jack in the morning," Angel said.

The next morning, Jack called the bank president with the credentials for the courier and thanked him for allowing the transaction to be handled in that way. With his health being what it was, it would have been painful for him to come downtown.

As soon as Jack had made his phone call, Alex slipped out back and called Luis with strict instructions about the transport and delivery of the money. The plan was now set.

CHAPTER FORTY-SIX

Charles called Colby and told him about his conversation with the witness on the sailboat. He felt sure, he said, that Alex had returned to Chub by boat and kidnapped Jack. He had no idea where he might be taking him. He suggested that Colby and Nathan get back to Chub, where they could put their heads together to come up with a plan.

Colby said they could get a ride on Nathan's company helicopter and be there within the hour. Charles told them to hurry.

Only about thirty minutes had passed when Charles heard a helicopter approaching the airport. He radioed Oscar to pick them up and bring them to the yacht. Ten minutes later, Oscar pulled up and dropped off Colby and Nathan. Charles led them to the yacht, and they all took seats on the aft deck. No one knew where to start, so everyone was silent until Charles finally spoke.

"We searched both marinas and found nothing out of the ordinary. Alex would have had to have left the hospital, made his way to the marina, and stolen a boat, but no boat was missing. That tells me he had an accomplice. Someone who had access to a boat and was part of the regular fishing fleet. We need to find out who that is."

Colby was the next to speak. "But how? There were at least twenty or thirty fishing boats that left the marina this morning, going in all different directions. Alex would have had to commandeer a boat and force the captain and crew to take him to Chub. But that seems unlikely."

"Well, how else could he have done it?" Charles asked. "Unless the captain was the accomplice and part of the plan. But I don't think Alex would have planned ahead for that. Because he thought you and Hunter would be dead in the water at Walker's Cay by then. When he found out at the hospital that you and Hunter weren't dead after all, that called for a drastic change of plans with no time to spare. Who would he have contacted at that point?"

Everyone was frustrated with no clear ideas about where to go or where to look. Even Nathan, who was the professional spy in the group, didn't have an answer.

Colby was restless and couldn't just stand there, so he started pacing around the boat, trying to come up with *something*, and that was when his phone rang. He pulled it from his pocket and was surprised to see it was his friend from the Nauti Rooster, Mark Azar.

"Hi, Mark."

"Hello, Colby. How have you been?"

"I've been better. How about you?"

"I'm doing fine. Back in Miami, and I've come across some interesting information. I know this is going to sound strange, but would you happen to be missing your father?"

Colby stopped in his tracks. "What did you say?" He rushed back into the lounge and put his phone on speaker.

"Your father. Is he there with you?"

"No! He is missing, Mark, and we believe that early this morning he was kidnapped by his captain. Mark, what do you know?"

"I got a call from one of my contacts that my cousin is being paid to pick up money from a bank and deliver it after some of his contacts forced a kidnap victim to arrange for a withdrawal. If you remember, he is the one who was causing the family some problems and had the little skirmish with your brother at the bar. I've been keeping tabs on him. My contact said the kidnapping victim was a wealthy man who owned part of Chub Cay. I knew that your dad was one of the partners and wanted to check in with you. How can I help?"

Charles stepped closer to the phone. He had a hunch. "Hi, Mark. This is Charles Westcott. Are you near the marina?"

"I am, about five minutes away."

"Can you do us a favor and see if there are any Hatteras fishing boats registered in Houston, Texas?"

"I can. Give me about ten minutes, and I'll call you from the dock."

"Thank you, Mark. Talk to you then." Colby hung up the phone, and he and Nathan looked at Charles for an explanation.

Charles poured a cup of coffee and sat on the couch. "I got to thinking about how nothing seemed out of the ordinary either here or in Nassau. Alex had to have had help, or someone would have noticed an injured, desperate man who was on the run. And who would that help have come from? It certainly wasn't a boat owner, and I don't think a captain would risk his job to help someone like Alex, especially if there was criminal activity involved. I was about to call Paul Keen, one of Jack's friends from Texas who has a fishing boat in Nassau. I wanted to ask Paul if he would check around, and then I remembered he'd gone back to Texas. Usually, that is when the captain and crew take leave. I know one of Paul's mates is friends with Alex and has filled in a few times on Jack's boat. So now I'm betting Mark will find a sixty-foot Hatteras named Oilman docked at the marina."

They were discussing this as a possibility when Mark called back. Colby put the call on speaker.

"I searched the entire marina and didn't see a Hatteras or any other fishing boats registered in Houston," Mark reported.

A dejected silence fell upon the group.

"However, I did find a Hatteras registered in Austin, Texas, that is moored not far from my cousin's boat storage facility. It's named Oilman."

It was the connection they were looking for, and now they understood how Alex had pulled it off. He must have had help from the mate, who wouldn't have seemed out of place at the Chub Cay marina. The man could have easily lured Jack on board, and no one would have paid attention to the boat leaving the harbor. Now they needed to figure out if Jack and his captors were still on the boat.

"Mark, can you have someone find out if they still are on the boat?"

"Yep, I still have one of them down there. Let me call him, and he can find out. Give me a few, and I'll call you back."

Just a few minutes later, Mark called back with his report.

"They aren't on the boat, but they can't have gone too far. The air is on, and so is the TV. Since my cousin is involved in this, I know all his contacts and have an idea where they might be. Why don't the three of you get over here as quickly as you can, and we can figure out where to go from here. Do you need me to send someone for you?"

Nathan answered that he had a helicopter standing by and that the pilot knew the area. He said to give us about forty-five minutes to get there. Mark said he would be waiting at the westside helipad.

Charles called Oscar to shuttle Nathan and Colby to the airport. He told them he had to run by his condo to pick something up and would meet them there. About fifteen minutes later, they were in the air, heading to Miami.

On final approach, they could see a Suburban with all the doors open parked next to the helipad. As soon as they landed, they jumped into the Suburban, and Mark directed his driver to take them to the marina.

CHAPTER FORTY-SEVEN

On the way to the marina, Mark told them he had received more information while they were flying in, and as he suspected, the meeting place would be the apartment he had mentioned. It seemed the handoff was going to be the next day at one, which was not what they were hoping for. Colby could not stand the thought of Jack having to spend the night with Alex and wanted to bust into the apartment near the marina right then. Or at least call the police and let them handle it.

But Charles and Nathan both felt they should wait and let the deal happen. Alex had to be desperate by that point with nothing to lose, having already attempted double murder. If cornered, they were afraid he might harm Jack. They needed to wait till the exchange to apprehend Alex and Angel.

Colby reluctantly agreed.

Mark offered to put them up at his house, which was a few blocks from the marina, but they all agreed they needed to be a little further away than that. Somewhere there was no chance anyone involved would see them. Mark said he would have one of his men stay at the dock and make sure the Oilman didn't leave the harbor. He then pulled out his phone and found a hotel about five miles from the marina. It was a Motel Six, and he made three room reservations in Nathan's name.

He dropped them off and said he would pick them up in the morning at eleven. He added they should call him if anything happened during the night. They thanked him, and Nathan went inside and got the keys for the rooms. It would be a long night, and it was doubtful they would get any sleep.

Colby opened the door to his room, and the first thing he did was take a hot shower. His muscles were tense, and the stinging water soothed them. His stomach growled, reminding him he hadn't eaten since going overboard at Walker's Cay, but it was too risky to call for a delivery. So they all went to bed and waited for the morning.

Colby thought about calling Aubrey, but he changed his mind. She'd called a few times, and he felt bad for not answering. He decided to send her a text that he was exhausted from fishing all day and all night and was going straight to bed. It was sort of the truth. He would call her the next day and explain. In less than fifteen hours, hopefully, it would all be over.

The next morning, they met in the lobby at eleven. Colby and Nathan were surprised to see Charles dressed not in his usual linen suit but in jeans, boots, and a Western shirt. He had a holster around his waist holding a Colt .45 1911 semiautomatic handgun. On the holster's belt hung a Cinco Peso. They all walked out the front door and got into the waiting Suburban.

They got to the marina and set up surveillance behind a few boats located near the warehouse. They had been there about two hours when Luis, Mark's cousin, drove into the parking lot. He exited his car with two suitcases and, after scanning the area, walked toward the door of the boat storage building. It was time to see this to an end. Colby and Nathan pulled their handguns and, along with Mark, were about to head to the door when Charles told them he was going to stay back. He wanted to make sure, he said, no one came in after them.

Just as Luis opened the door and walked in, the three of them rushed in behind him.

Luis turned toward them, confused. "What are you doing here?" he asked, focusing on Mark.

None of them answered. Mark put his finger to his lips, motioning for Luis to be quiet. Nathan pointed to Colby and then Mark, indicating a direction each of them should take as they spread out, canvasing the boathouse in search of Alex, Jack, and Alex's accomplice. Nathan and Colby searched the perimeter and then checked the boats. Mark checked the offices and bathrooms, finding no one there. They met back by the door and Mark asked Luis, "Where are they?"

Still confused, he answered, "I have no idea. I'm just following instructions. They told me to bring two suitcases here and have Juan meet them at the dock with the suitcases with the cash inside. I took out my commission, and that was the plan. Why are *you* here, and what is going on?"

They all stood in silence. They had been fooled and should have seen it coming. It appeared Alex must have figured they would eventually discover he had taken the Oilman, and the logical place for him to escape to was Miami, where he would be at home.

Further up the dock, Alex, Jack, and Angel were boarding the Oilman. They quickly tossed the lines and backed out of the harbor. In their haste to depart, they failed to see that someone was sitting in the shadows of the aft deck.

Alex jammed the throttles forward and set a course to travel south. They were ten minutes clear of the marina when Jack spoke.

"You said if I got you the money, you would let me go. Why are you doing this, Alex?"

"Jack, you really didn't think I was going to let you go, did you? There are too many things that could have gone wrong, and we couldn't afford to take that chance. Oh, but don't you worry. We won't need you much longer," Alex told him with a sneer.

"Where are we going?"

"*We* are going to Cuba, but I'm afraid *your* final destination will be elsewhere. You have spent your whole life on the water, so don't you think it will be a fitting end for you to have a burial at sea? Do you really want to spend your last days stuck in a hospital bed, sucking down morphine to keep you out of pain? I'm actually doing you a favor," he said in a tone of no remorse.

"Alex, it is not for you to decide where I want to spend my last days. Please let me off this boat. You can put me in the life raft and continue on to Cuba. I did what you wanted."

"Just sit there and shut up. This is how it's going to be, and there is nothing you can do about it."

Alex kept pushing the throttles to their limits and watched the radar. Angel stood next to him and didn't say a word. Thirty minutes went by, and the edge of Cuba appeared on the radar screen. Alex pulled the throttles back to idle and removed a canvas bag from under the helm. He unzipped it and pulled out a revolver and a bottle of bourbon. He twisted off the bottle cap and threw it overboard, taking took a long pull from the bottle. He handed it to Angel, and Angel did the same.

Then Alex turned to Jack. "You were always preaching to me about not letting alcohol control my life. What do you know about life? I watched all your rich friends drink until they stumbled to bed, and you had the nerve to tell *me* that I shouldn't drink, that it brings out the worst in me? I'm betting you never gave that high and mighty speech to any of your friends. It wasn't the alcohol that brought out the worst in me, Jack. It was your ungrateful family and arrogant friends, who didn't give a damn about me. That's what brought out the worst in me. But those days are over." He took another drink. "Get up and move to the back of the boat," he yelled.

Jack slowly got up and walked to the stern. Alex took another drink and was already feeling the effects of the bourbon as he raised the revolver toward Jack. "Before I do you a favor and end your life, I'm going to give you a chance to say any last words, not that anyone will ever hear them." Alex laughed and handed the bottle to Angel. "So, got anything to say?" Alex sneered, pulling back the hammer of the revolver and pointing it at Jack.

Jack stood silently.

But from the shadows of the stern came a voice. "He may not, but I do."

Alex spun around in disbelief. Charles was standing there with a gun pointed at him. Alex moved to point his gun at Charles, but it was too late. With precise aim, Charles shot the gun out of Alex's hand. The gun hit the deck, and blood poured from a hole in Alex's hand.

With a guttural yell, an enraged Alex charged toward Charles. But before he could reach him, Charles put two more bullets into the center of his chest, propelling him to the rail of the boat. Alex's face was a mask of sheer fury as he rolled over the rail and into the sea.

Angel dove for the revolver, but as he turned toward Charles with the gun in his hand, his white shirt turned crimson. He stumbled to the side and tried to hold on, only to fall overboard, and soon he was floating a few feet from Alex. Charles walked to the rail and emptied his gun into both of them. Within a few seconds, both began to sink.

Calmly, Charles holstered his Colt .45, the companion that had been with him since he joined the Rangers. Then he turned to Jack and said, "Let's go home."

CHAPTER FORTY-EIGHT

C harles piloted the boat back to the marina and immediately took Jack by helicopter to check on my brother.
After six hours of surgery, the surgeons had been able to
repair the damage to his cranium. Fortunately, the bullet hadn't
penetrated his brain, and the doctors saw no reason he wouldn't
make a full recovery.

Jack remained by his bed until he woke up the next morning.
Hunter's first words were "Where is Colby? Is Colby okay, Dad?"

Jack smiled and, with a warm and grateful heart, told him his
brother was just fine.

Charles, Nathan, and I met with the authorities and gave a
detailed account of what had happened. With the involvement of
a semiretired CIA agent, along with the testimony of a decorated
Texas Ranger, the investigation was wrapped up in a matter of
hours. There was no search for the bodies of Alex and Angel, and
Nathan managed to keep Mark out of the investigation. Mark
promised the family would deal with the actions of his cousin.

Mentally and physically exhausted, I wasn't in any shape to fly
my airplane, so I caught a flight back to Atlanta on the company
jet with Nathan. They dropped me off in Sandersville.

Other than a text, I had not talked with Aubrey since the ordeal began—and I had missed about ten calls from her. I had tried to call her while I was in Miami, but her phone had gone to voicemail. I left a message I was on my way home and would be there that afternoon. I knew I had a lot of explaining to do.

Before I jumped in my truck to head home, I peeked in the hangar to see that my Cessna 310 was safe and all in one piece. Seeing it made me think about the boys, and I wondered how their practice flights were going. Later I would have to figure out a way to get the 182 back to Sandersville.

On the way home, I sent Aubrey a text that I would be home in twenty minutes. She replied that she would be waiting. Nathan, she said, had called and filled her in on everything that happened. I was not surprised. He knew I would get emotional and probably upset her with the details of how close we had come to being killed. It was nice of him to prepare her for what was sure to be a hard conversation.

—

When I pulled into the driveway, she was standing on the porch. She was as beautiful in that moment as she had ever been, and it was too much. I got out of the truck, made it the few feet to the well house, and broke down. Seeing her brought home the reality of how I had almost lost the chance to have a future with Aubrey and our baby. She ran to me, wrapped her arms around me, and we sank to our knees and just held each other. In a weak voice, I told her I was sorry, that I never wanted to be apart from her again.

Charles had returned to Chub, but he flew back to Nassau to support Jack, who had remained with Hunter. It took a few weeks, but Hunter improved enough to get clearance to go home. He had his pilot pick him up and fly him back to Texas. Jack wasn't far behind.

A month later, on a Monday morning, Aubrey and I held our breath at the long-awaited appointment to check on the baby's progress. Emotionally exhausted after weeks of waiting, we nervously watched as the doctor performed the ultrasound. I held Aubrey's hand and tried not to throw up. It took longer than the first one, and we waited quietly as the doctor finished. Then, without saying anything, he pushed the ultrasound cart to the side of the room and pulled up a chair.

With a remote-control device, he brought the images of our daughter up on a large screen across the room. The room was silent as we looked. Then, with a stoic expression that turned into a smile, he said, "Your daughter's brain is developing exactly as it should, and what we now know to have been a cyst has completely disappeared."

I let out a shout and grabbed Aubrey for a kiss, then I hugged the doctor.

"In about four months, you should deliver a healthy baby girl," he said with a big smile stretched across his face.

Elated, we left the doctor's office, taking time to thank God for answering our prayers.

Jack stayed on the yacht for another couple of months, and when his health began to fail, he knew it was time to go home. He had the crew pack up his personal belongings and spent a couple of days saying goodbye to all the people on the island who had meant so much to him. The morning he departed Chub Cay for the final time, everyone on the island who had ever been a part of his life was at the airport to see him off. There were hugs and tears and smiles and laughter. Jack had been a light, a source of joy, and he would be missed.

As his jet departed, he looked down one last time and smiled. Chub Cay had been his place of peace, a place where he found refuge from the stress life can bring, and Chub Cay had been the place he finally got the chance to reconnect with his son. Flying back to Houston, he thought about the next few months and the challenges they'd bring. He thought about Colby and Aubrey and their baby on the way. Then he closed his eyes and asked God for one more favor.

EPILOGUE

On August 18 at University Hospital in Augusta, Georgia, at 5:23 p.m., Aubrey delivered a beautiful baby girl. We named her Jacqueline Grace, and we would call her "Jackie." She looked just like a little angel. With her in my arms, tears rolled down my cheeks as I thought of another father, one who had held his baby son forty-seven years before, knowing he might never hold that son again. Thankfully, he did.

We took her home and settled into our life as parents. With my new duties of changing diapers and getting up at all hours of the night, I didn't spend much time at the airport, but I didn't need to. The Mario Brothers had passed their multi-engine instrument check ride and decided to enroll in a professional flight school in Florida.

A few months later, their car packed to the gills and headed to Daytona, they stopped by the airport to say goodbye and thank me for everything I'd done. As I waved goodbye to them, my phone rang. I pulled it from my pocket to see it was Hunter.

It was a week away from Thanksgiving, and Aubrey and I had planned to spend the holiday with Jack in Houston. Jackie had just turned three months old, and it was time for her to meet her grandfather. I had just talked to Hunter a few days earlier, and I had a sinking feeling about why he might be calling.

"Colby, Dad isn't doing good. I think you might want to get here as quick as you can."

I told him we would leave early the next morning. He said he would have the Gulfstream 650 waiting for us at the Sandersville airport.

—

We arrived at the airport the next day to find the big jet parked on the tarmac with the steps already down. I pulled my truck into a parking space in front of the FBO and began to unload our luggage. When I looked up, a man in a blue suit was walking toward me. I set down our bags and met him with an embrace.

"Good to see you, Charles, and thanks for picking us up."

He smiled and nodded. Then he grabbed our luggage, taking it to the baggage compartment while I helped Aubrey with the baby.

After everything was secure, we strapped ourselves in and expeditiously departed Kaolin Field.

In the air, I took the baby from her car seat and sat next to Charles. I held her out to him, and I could tell he was unsure about how he should respond. In a quiet voice, I asked, "How would you like to hold your goddaughter, Charles?" He gently took her from me, and when she smiled at him, I saw a tear roll down his face. It was the first time I had ever seen Charles show emotion.

"I have never held anything so beautiful." He rocked her for a few minutes and then gave her back. I put her back in her car seat and retrieved a special item that I'd brought. This time I was the one handing an envelope to him. It held a list of godparent duties and described the role a godfather played in the life of a child. I had grown close to Charles. He was a good man, a natural protector, and it was important to me that he be a part of Jackie's life.

I handed it to him and said, "If you accept this, you will have the wonderful opportunity to help shape this child's life. To be there for her baptism and mentor her in ways you think would be useful to her."

He opened it and read it, then he put his arm around my shoulders. "I will proudly uphold these duties and responsibilities. Thank you and Aubrey for this honor."

He got up and gave Aubrey a hug, and she thanked him enthusiastically.

The flight was two hours, and when we landed, we were met by a black car. I was pleasantly surprised to see Oscar was our driver. He loaded our bags and then drove us to Jack's.

After the drive from the airport, we walked into a large Mediterranean-style house, and Hunter was there to greet us. He smiled and gave me a big hug before I introduced him to Aubrey and Jackie. He hugged Aubrey and told her she was much prettier than I had described. Then he looked at Jackie and told Aubrey, "She is beautiful, and thank God she got your looks." We all laughed, and then he got serious. "Don't be shocked, Colby, by his appearance. He has lost a lot of weight."

We quietly entered Jack's bedroom, where we found him in a hospital bed, hooked up to a myriad of tubes and wires. He gave us a weak smile and motioned for us to come closer. He had indeed lost weight, but his warm, blue eyes were still full of life.

Aubrey walked over with Jackie. "Hi, Jack. It's a pleasure to meet you, and I would like to introduce you to your granddaughter, Jackie. Would you like to hold her?"

He managed to sit up a little and said he would love to. Aubrey placed Jackie in his arms, and I noticed it right away. Around Jack's head and shoulders was a peaceful blue and glowing aura, a physical sign of the love he felt for my little girl. He rocked her for a minute and then began singing her a hymn.

"When peace like a river attendeth my way,
when sorrows like sea billows roll;
whatever my lot, thou hast taught me to say,
It is well, it is well with my soul."

She smiled and stared at him, and I felt myself getting choked up, knowing this would be the only time they would ever be together. I pulled my phone out and took a few pictures so I could show her when she was older.

When he got tired, Aubrey gently took her from him, but she didn't want to go. All of us held our breath when she reached back for him.

It was a moment.

Then Aubrey left the room, and Hunter and I moved to opposite sides of the bed and held his hands. He had tears running down his cheeks from the experience of holding his only grandchild. He motioned for me to hand him a cup of water from a tray on the bedside table. He put the straw in his mouth and took a sip. Hunter and I waited quietly.

Then Jack handed the cup back to me and said, "It was always in my dreams that one day this would be possible—the three of us together. Although when I dared to imagine this, you two didn't know each other, and I had not seen Colby up close since I held him the week he was born. Now, I have my boys with me. I want you both to know how much I love you. I want to say I'm sorry for not being there for you, and I hope you both can forgive me. I wish we could have had years together, but I wouldn't trade anything for the short time we've had. I have a last request for both of you," he said, squeezing our hands lightly.

"I want you to spend the rest of your lives loving and taking care of one another. I want you to build the bond that I wish you could have had the opportunity to build many years ago. It's important to me that you do more than just talk every now and then. I want you to truly be in each other's lives. Can you promise me that? If the two of you can do that, my life will have been a success."

I don't know who made the first move, but Hunter and I reached across Jack, took each other's hands along with his, and squeezed them together as one. We told him we had already built a bond that would keep us together always. Our time fighting for our lives in the water had forever sealed that bond.

With a smile, Jack closed his eyes, and later that Sunday morning, he left us.

Hunter took it hard, laying his head on Jack's chest and sobbing. That was too much for me, and I left the room to walk outside to the garden in the back. There, I settled on a bench and wiped my eyes.

I thought about all the things that had happened in my life in such a brief span of time—and what I had learned from them. I'd learned to live in the present and to let go of things that happened long ago. I'd learned to have the courage to accept the changes that life brought. I'd learned that changes came with gifts: a baby at middle age, even a new brother in a safari suit. I'd learned to live with empathy, to recognize the needs of others, and to be a blessing and a comfort to them. Most of all, I'd learned to cultivate a sense of peace and joy to carry deep within my soul. I'd learned to always strive to be a better person.

If I could continue to do these things, as Jack did, I would be able to call my life a success.

About the Author

James Campbell grew up in Atlanta and earned degrees in journalism and business from the University of Georgia.

He loves incorporating his real-life interests into his fiction, including flying airplanes, racing cars, and romance. While he is more of an authority on the first two, he hopes readers will enjoy how the three come together in the adventures he creates.

James is the author of *Mandatory Role, Mandatory Flight,* and the third of the trilogy, *The Reunion.* He currently resides in the Georgia towns of Warthen and Madison.

To reach James with any comments or reviews, visit his Facebook page. Facebook.com/JcampbellAuthor.

CPSIA information can be obtained
at www.ICGtesting.com
Printed in the USA
BVHW070440150522
637018BV00001B/4